This book may be returned to any Wiltshire
library. To renew this book phone your library
or visit the website: www.wiltshire.gov.uk

Wiltshire
COUNTY COUNCIL

CHILDREN, EDUCATION & LIBRARIES

LM6.108.5

Strategic Book Group

Strategic Book Group
P.O. Box 333
Durham CT 06422
www.StrategicBookClub.com

ISBN: 978-1-61204-522-1

Book Design: Suzanne Kelly

ALSO BY MARTINA NICOLLS

*The Sudan Curse*
*Kashmir on a Knife-Edge*

*For Colin Barry,*
*my university mathematics lecturer—*


*And for everyone in my life who guided my*
*chariot in both the right and the wrong directions,*
*so that I would know one from the other.*

# TABLE OF CONTENTS

# PROLOGUE

I changed my daughter's name when her mother died. Under different circumstances, my daughter could possibly, and in all probability, have had an altogether different life. Whether her fate was pre-determined at birth, or whether that one modest act of mine, a month after her birth, altered her course in life, I'll never know.

Her mother brooded interminably and lovingly over the choice of her child's name. She finally selected one signifying a heavenly body: a star. By accident, after my wife's death, I discovered the name was also one of a fictional woman who conceived a baby after an adulterous affair. I never intended to erase all memory of my wife, but, shocked and in haste, I changed my daughter's name to Prudence, symbolizing wisdom, intelligence, and foresight: a foreseeing of the future. I thought it was perfect.

I confess that I had an interest in the art of numerology. As a mathematician, I did not view it as a science, but its appeal seemed logical to me. Each alphabetical letter is allocated a numerical value. The individual letters in a person's name, when assigned a number and added, form a core number that numerologists say has substantial significance; the core number may have manifestations, beyond human understanding, of a person's character, personality, and the person's subsequent destiny. My daughter's previous name, according to numerology, indicated she would be responsible, careful, conventional, and reliable. The name, Prudence Bari, was altogether different. The character of Prudence would be a leader, a planner, and a high achiever with strong, sound judgment. These were characteristics I admired.

If that were the end of it, then there would be no controversy. Detractors believe numerology to be supernatural. I do not see it that way. I was, and still am, a deeply religious man with scientific abilities, and I prefer to acknowledge numerology merely as a computational hobby. I learned of numerology after I had changed my daughter's name, and this is my torment—had I changed her name for better or for worse? Did my decision affect my daughter's future? Had I not changed her name, would she have developed the same characteristics and have had the same destiny? Many could argue that her destiny was not a result of my decision to change her name. Many could argue that all of my decisions, indecisions, actions and inactions, throughout her whole life, and perhaps those of everyone she interacted with, may have influenced her destiny.

Words and their meanings are not my forte. Mathematics is my strength. I will never forget the amazement with which I read *Cours d'analyse* and realized, for the first time, what mathematics really meant. In my twenties I was a mathematician with a genuine passion for numerical computations and calculations.

At the age of thirty-six I suffered the common fate of many mathematicians: steady mental deterioration. The mind rarely improves after the age of twenty-five or thirty; at least, for me, this was true. All the same, I've had more reward than was due to a man of my particular ability. I've had a comfortable life.

In my antique, mahogany escritoire I still keep a leather box of mementos and, from time to time, I read the stained newspaper clipping dated July 24, 1942, to remind me of my slight achievement:

*NEW VERSION OF EUCLID'S ELEMENTS*
*Adelaide mathematician, Dr. Leonardo Bari, has recently completed a new version of Euclid's* Elements. *Euclid, the Greek mathematician, wrote the work of the* Elements *in 13 books, of which nine deal with plane and solid geometry, and four with number theory. Bari, while making only inconsiderable additions to the content of the* Elements, *has endeavored to remove difficulties*

*that might be felt by learners in studying the book, as a modern editor might do in editing a classical textbook for use in schools. There is no doubt that this edition will be enjoyed by his Adelaide students for whom it was written, as well as by all Australian students in the future who will use it almost exclusively as part of the secondary school curriculum.*

The new version of Euclid's *Elements* may have contributed in a small way to my students' education at the time, but geometry, like me, soon faded from the curriculum.

It is plain now, at seventy-five, that my life, for what it is worth, is finished, and nothing I can do will notably increase or diminish its value. In retrospect, it seems absurd to suppose that I could have done better, even though I've never accomplished anything of great note. No mathematical achievement of mine has made, directly or indirectly, for good or ill, the least difference to the world.

My one achievement, for which I am immensely proud, is that I have produced a daughter of exceptional mathematical genius. I never wanted her to be anything but a mathematician because mathematics was familiar to me. Perhaps it was inevitable that my daughter followed in my footsteps. It did not take her long to surpass my capabilities, but unpredictably, she defied all expectation to become one of the world's most noted mathematicians.

It is said that in every generation there is one great mathematician and the rest don't do any harm. My daughter was that great mathematician. Did my daughter's success entitle me to bestow success upon myself? I would like it to be so, but in all rationality I cannot draw such a conclusion. In the mathematical fraternity, no one can be fooled. There is never the remotest possibility of greatness being the pinnacle of an otherwise uninspired person because all mathematicians recognize genius immediately. To that end, my inclination to change my daughter's name before she had assumed an altogether different identity and to raise her as a single father, in the only manner I knew, was vindicated. In short, the end justified the means. Or did it, for the end came much too soon?

I'm not afraid to take ultimate responsibility for my daughter's destiny because I'm her father. So, it is here, within these pages, I will be judged.

# SEPTEMBER 28, 1969

I heard Prudence's Fiat turn into the driveway. Instead of waiting for her key to turn in the lock, I shuffled up the hallway in my comfortable brown slippers and unbolted the door. I held it ajar to wait for her like a puppy eagerly awaiting its master.

It was not Prudence. A robust policeman stood at the entrance.

"Dr. Bari?" the voice boomed.

"Yes." I peered inquisitively into his Herculean face.

"Is this the residence of Prudence Bari?" He had removed his hat and held it in his strong hands. Blue veins protruded from his skin.

"Yes."

"Is she at home, please?"

"No, she's not. I'm expecting her soon. I thought you were Prudence."

"Have you seen her today, sir?"

"Fleetingly. She's been in and out all day. What's this about, officer?"

"Does she own a yellow Fiat 500?"

"Yes, she does. Was she speeding, officer?"

"We found the car in a vacant block, southwest of the city."

"It must have been stolen. Perhaps Fabian has picked her up, or she might be taking a taxi home. She'll be here soon, officer. I've been waiting for her. It's getting late and she said she'd be home by now."

"Dr. Bari, we'd like you to come with us to the police station. We'll go the hospital first." A taller, thinner policeman stood behind the burly man, almost obscured from view.

5

"To report the stolen car? Is that it? Why don't we wait for Prudence? I'll put some shoes on. Come inside and wait with me!"

"Dr. Bari, you can wear your slippers to the police station. We'd like you to come with us straight away. It's getting late and we'll have you back home by midnight. You see, and we're sorry to say this, but your daughter may have been—she may have had an accident. Come with us," he said firmly and insistently. Positioning themselves on either side of me, they gently maneuvered me to the blue and white police car.

"Accident? Perhaps you're mistaken. She'll be home soon. She was driving a friend to the airport." My body did not have the strength to resist their guiding hands.

"Let's hope we are mistaken."

As I slid into the back seat, I tried to recall Prudence's appearance, but my mind was fixated on the word "accident." Had she been struck by another car? Had she driven recklessly and caused an accident? Visions of crumpled vehicles flashed through my mind like a newsreel. What was she wearing? Where was Prudence? Where had they taken her?

The policemen escorted me into the bowels of the hospital. No one spoke. Solemn and silent, we marched in triplicate. A sign directed us to the mortuary. I felt nauseous and was about to faint. Just in time, a white-coated doctor put his arms around my shoulders and spoke to me, but I can't remember what he said.

A green, plastic sheet covered a body on a sterile metal trolley in a stark, cold room. The stench clung to my nostrils. It was a particularly fiery stench: the fetid odor of burnt flesh. I gagged and held my hand to cover my nose and mouth. The doctor ushered me quickly out of the room and into the arms of policemen. I purged my insides onto the polished floor near their shiny shoes. I heaved so violently I couldn't control the spasms. The policemen were true gentlemen; they guided me into an ablutions room where I splashed water over my face and into my bilious mouth. I hadn't even seen the body, but I was sickened to my stomach. Surely it was not Prudence. They must be wrong. They've got it all wrong!

# COMMISSIONER'S COMMENTARY

The first time I saw Leonardo Bari, two of my men were leading him into the police station: the police headquarters to be exact. Bari appeared confused. The color of his skin surprised me. It was pasty gray, almost matching his trousers. In a word, he looked frightful.

The night was hectic due to a spate of burglaries during the week. Victims were filing complaints, suspects were being questioned, and there was a continuous tide of people coming and going. Regrettably, Bari was required to wait an hour before I could speak to him. When I did, he was bent forward with his face buried in his hands. One of my men tapped Bari on the shoulder, which made him look up at me. His eyes were bloodshot and swollen. I introduced myself as the commissioner of police. He didn't move.

I was civil and cordial. I am not an aggressive authoritarian, and, besides, I felt sorry for the man. I hasten to add that this wasn't an interrogation of Dr. Bari; it was merely an initial data-gathering session to ascertain whether the body near the burnt car was his daughter. Prudence Bari was a celebrity in this city, so I took an immediate interest in the case. Besides, I liked her. I liked her a lot. Consequently, I wanted to treat her father with respect: the respect he deserved. I would never want his fate, not for a million pounds, or even a million new dollars.

I should point out right now that my commentary is not official in any way, shape, or form. It is 1970, and the Prudence Bari incident is over: wrapped up and resolved. I'm merely adding my own impressions and memories to this journal, written by her father. He died of natural causes a year after his daughter's death, although many said he died of a broken heart.

A cadet officer, on routine duty in Bari's street, went to the scene when his neighbor found him dead. The neighbor, Franco Visconte, had become concerned after not seeing his friend for a few days. Anyway, the cadet found the journal near the old man's dead body and retrieved it as evidence in the event that his death was unnatural.

Maybe the journal was Bari's way of leaving a legacy in memory of his daughter. As for me, notoriety is not what I'm seeking. Nonetheless, when I read Bari's journal, I felt compelled to write. It's hard to explain why: to find order and sense to the tragedy; as a cathartic way of handling the situation, perhaps; or even as some sort of closure. Naturally, as commissioner of police, I had information about his daughter's case that was not known to Bari. What struck me most, apart from what was written in the journal, was what was not—whether from circumstance, ignorance, or denial. Consequently, I felt compelled to set the record straight, or at least provide additional information on the events leading up to his daughter's last year and last day: September 28, 1969.

So there was Bari, looking up at me. What was I to make of his expression? He appeared gutted, completely devastated. I thought it best that he shouldn't return to the mortuary to view the body. Instead, I asked Constable Hallett to bring me photographs of the accident scene, known as the crime scene. There's sometimes a fine line between the definition of "accident" and "crime," but, due to the horrific injuries the body incurred, we regarded it as a criminal case. It would remain that way until proven otherwise.

Constable Hallett placed the photographs on the table. I sorted through them, removed the ones that were either too graphic or of poor quality, and put them, face down, in a pile. There were scarcely a handful of acceptable ones remaining, and I put them in front of the old man so that he could identify the body. I'd already arranged for an autopsy and a check of dental records, but I was hoping to get immediate confirmation from Bari. In my mind, I was sure it was his daughter; she was an unmistakable identity, after all.

I offered Bari tea or coffee. He didn't speak or move, so I ordered Constable Collins to make coffee for him. One photograph showed an orange and black, patent leather handbag on the road. It was open and some of the contents had spilled out: lipstick, money, a mirror, a notebook, a gold pen, and some pencils. Bari nodded when I asked if it was his daughter's handbag. The next photograph showed a pair of bloodied, sooty legs, with black shoes nearby. He stared speechlessly at the image for a long time. I had to ask him again whether the shoes were his daughter's. The old man placed his right hand over the photograph and closed his eyes. Soon afterwards, he removed his hand and slid the top photograph underneath the bottom one. The next photograph revealed a charred slender hand with shredded flesh, clotted with blood and carbonaceous sediment. It was the right hand: its wrist broken and distorted. Serrated, orange lacquered fingernails appeared as though they had been ripped off. On one finger was a beautiful gold and topaz ring.

"Italy. It was from Italy." They were his first words. "Please don't let it be Prudence," he said. Then he repeatedly uttered *no, no, no*, shaking his head vehemently. If it weren't for him declaring that it wasn't Prudence, I would've ceased questioning him, for the time being, but I had to persist to be certain of the identification. He kept saying it was someone else. I didn't know whether he was hoping it was someone else, whether he believed it, or if he were actually telling the truth. Coherence was not forthcoming. In fact, the opposite occurred.

I remember his words: "It's not Prudence. It's my daughter. Florence. Palazzo Vecchio. Girolamo Savonarola, the mad monk. The burning."

I looked at Constables Hallett and Collins. Without speaking, I knew that they were no wiser than me. Quite frankly, I was confused. Initially, I thought he meant he had two daughters: Prudence and Florence. I sought clarification from him, but nothing he said made sense to me. Bari babbled, "The burning of her clothes. The bonfire of the vanities. The burning. Girolamo in Florence. All over again. Phaethon and Girolamo.

9

History repeats, over and over. The signs were there, but I didn't see them."

He stared at his hands. "Helpless hands," he whispered. They were shaking, and he held them together, tightly, to control the tremors. Not calloused and dry, they weren't the hands of a laborer, but neither were they delicate. I would say that they were a gentleman's hands, if you know what I mean.

With his eyes closed, he rocked back and forth muttering, "Phaethon in his father's chariot is pulling a fiery comet across the sky. It's colliding with Earth. Eruptions. Flaming tongues. Meteoric flesh. I can see the face of Girolamo."

Who was Girolamo? I certainly had no idea. I shook Bari slightly and stared right into his face. As if he had woken from a dream, he spoke lucidly for the first time. He explained that Girolamo was a mad monk, excommunicated for protesting religious corruption. Eventually, the monk was tortured and hanged for heresy; his opulent clothes were set alight. Unexpectedly, Bari reverted to rambling. "These are the images of science and religion: two faces of reason. Two faces of reason: science and religion. But now they are one: Prudence burning for the transgressions of her father. It was an inevitable death. I should've seen it coming because it was written in history. Why had I not foreseen it and changed the inevitable? Death should've been mine. I was the one who charted her destiny."

His untouched cup of coffee was cold. I was frustrated and remember whispering to Constable Hallett that Bari was confused. I ordered Hallett to record the identification of the body as Professor Prudence Bari. The dental records would confirm it anyway. We had already planned to ask Prudence's manager, Fabian Rossi, to identify the body too.

I expressed my gratitude. He seemed to look through me when he said, "Oh God, turn me into a chariot of fire to burn in hell, unforgiven, forever."

# SUSPECTS

Yesterday was too much for me. Admittedly, I was ineffective in assisting the police identify the body. In all honesty, I didn't want it to be Prudence, and I could never have acknowledged that it was. It seemed incredulous to me that she was so vibrant during the day, but by the evening she was gone.

Without warning, after midday, two police officers knocked on my door to take me back to headquarters for further questioning. I wasn't sure how helpful I'd be to their investigations because I couldn't remember anything. Unfortunately, I had no choice but to accompany them. Sitting in the interrogation room, I felt nauseous. All I wanted to do was go home, lock the door, and never see anyone, ever again.

"I, I'm okay. I'll try to answer some questions, commissioner," I stammered.

"Fine, Dr. Bari. Tell me to stop if you need a break. Fabian Rossi has identified the body, so we must proceed in determining how this tragedy occurred and who was responsible."

"Yes, he rang me this morning," I said. I looked around the bare room, noting every hairline crack in the flaking plaster, and every smudge mark on the paintwork. The commissioner of police sat opposite me in the depressing, soulless room.

"You do understand that we're considering foul play, rather than an unfortunate car accident?" he asked.

"Yes. Fabian explained everything," I answered.

"Dr. Bari, can you think of any possible suspects, however remote, even if you don't think they could've done it. Take as long as you like."

The commissioner was a serious, imposing man with a ruddy complexion, a receding hairline, and small dark eyes. His fat fingers looked like sausages. My hands were slender, appearing frail and diminutive next to his.

I sighed out of weariness and sleeplessness. "If Darren Hicks were alive, he'd be my first suspect. He worked at the university with Prudence, but in a different department. Actually, I don't think he worked; he was just there most of the time. He didn't like Prudence. He was always defensive and paranoid. Everyone hated him, he said, because he was gay. But he had it all wrong. People didn't hate him; he hated everyone. He hated Prudence because he was jealous of her. She befriended Cyril Silverman, you see, another lecturer in the music department. Cyril and Darren were lovers, and Darren was jealous of Cyril's friends. I always thought Darren influenced Cyril in some way, even though Cyril was considerably older. Strangely, Cyril wanted to please Darren, I think. But, of course, Darren is dead, so he's out of the equation." I stared at the wall. What more could I say?

"What do you think of Cyril?"

"I've known Cyril for a long time. My daughter liked him a lot. When I first met him, I liked him too, but he changed over the years. In public he said terrible things about Prudence, but when he was with her, he was charming. Sometimes he was almost too charming. He's not a bad person, really. I know he was angry with Prudence about Darren's death. He blamed her, but of course she didn't do it. Darren killed himself in prison: suicide. Cyril never used to be such an angry person, not before he met Darren. Cyril changed and became angrier and angrier. He began to protest against the government, and then he organized student demonstrations. Students looked up to him and followed his lead. He's a lecturer and should have been a better role model. I—I became more and more disappointed with him. But for all his faults, I can add that if Cyril says he didn't kill my daughter, I believe him."

"Is he capable of persuading someone else to murder for him, do you think?"

It was a question not worth consideration. "Maybe he could, but I doubt it. Surely people know the difference between right and wrong. I've heard people say he has a band of followers, and they would do anything for him, especially university students. I'm not saying all university students are susceptible to influence; I'm just saying that some might be. It's hard to believe that even susceptible students would kill on someone's behalf. Impossible! Cyril may have been like Svengali, but he was no Charles Manson. I just can't believe he'd incite violent murder, or do it himself. Perhaps the drugs made him do it. He took drugs, I'm sure. Most young people do now, don't they?"

"Really? What makes you think he was a user?"

"His behavior and appearance changed, especially his eyes. When I first knew him, they were blue and sparkling and alive, but recently they looked dull. He used to be friendly, but recently he had mood swings—one day aloof and the next day angry—which are symptoms of drug use, aren't they? Besides, he told me."

"Did he ever physically attack Prudence?"

"Never! He was angry with her, sure, especially when Darren killed himself, but he seemed to calm down when I spoke to him. He was, after all, a rational man. At least he used to be. He definitely never hurt Prue."

"Could anyone else be a suspect, Dr. Bari?"

"No, I can't think of a suspect. Fabian Rossi, her manager, is a wonderful man. Prudence and Fabian were a productive team, working in concert; they even went overseas together. They were on the same wavelength, you could say. They admired and respected each other. Fabian wouldn't harm her in any way. He is definitely not a suspect, and neither is Oswald Danes. He's a farmer. I suppose you could say Prudence and Oswald were in a relationship. They've known each other for more than twenty years. He's not a killer. He loved Prudence. By the way, he telephoned me this morning and said the police had already questioned him. I was surprised. How did the police know about him?"

"Fabian Rossi gave us a few names, and we have already begun inquiries. Oswald said that she refused his marriage proposal. Did you know about that? How do you think he felt about it?"

"Yes, I knew about the proposal. I overheard Oswald proposing to Prudence, but don't tell him that. He didn't want me to know. She refused him, but they agreed to remain friends. He was upset, naturally, but not angry. Not violently angry. Not angry enough to kill her like that. He wasn't a maniac. He was a meek and mild farmer. Prudence had feelings for Michael, Michael McShane, I think, from Ireland. Perhaps she was hoping that they'd live together. I don't know. She didn't say so to me, of course. I'm merely hypothesizing." I wanted the questioning to end.

"Farmers kill things, Dr. Bari. Oswald was a farmer," the commissioner said, without stating the inference.

"Oswald grew potatoes. You can't kill potatoes. He wouldn't hurt anyone or anything. He wouldn't hurt a fly, literally."

"Tell me about her Irish friend." The commissioner checked the tape recorder.

"Prudence was fond of Michael, but they didn't see each other much. They saw each other recently because he's in Australia now, on vacation. I met him in his hotel. He's a very dark, brooding man: a tragic figure really. Lonely, I think. There is something about him that is definitely appealing. In that respect, he is much like Cyril, but in a different way. They are both interesting people. I imagine Prudence would think Cyril is interesting in a sexual way and Michael is interesting in a global way: well-travelled, creative, poetic, and intense. Prudence would've been quite attracted to Michael and his intellect. He lived somewhere in England. I'd have to look up his address. No, it wasn't him. He had no motive."

"Keep going, you're doing well."

"There's Polly, the flibbertigibbet. Polly Smith is a student. She's very talkative, but sweet and naïve. She's too self-absorbed to know what's happening in Prudence's life, or anybody else's for that matter. In any case, I don't think Polly saw Prudence lately. Raphael and his girlfriend, Julia, were also Prudence's students. I've never met Julia, but I've seen her. She's very beautiful. Good looking is how you'd describe that couple. I used to see Raphael more when he first started university, but not recently. Prudence liked his looks. That's not to say that there was anything between them, because I'm sure there wasn't. He was just a boy, but she liked his looks. He's a younger version of Michael, but not as intense. Not that I can say with any certainty. Anyway, Raphael would have no reason to hurt Prudence."

"Are there any other students whom we might question?"

The commissioner looked directly into my eyes. I was disturbed by the intensity of his stare and cast my eyes at the table. "Innes Cartwright was deeply infatuated with Prudence. He wrote her letters. I know where she kept them, and I can show you if you want. Whether she wrote back or not, I don't know. She didn't say. He's a very frail, delicate, sensitive boy. He couldn't cope with his studies, although he was very gifted. He just couldn't handle pressure of any sort. Innes wanted to quit science to study theology. I suppose he'll start next year. Ultimately, he wants to be a priest. I heard him say so to Prudence. He's deeply religious and wouldn't hurt her, I'm sure. I think that's about it. I don't know all of her students and friends. I'm getting tired now. I just can't think of who could've committed this horrendous act. It's beyond me."

"I'd like to ask you just a few more questions, Dr. Bari. Is there anyone else, no matter how remotely attached to Prudence, who would have the potential to harm her? Is there anyone who disliked her?"

"Prudence saw Arlene Bernie, the actress, recently. They were good friends though, not enemies. She visited Arlene in Melbourne. They keep—they kept in touch through letters and phone calls. Arlene is a lesbian with a partner. I can't say whether Arlene fancied Prudence or not, but I think not because Prudence never mentioned it. One person who did dislike Prudence was a journalist called Philip Brownley. He heckled her at one of her public lectures, but that was a long time ago—about three years ago. She didn't press charges. He admitted his stupidity. I know they were on friendly terms recently. In fact, Brownley actually revered her. He put her on a pedestal, he did. He's another meek man and wouldn't do anything hurtful to her. His anger was expressed with words

15

and not violence. Another journalist who disliked Prudence was Diana Dray. She was downright vitriolic. I never liked her, or her newspaper column."

"Did you know her, Dr. Bari? Have you ever met her?"

"Oh no! No. Never. I just read her critiques. Rudeness was her forte. She was discourteous to everyone, especially Prudence. I think Miss Dray didn't like intelligent women, or she was jealous." I shouldn't have mentioned her at all. I was clutching at straws, at anything that entered my head.

"Did Prudence know her? Had they ever met?" He fiddled with his pen, spinning it between his fingers.

"I don't think so. I don't think there was any personal vendetta in Miss Dray's comments. All public figures were cut down by her."

"Dr. Bari, it appears that you think none of your daughter's friends or acquaintances committed her murder."

"Why would they? I can't understand the motive for a violent murder. If that's what it was. What if it was an accident? Maybe Prudence crashed the car and it caught alight? Your hypothesis of murder sounds erroneous to me. What could be the motive? Was someone jealous of her success? Was it anger? Was Cyril angry over Darren's suicide or was Oswald angry at her refusal to marry him? Was it revenge? I don't know, commissioner. I just don't know." I know I raised my voice.

"The car was not damaged, Dr. Bari. Unrequited love is often a strong motive for murder, even for meek and mild people," he mused.

"I don't think so. I don't think so," I replied adamantly. I didn't know whether the commissioner was referring to Fabian or Oswald, and I did not ask.

"Did you kill your daughter, Dr. Bari? We have to ask, you understand."

He did not shift his gaze from me, but I was focused on his dark brown hair, greased flat to his head and combed in place. His hair was controlled and curtailed, quite unlike mine. I did not oil my hair anymore, preferring the natural look. Besides, it was an unnecessary luxury that I could do without. The commissioner had to ask. Was that why there was no emotion in his voice? He didn't seem accusatory in any way.

"I loved her. I adored her. I worshipped her. I'm lost without her. We loved each other, commissioner. Anybody would tell you that." Why was I so defensive? It was a standard question that he surely asked everyone he interrogated in situations such as this. I tried to take deep breaths to calm myself.

"Did you love her too much, Dr. Bari?"

"What do you mean? How can a father love his daughter too much?" How preposterous, I thought. I wanted desperately to go home.

"Were you jealous of her success? Were you jealous of her relationships with men? Again, I have to pursue this line of questioning. Everyone's a suspect, Dr. Bari. We have to ask."

"I don't think so. I wanted her to be married. I did want her to marry."

"You did? To Oswald?"

"Yes, of course." I paused. "Well, to be truthful, I would've preferred Fabian to be her husband because he's Italian like me, but they weren't a romantic couple. Oswald was a kind man and a suitable husband, I suppose."

"Were you jealous of her success?"

"I would never have been as successful as Prudence. She was naturally gifted."

"Fabian mentioned that Prudence was going to buy a house. She intended to move out of your home. Did you know that, Dr. Bari?"

"Prudence didn't say anything to me, and neither did Fabian. I can't think why she would want to move out. It seems odd to me." I wracked my brain to think of signs, of inklings of Prudence mentioning the purchase of a house. It was unnatural of her to keep an important decision like that close to her chest.

"Fabian and Prudence had been looking for a suitable place," the commissioner said smugly. He raised his eyebrows when I looked at him.

"Together? Were they just looking together or were they going to move in together? What are you implying? There wasn't anything romantic between them. He would have told me. She would have told me. Besides, they seemed tense after they returned from Europe. No, I think you've got it wrong," I said emphatically.

"You tell me. So you didn't know anything about this house hunting episode?"

"Nothing! I didn't know anything."

"What if Prudence had moved out?" he scrutinized.

"I, I haven't thought about it." I was uncomfortable with the question and hoped it didn't show.

"Okay, Dr. Bari. I think we can finish here. We'll contact you if we need to. Thanks for being cooperative. I appreciate it. You'll make yourself available for further questioning, won't you?"

"Yes, commissioner."

At home, sapped of every ounce of energy, I felt useless. I hadn't assisted the police at all. I felt embarrassingly imperceptive. Had I missed the nuances of people's actions and behavior? Had there been a violent murderer in my home? Had I looked into the face of my daughter's murderer? Had I failed to protect her? Perspiration ran down my face. In the bathroom I wiped myself dry. Looking into the gilded mirror, I saw a lost face: the face of one removed from ordinary humanity. It was white, weak, a mere mask, as though the spirit had fled long ago.

*Credevo sia dolce sognare;*
*ma il sogno e uno specchio, che intero mi rende,*
*che sa smascherare*
*l'intimo vero.*
*I thought dreaming was sweet;*
*but dreams are a mirror, making me whole,*
*revealing*
*my intimate truth.*

# COMMISSIONER'S COMMENTARY

The press gallery was inundated with people: lawyers, journalists, media representatives, and security guards. I hated appearing on television because it distorted my size, making me look too rotund. Microphones were directed at me as I faced the crowd.

Everyone had the same question: "Is the deceased Prudence Bari?" I cautiously stated that the body had been positively identified as Professor Prudence Bari, but we were verifying this against dental records." Almost to a person, there was visible distress. Reporters had feelings too, after all.

"Do you have a suspect?" they asked in unison. Initially, we detained Cyril Silverman for questioning. He was evasive, surly, and uncooperative. Without definitive evidence, we were required to release him. Surveillance of him was not out of the question, nor further inquiry. Silverman had no alibi and, in my mind, plenty of motive. I didn't like him at all. I'm not an aggressive man, but, personally, I wanted to slam him against the wall to force him to speak. Fortunately my inner rage didn't manifest itself. Perceptively, Bari indicated that the English lecturer was experimenting in drugs. Silverman certainly seemed in a heightened state when I questioned him. In any case, my answer to the press was that, at this point, we were investigating a number of leads. Quite frankly, we had nothing: lots of speculation, but nothing concrete.

A journalist asked about the motive. It was too early to tell, I responded. He persisted, asking for speculation. My officers had theories, but I wasn't about to tell the press. The media fired a volley of motives, hoping to gain a response: Jealousy? Jilted lover? Robbery? Blackmail?

The next question related to evidence. My squad took immediate steps to cordon off the area to ensure evidence would not be compromised. This was normal procedure in cases of foul play. One of the most important pieces of evidence was, of course, the body. An autopsy was underway. All I knew, from preliminary evidence, was that a woman bearing resemblance to Prudence Bari was physically injured and that she received burns to the upper part of her body, predominantly her face. It appeared that her hair was set alight. The exact cause of death was yet to be determined.

The press, naturally, wanted more information than I could give them. I honestly didn't know a lot at that early stage, but even if I did, I knew better than to reveal too much.

When I returned to the office, the results of the autopsy were on my desk. The body was female, Caucasian, five feet and two inches, fair-haired, and fortyish. The forensic pathology report indicated that there were no signs of sexual assault, although the killer attempted to cut off Professor Bari's clothes, possibly with a thin-bladed knife, lacerating her upper body. Both arms and wrists were broken, and a number of ribs, probably due to the weight of a knee against her chest. The radius of the left forearm was shattered in four places and the ulna suffered an almost complete transverse fracture: injuries consistent with the arm being violently twisted behind the victim's back. She must have struggled with the killer because her fingernails were torn off. The killer subsequently set fire to her hair. Her upper body was extensively burned making her barely recognizable.

The forensic pathologist concluded that the victim was lacerated first, and subsequently burned. The characteristic heat-stiffening, pugilistic pose implied that the body was exposed to intense heat. The arms were extended from the shoulders and the legs were flexed. Her forearms were partially flexed, accentuating the pose of a boxer. The cause of death, the coroner noted, was burns indicated by the presence of particles of carbon in the air passages and lungs. Mr. Fabian Rossi positively identified the body as Prudence Bari.

More determined to solve the case, I scrutinized every detail of the photographs taken at the crime scene, and during the autopsy. Evidence indicated a sole killer. Cyril Silverman seemed a likely perpetrator, but maybe he wasn't directly involved. He may have coerced a disciple to instigate the crime. Nothing in his statement, at the time, proved his connection. I wasn't wholly convinced by his answers, but he revealed little, refusing to respond to most questions. Nothing seemed, so far, to make sense. All I knew was that someone was dreadfully angry and incredibly malicious. That implied, to me, a hate crime of exceptional personal intensity.

# PRUDENCE 1966

It was in 1966 that the trouble started. If I think hard enough, the first time Prudence received criticism was soon after her return from Europe. Realization was twofold for me; not only did I begin to note condemnation of her, but I also recognized the depth of her fame.

Anyone would tell you that my daughter's hair was striking. Some even said it was a "beacon of light" or her "signature." I was obsessed with her hair. Throughout her childhood, I enjoyed brushing, combing, and styling it. Youthful ponytails and plaits transitioned into sophisticated chignons, French braids and Brigitte Bardot beehives. Prudence always said I should have been a hairdresser, not a mathematician. I was styling her hair on the night of her inaugural public lecture in Adelaide. That is when the trouble started. Maybe trouble had been brewing earlier, but it was that evening when it first came to my attention.

Backstage on the night of her public lecture, I teased her auburn hair at the crown for height and allowed her curls to coil untamed across her shoulders. Her thick fringe met her high-arched eyebrows revealing her green eyes that flashed with the alertness of traffic lights. My pin-up idols were actresses Sophia Loren, Gina Lollobrigida, and Brigitte Bardot, and I would replicate their hairstyles on my daughter. One of my favorite styles was Bardot's *choucroute*, or sauerkraut hairstyle, although I am not familiar with the reasoning behind the name. It was a less severe beehive with more waves: a style that flattered both Brigitte and my daughter. Prudence did not have the tumescent scarlet lips or buxom, heaving chest of Bardot, but she did have the same flawless skin with high cheekbones and the appearance of a film star. Although beautifully desirable, all my favorite starlets—Brigitte, Sophia, and Gina—were good Catholic girls, which pleased me greatly.

"Don't you need a brassiere underneath that tunic?" I taunted her. "Do you want your hair higher at the back? Shall I add more styling spray before you go on stage?"

"No thanks. We've burnt our bras, remember?" She laughed loudly. "I'm just teasing! This halter style doesn't look good with one anyway. Emmanuelle Khan designed it as part of Missoni's collection. Khan calls it 'The Droop.' Don't you just love the texture, papa? Feel it. It's the new material, Lurex. Machine-knit garments are all the rage in Europe now."

She ran her long fingers, left and right hands in paralleled unison, from her breasts to her slim waist, pausing to accentuate the fabric's fluidity. The two-toned green tunic shimmered with every movement. With her bare, square shoulders exposed, the tunic conically wrapped itself around her in an optical display of texture, shape, and color that was typical of the new fashion. Emerald and lime scalloped layers flowed over matching flared hipster trousers. It was stylish and totally eye-catching. As an elderly Italian man, I admired style, but I had not yet become accustomed to the polychromatic apparel of the current times. I confess that magazine pictures of her in a shamelessly revealing ball-gown had me so enraged that I couldn't articulate my feelings for days. It was such an ostentatious display of flagrancy that I tore the pages into confetti. Prudence reprimanded me for over-reacting and showed me the photographs that were not published. I realized then that there were different levels of indecency, and it was all a matter of perspective, and a sign of the times.

My daughter's attire was a personal statement of her individuality. She experimented with contemporary colors and fashionable fabrics. In contrast, the audience wore monochromatic somber suits, evening dresses and gloves: garments that demanded protocol and formality. There were no Avenger cat suits, Quant mini-skirts or polka-dotted, stretch-knit hosiery among the businessmen, mayoral representatives, scientists, and researchers in the auditorium.

"Prue's on now, Leon! Leonardo—hurry! Come on! It's time to be seated." A dark, hairy hand closed around my left shoulder; the other slid gently under my right elbow. Fabian, my daughter's affable and organized manager, ushered me out of her dressing room.

"Ladies and gentlemen! Ladies and gentlemen! We are presenting to you tonight a discourse entitled *Science: The Language of Truth or Rhetoric?* Beckman Brothers are proud and privileged to bring to you a most remarkable person. She is chair of the prestigious Cabrini Mathematical Institute in Milan, winner of this year's Turing Award, author of the acclaimed book *Conical Sections and Classical Lines*, a mathematician, an astronomer, and a physicist. Here, in her home city of Adelaide, after a long stay abroad, I present our own Professor Prudence Bari. Please make her welcome."

My daughter flowed onto the stage like iridescent lime viscose, her eyes penetrating the audience. At the podium, she flicked her russet hair backward to uncover her oval face. Quickly, I seated myself slightly left of center, a third of the way from the stage. I calculated that the position was as close to visual and acoustic perfection as I could reasonably expect in this aged, yet majestic, theater.

The audience's deep drones and high-pitched voices melded into muted mutterings. In front of me, two elderly males nudged each other with boyish zeal. Stunned and incredulous stares fixated on my daughter. Her long crimson fingernails were visible as her slender hands gracefully touched the papers on the lectern. She did not look down. I felt, in my mind, that her green eyes were looking directly and solely at me. This was a lecture to her most ardent fan: her father.

"It is indeed an honor—"

Before she could finish her first sentence, a coarse voice shouted at the stage. "Repent your sins! Repent your sins, you scarlet woman! Repent! You hussy!" An immaculately dressed man stood erect with his fist in the air. The shocked audience gasped and screamed. Two security guards emerged from the shadows of the left wall and descended the aisle. One clambered over seated dignitaries and the other rushed onto the stage to stand in front of Prudence. The man seated next to the heckler grabbed his jacket, pulling him backwards. The security guard wrenched the heckler's arm behind his back, making him wail in pain. Threatened with eviction, the heckler acquiesced and was promptly released. It was, in my humble opinion, as if a Roman soldier had placated a lion in the Colosseum, before the eyes of my regal daughter. The middle-aged heckler sank into his seat sheepishly, picked up a notebook from the floor, rested it on his lap, and fumbled for a pen in his breast pocket. Embarrassed, but not enough to slink out of the auditorium, he fidgeted with his pen. The security guards resumed their positions.

Throughout the ungentlemanly interruption, Prudence remained detached and calm as the audience composed themselves: coughing, shifting in their seats, and tut-tutting at the disturbance. The emcee waited in the wings, ready to re-introduce Prudence, but she merely shifted her papers and commenced speaking. "It is indeed an honor to be here in Adelaide to see my father, distinguished guests, colleagues, students, friends, and interested individuals in this auditorium. Tonight, I'm presenting my view on the language of science. Is it the language of truth or is it merely rhetorical? I will commence my scientific discourse with Plato's view that 'the truth is out there.' I believe that science is the language of truth, and I will substantiate this claim by examining the Platonic view of objectivity, rejecting the notion that scientific discourse is rhetorical. Through a dualist vision of logic and aesthetics, objectivity is the course to truth." She paused briefly.

"First, I'll discuss rhetoric. Rhetoric, originally the practice of oratory in ancient Greece, encompasses the use of language, written or spoken, to inform or persuade others. The classical rhetoricians of the Sophists, such as Georgias, and the Romans—Cicero and Quintilian—emphasized the importance of presentation, style, and delivery of public speech. Aristotle, too, believed that it was important for a speaker to possess the ability to persuade the emotions of the audience. The classical rhetoricians, therefore, viewed all language as rhetoric, includ-

25

ing scientific language. They also viewed all language as an essential component in the search for knowledge and reality, but adopted the relativist view that absolute truth was impossible. Absolute truth, they believed, was 'unknowable' and 'non-existent.' Plato rejected this view and that of the Sophists."

"My view is that science is the discourse of truth," Prudence continued. "Plato believed in a Socratic view that truth existed and ultimate truth was attainable. He believed that the language of science was the language of truth. Plato defined the terms 'false rhetoric'—that of Georgias—and 'true rhetoric'—that of Phaedrus, a pupil of Socrates. He adopted the Socratic notion of the beautiful and aesthetic form of knowledge and truth. Plato also espoused feminine values of truth, such as, and I quote, 'a world-conquering goodness, ready self-sacrifice, warm-heartedness and devotion.' It is also my view of truth."

In my line of vision, two women locked their heads together like conjoined Siamese twins, and whispered disapprovingly. One said, "Feminine values of truth? She must be one of those new feminists," and the other answered, "She's not wearing a bra either." The young heckler, two rows in front of me, remained silent. Intermittently, he glanced behind him at the security guard.

As my daughter's voice continued, I reflected on her phrase, "feminine values of truth." Never contemplating the influence of gender on science, I wondered whether it could be so. It seemed unfathomable in physics and chemistry, but feminism in nature seemed plausible. All things in nature were balanced with an equal but opposing element, such as black and white, day and night, and good and evil. The inclusion of male and female seemed atypical to me, but not too ludicrous. I was prepared to concede that it might be so. Male and female, masculine and feminine, man and woman, boy and girl, virile and nurturing, hard and soft: on and on my mind wandered.

The years Prudence spent in Italy studying mathematics and astronomy predetermined her meteoric rise from Australian anonymity to European prominence and lionization. Italy was where I spent my youth, and I wanted so desperately for my daughter to have the same educational experience. I yearned for her to understand the culture of ancient Italy, to reside amongst the architectural splendor of Rome and Milan, and be imbued by the language and essence of Europe. In no way do I regret spending money on educating her in science, mathematics, art, and history. My daughter not only grew into the most beautiful Roman goddess, but she spoke like one too. Deviating from feminism and science, my mind meandered into a timeless state, beyond contemplation and toward sleepiness. Just when I felt myself slipping into a void of semi-consciousness, my nodding head snapped back, forcing me to focus on my daughter.

"I support the Platonic view that scientific discourse is arhetorical and therefore is the language of truth. My view is based upon Platonic theories of objectivity and aesthetics espoused by many traditional and contemporary philosophical scientists. Classicism characterized the culture of Greece and Italy until the Enlightenment in the 18th century. Scientists of the classical era, such as Roger Bacon and Galileo Galilei, stressed the importance of obtaining knowledge through precise, quantitative experiment, and observation. The philosophers of Galileo's era also expressed an arhetorical view of science. They believed that if humans wanted to understand science and nature they must consult science and nature, and not the writings of Aristotle."

"Scientists and philosophers of the Enlightenment and Romantic eras rejected rhetoric in discourse," she continued. "English philosopher, John Locke, and German professor of logic and metaphysics, Immanuel Kant, also opposed rhetoric in the search for truth. On the other hand, Kuhn, the modern rhetorician, believed that when a scientist used language that reflected perception, a scientist was, by definition, engaging in rhetoric. The reemergence of rhetoric in the modern and postmodern eras was not supported by all scientists and philosophers. Werner Heisenberg, quantum physicist and 1932 Nobel Prize winner, took the view, which he regarded as Platonic, that science, and mathematics in particular, was the essence of reality. He felt that mathematical order had an objectivity that could seek the truth. I support the dualist Platonic vision. First, that knowledge, which is gained immediately by perception, is unaffected by other beliefs. Second, I believe in the acquisition of knowledge that is not immediate, but is mediated by various thought processes in which other beliefs are involved. I agree that scientific discourse cannot be totally value-free, however, I believe that it aims and strives to be objective. A strong point in favor of objectivism is that scientific inquiry can have unintended consequences. For example, when Alexander Fleming found mold on his staphylococcus cultures on September 28, 1928, he initially threw them away. He picked them out of the garbage bin to show a colleague the spoilt cultures and noticed that the mold had destroyed some of the staphylococci, thus revealing its bacteria-killing property. Fleming called the mold *penicillium*, Latin for the more commonly used word 'penicillin.' The Australian doctor, Edward Florey, experimented further with penicillin that led to the discovery of its therapeutic potential. This demonstrates that a scientist may be a proponent of a theory, but his or her scientific inquiry may produce quite unexpected results, often leading to a discovery. Hence, scientific realists, and Platonists, emphasize the assumption that the physical world is the way it is independently of our knowledge of it. Realists do not support Platonic propositions; rather, they oppose rhetoric and support the doctrine that theories have an objective existence. However, there is another argument supporting the Platonic view of scientific discourse as the language of truth and not rhetoric, and that is the mysticism debate."

There was, throughout the auditorium, an audible and united inhalation of breath. Three balding males, to my right, shook their heads in unison, and one echoed their views, "Mysticism? What's that got to do with science?"

"Philosophical scientists have increasingly publicized their views on mysticism," Prudence resumed. "Mysticism is religious belief or spiritual existence based on direct, intuitive communion with the divine. I'm not espousing any particular religious or spiritual beliefs. Plato's vision of intuitive communion with the divine is based upon the good, the true, and the beautiful notions of science, mathematics, and nature. They are the fabrics of his view of reality. Such terms as 'elegance' and 'beauty' recur regularly in the works of philosophical scientists, such as Einstein, Heisenberg, Eddington, Jeans, Bohr, Wald, Bohm, Prigogine, and Richard Feynman, last year's Nobel Prize winner for his work on quantum electrodynamics. I admit that mysticism is no substitute for scientific inquiry and logical reasoning, but I believe it is a contributor to the search for truth and reality. Mysticism can be the shortcut to truth or a 'direct and unmediated contact with a perceived ultimate reality.' It is often the pathway to an inspirational idea. We may even call it intuition. Something in the scientist's environment may trigger a line of thought that leads to a moment of inspiration: to the moment of truth. This is not only the case for scientists, but also for artists, architects, and writers: in fact, everyone. Everyone has that divine spark of inspiration in his or her daily life, but for some the inspiration leads to greater consequences."

A man in a brown plaid suit, three rows in front of me, caught my attention. His light brown sideburns, protruding ears, and prominent chin were familiar to me, so I maintained my stare, waiting for a spark of inspiration. It came to me some moments later when I recognized the person as Richard Smythe, a well-known radio and television celebrity. He was seated between a man of similar age, with wavy, dark hair, and a younger fair-haired woman in her twenties, who most definitely was not his wife. It was difficult to determine which one was his companion.

"In conclusion," Prudence said, "all discourse, whether scientific or artistic, is formulated on philosophical theories of communication, all of which are expansions or rejections of previous theories, and all of which are open to debate. The major debate in the case of scientific discourse centers on each theorist's perception and definition of objectivity and truth. I have focused my discussion tonight on the theories and views of mathematicians and physicists, in particular, for two reasons. The first reason is for their long-studied theories on the links between humans and their physical world. The second reason is their continual search for the ultimate and definitive explanation of existence—of how life started. In this regard, many mathematical and physical scientists have adopted the view that truth exists and that it is possible to search for the ultimate truth. An objective, analytical, and dialectic structure of inquiry and discourse can progress this search. Furthermore, Platonic theories are evident in their approach to scientific inquiry: that logic and aesthetics can both be employed to achieve objectivity. Mathematics and science are not impersonal, cold, dry, and void of beauty. They are intuitive and aesthetic. They have feminine as well as masculine values. They are elegant, and they are, indeed, beautiful. Thank you very much ladies and gentlemen. Thank you."

The capacity crowd stood united in praise and admiration. The thundering, rapturous approval of the students in the rear seats smothered the muted, gloved applause of the front-row dignitaries. At the close of the lecture, my daughter mingled in the crush of the crowd, signing autographs and embracing colleagues and students. As the heckler approached her, a security guard moved forward to intervene, if necessary. The heckler was no cause for concern. He merely apologized for his outburst and introduced himself as Philip Brownley, a freelance journalist. Prudence smiled and invited him to contact her manager if he wished to interview her. Fabian stood alert behind the crowd, his large hands clasped together in front of him. My eyes followed the heckler as he moved toward the exit.

Richard Smythe placed a hand on Prudence's shoulder as he leaned closer to hear her conversation. His hand slid down Prudence's back to her buttocks as he kissed her affectionately on her temple. His companion, the young blond woman, interrupted Richard's flirtations, edging him away from my daughter. Richard left the theater with the woman tottering on high heels beside him.

Prudence extended an arm to pull me toward her. Kissing me on the right cheek, she whispered, "I'm hungry. I thought of a big bowl of pasta every time I looked at you. Papa, let me talk to Fabes, then let's go home to eat."

Whenever Prudence was in town, she lived with me in my Federation house in St. Peters, an affluent and cosmopolitan inner suburb of Adelaide, the capital city of South Australia. The red-brick home of the 1920s represented Australia's quest for a distinctive order of architecture. The raw brickwork of red clay was in vogue at a time when I had settled into the Australian way of life in my thirties. I was teaching geometry to high school students when Prudence was a young girl. She was born in Adelaide in 1924, when I was thirty years old. At the time, I rented a modest apartment in Brompton, a none-too-wealthy suburb with a proliferation of migrants, like me. It was a close-knit community, and when my wife died there was no shortage of surrogate mothers to help me raise my daughter. My sister, Blanca, established a day care roster to ensure Prudence was never without a guardian to attend to her. But, of course, after I finished work each day, at about five o'clock, I would assume all responsibility for her welfare. When Prudence was seventeen and studying overseas, I purchased this house, my first home. A brick house was the symbol of material success in suburban hierarchy, and hence the purchase represented a considerable step up the socio-economic ladder. In a way, having acquired the "Great Australian Dream," I also felt decidedly more Australian.

I was particularly fond of the characteristically steep-pitched, multi-faceted roof with its spires, dormers, and false gables, and I was passionate about the leadlight casement windows and the ornate brass knocker. The house stood in its own plot of land, a square block in which I planted vegetables in the back garden and Italian lavender in the front. There was an air of roominess and privacy about this home that I had not experienced before, yet it was side by side with other houses of similar size, shape, and architecture. It was a symmetrical house in a symmetrical street, and this satisfied my sense of order. I knew nothing whatever about buildings and construction; I had never lifted a hammer in my life. However, I knew about aesthetics and lines of perspective. When I viewed the house for the first time, I stood in front of it on the left-hand side and walked in a large semi-circle to the other side. All the while, I eyed the house to see its changing composition, just as one would do when viewing a piece of artwork. The geometric form of the man-made

31

structure looked marvelous to me. I surveyed the inside with the same mathematical eye. The rooms of right angles, the windows of exemplary proportions, the thick insulating walls, and the straight line of a wide hallway, combined a true sense of topography with a strong sense of shelter.

Prudence was not, however, fond of this style of architecture. She disliked the narrow, dimly lit hall that ran through the center of the house with rooms symmetrically positioned on either side. She said the house looked like an English dormitory for girls. More so, she detested the position of the bedrooms that faced the neighbor's wooden fence. For me, the style and dimensions were unpretentious and fundamental, not frivolous and extravagant. When I moved in, I filled its empty rooms with comfortable and comforting contents.

The best room in the house was the dining room. It was the room that had the most expensive furniture and the room that was used the least. It was dedicated to Sunday dinners and formal functions. Twelve stiff, high-backed chairs with sherry-colored, velvet upholstered seats guarded a sturdy mahogany table. A projecting fireplace with a cast iron grate edged one wall. Patterned tiles flanked the grate leading to a weighty mantel inlaid with beveled, rhomboid mirrors. Gild-framed Italian Renaissance and Baroque paintings adorned the high walls. It was a magnificent room, but I always ate my meals in the kitchen.

Status was not important to me: quality meant so much more. The built-in kitchen cabinets and sideboards were fitted with leadlight doors. The labor-saving appliances were clean, efficient, and functional. The warm, timber tones of the kitchen table were reflected in the browns and grays of the bench tops and window awnings. Original buttery linoleum tiles had streaks and scrapes of caramel colors, evidence of a well-used and much-frequented area. Potted plants, presents from Franco, bent heliotropically toward the windows, searching for daylight. It was a small, social room.

My favorite room was the living room where I had my well-worn, button-backed, brown leather armchair and ottoman, my writing desk, the piano, classical marble busts, and two comfortably large settees. Ceiling-high mahogany bookshelves were crammed with a lifetime's eclectic collection. A porcelain lamp sat firmly on the ball and claw mahogany lamp table, strategically positioned between two settees. A matching coffee table with a smaller circumference complemented the furniture. The largest table held a second porcelain lamp and an assortment of wooden picture frames displaying stages of Prudence's development and achievements. The coffee table was often covered in a varied array of reading material. It was in this room that I modernized the three Euclidean works: *Elements*, *Data* and *Optics*. It was a cozy, darkened room in a largely unlit house.

My choice of furniture and décor were also unpopular with Prudence. She would regularly suggest that I change with the times and purchase new and fashionable pieces, which I had resisted for many years. Often she would threaten to remove the long strip of threadbare burgundy carpet in the passageway. She had an idea to replace it with polished floorboards coated with Estapol, the latest clear, gloss paint designed to produce a bright, "natural" wood finish. I liked the warmth and texture of the carpet, and it stayed. It was altogether a comfortable home, resisting and defying the plastic vinyl, stainless steel, modern, and sparse look of the new generation. The décor was, very much, that of an elderly man.

It was here that Prudence came after university lectures, interstate and international visits, and public speaking engagements. It was here that she came for peace, harmony, and tranquility. It was her home too. In this house, we enjoyed each other's company the most.

Though she owned a little automobile, she thought it "more convenient" to take a taxi after her lecture from the auditorium, less than three miles from our home. I thought it rather extravagant.

The shrill ring of the black telephone greeted us when we returned home. Prudence rushed along the hall to the semi-circular telephone table butted against the wall below a tall, rectangular mirror.

"Hello, Prudence here.—Yes, Oswald, I'm fine, but rather tired though. How are you?—No, no, I'm staying in tonight, without visitors. I haven't seen papa in months and I've only just returned from Milan two days ago. I want to spend time with him before I leave for London next week.—No, I'm having one of papa's pastas.—No, it's not raining here. Not a drop.—I can't.—No, another night then. I won't be in London long, and I'll see you when I get back in about three or four weeks. Bye!" She firmly returned the receiver and smiled at me. "Did you hear that, papa? I'm staying in tonight. You are going to make me my favorite mushroom fettuccini, aren't you?"

As I was slicing the mushrooms, Prudence emerged from her bedroom, singing, *"These boots are made for walking, and that's just what they'll do."* She danced down the hallway. She had removed the lime green outfit and changed into pink stockings, white knee-high vinyl boots, and an oversized purple, long sleeved sweater.

"I'm glad it was an early session tonight," she said. "Shall I stir the pasta? I'm starving. When are you going to get some modern stainless-steel pots? They're lighter than cast-iron." She encircled me with her arms and squeezed tightly. The base notes of Chanel's *Cuir de Russie* were familiar and comforting: the scent of luxurious hedonism, of decadence with elegance. We prepared our late supper together and talked endlessly of European politics, operas, and art exhibitions.

# CRITICISM

When I arose the next morning, Prudence had already been to the corner store to buy the newspaper, eggs, and milk. She was sitting at the large, rectangular, wooden kitchen table with the morning sun streaming onto the newspaper print. Pop songs with inane lyrics vibrated from the radio.

"Your egg is boiling. Coffee is ready, milk is in the fridge, and I've given you the review section. I've already read it. Read the one by the heckler, Philip Brownley. It's okay. Then read Diana Dray's column. You'll love that!" Her tone was clipped and regimented. I wondered whether it was an Italian or an Australian trait.

"You've bought *The Australian*. Why do you pay so much for the national newspaper when the local one will do? How much did you spend? I'm sure everything is more expensive in cents than it ever was in pence. I just can't get used to this new currency. At least I get my eggs from Franco next door, which saves me money. They're fresh and I give him some vegetables in return. We like it that way, but you buy eggs at the shop. You must stop doing that. You're too extravagant with your money," I chastised her. Thrift was not in her nature, as it was in mine. Prudence's trait of habitual spending must have been inherited from her mother.

"I can afford *The Australian*," she retorted, "so just read it. Besides, the critics write for the national paper, and I want to read their articles. I keep telling you not to convert dollars and cents to pounds and pence. Just think in dollars and cents now. Eventually, using it will become second nature to you. Read the paper. Your egg is more than done. It'll be rock hard if you don't take it out of the saucepan immediately."

35

With my hard-boiled egg, a slice of toast, and a cup of strong, black coffee in front of me, I read Brownley's review of my daughter's presentation: "*Brilliant ... a fine piece of scientific discourse ... expanding the boundaries of contemporary thinking ... unusually gifted ... beauty and grace incarnate ... melodic voice ... standing ovation,*" I read aloud.

"Now read Diana's column." Prudence was engrossed in solving the cryptic crossword and did not raise her head to look at me.

"Leave the regular crossword for me to do, Prudence. Just do the cryptic one. I didn't see Diana Dray at your lecture last night. I don't like her column. It's always so—oh my goodness! It's terrible. Listen to this: *The androgynous form of Professor Prudence Bari took center stage in a controversial display of provocative propaganda. Flaunting feminist and mystical views of science, this strange seductive sorceress tempted the audience with the antithesis of Platonic truth and reality, fouling her den with magic rites and loose lovers, and manipulating the gullible and impressionable minds of her students and youth of today. Revolutionary and revealing, exposing her untethered breasts*"—I stopped abruptly. "I can't read any more of this. Oh, Prudence, it's awful." My chest, swollen with pride, had deflated, and my thin, gold-rimmed glasses were leaden on my nose and ears. The egg seemed to turn sulfurous, and I was nauseated by its smell.

"Don't worry about it. Diana always writes like that. She just writes to create controversy. It's why people read her column." She continued completing the crossword. The blue ink of the fountain pen dispersed into the fibers of the newspaper, distorting the letters.

I had ventured into the lexical sport of crosswords when I arrived in Australia in an effort to learn the complexities of the English language. It was a painstakingly slow process of assimilation. Nonetheless, I progressively mastered the Australian vernacular. Deciphering crosswords came naturally to Prudence. Systematically, she completed the white squares. Her sinewy hand guided the pen with perfect poise, while her body remained unmoved in concentration. Was she androgynous I wondered? The white sleeveless blouse revealed her taut arms. Admittedly, she wasn't voluptuous with womanly curves, such as a soft protruding belly and a bulbous posterior. She was muscled across the shoulders, arms, and back with a trim, slim figure as a result of the physical training I had instilled in her from an early age. I had encouraged her to undertake a daily routine of exercises, and she had benefited from this all of her life. Prudence had boundless energy and a *joie de vivre*. She was flirtatious and kittenish, but above all, she was intelligent and elegant. Was she seductive? How can someone be androgynous and seductive at the same time? Nevertheless, there was, some would say, seduction in her sparkling eyes, glossy hair, sensual mouth, and sunny, infectious disposition. Was she sexual? I had never thought of my daughter as being anything other than asexual. At forty-two years, she was unmarried and childless. She had never discussed marriage, or children, and this would appear to be strange for an Italian woman. Yet I had not, in any way, thought of her to be less of a woman.

"Do you love Cyril, Prudence?" I quietly asked.

She concentrated on the crossword. "Of course! What a stupid question."

"I mean, do you love him in the real sense?" I continued to probe. "What about Michael? Do you love him?"

"Michael who? Are you making up names?"

"Michael McShane? Have you been seeing him in England?"

"Yes, of course. I visit him often, as you well know. He's very special to me. Are you satisfied?"

"Do you love Oswald?"

"Why are you asking?" she demanded. "Is it because Diana Dray wrote that I have loose lovers? I don't even know what she's referring to, do you? Are you going senile, dear papa?"

I ignored her. "Why don't you marry Oswald? He's a good man. People are talking about you two. They say the two of you are getting married. Perhaps you ought to get married."

"I don't love him—in the real sense. How many times do I have to tell you that? Besides, I didn't think you were fond of him." The crossword was complete and she doodled in the margins.

"Marrying Oswald is better than never marrying. People are asking why you aren't married. Some people say it's because you're a radical feminist and dislike men. Some say that you're a lesbian. I hear them talk." I watched her face for signs of shock, defensiveness, anxiety, anger, or distress. There was none, only an air of exasperation.

"Have you brought any women home, papa? Girlfriends?"

"Of course not!" I exclaimed indignantly.

"So does that mean you're gay: a homosexual? Does that mean you love Franco next door? Really, critics like Dray are silly. One minute they say I have too many men and the next they say I'm a lesbian. They make things up. Why are you asking stupid questions?"

"You do see lots of men. Surely you like one of them. What about Cyril? Can we turn off the radio?" An Englishman was screaming the words, *I can't get no satisfaction,* and I cringed at the incorrect grammar.

"Cyril is gay. You know he loves Darren." She shook her head at me disdainfully. "Don't touch the radio, papa. The news will be on soon."

"What about Fabian? I like Fabian. He's nice, isn't he?" I turned down the sound and returned to the table to finish reading the paper.

"Yes, he's nice."

"Fabian is perfect; he's Italian. I think you should marry an Italian man. He's handsome, don't you think? Fabian likes you. We could all live together. Oswald's a nice man, but he's Australian, and he lives in the country. I like the city and you do too. You should be with a nice Italian man in a nice brick house in a nice suburb of Adelaide. What about Raphael?"

Prudence scrawled numbers on the newspaper and filled in the zeros. Eventually, she looked at me. "He's dark, exotic, and good-looking. I adore him because he's like a Greek Adonis, but he's my student. Haven't you got some gardening to do, so I don't have to listen to this nonsense?"

"Your favorite is Michael. I can tell. You love Michael, don't you?"

"Finish your breakfast, papa. I need to buy some things for my trip to London." Folding her section of the newspaper neatly in half, she placed it in front of me. She cleared the crockery from the table without speaking, turned off the radio, and danced down the hallway singing, *No, no, no, I can't get no satisfaction, I can't get no, I can't get no, hoo, hoo, hoooo—*

# COMMISSIONER'S COMMENTARY

Interrogating Philip Brownley was a tedious exercise. It was not only me who found him to be sycophantic and effusive in his adoration of Prudence; it was the joke of police headquarters. Imitations of Brownley's affected speech could be heard for weeks throughout the station, as well as his adopted nickname, "Brown-nose." For those not accustomed to the idiom, brown-nose originated from the expression "to kiss someone's bare butt," and consequently is the moniker for someone servile or obsequious. Surprisingly, it's not considered a vulgar term, although it's certainly not complimentary.

As it turned out, Brownley was initially so revolted by the rumors of Prudence being a lesbian he lashed out at her during her infamous science lecture of 1966. Justice had been meted out in the form of his public humiliation in the auditorium. Deservedly so, I thought. I can't say that I had much time for that man.

Lest I be seen to be totally heartless, Brownley did have some self-confessed respectable traits. These included his attention to detail, which aided his career as a journalist. He was also serious, honest, and faithful to his wife. By his own standards, he admitted that he formed immediate and intense likes and dislikes toward people due to high ideals of morality. In addition, he agreed that his sensitivities and insecurities were often his downfall. Moreover, he admitted a tendency to express his emotions passionately, and without a great deal of thought. From the interrogation, I formed a swift opinion that he was incapable of murder. My constables disagreed. They said such quick emotions could easily stoke the fires of rage.

I rarely discussed police work outside the station, but I was in need of a woman's intuition, and I spoke to my mother about a number of the suspects in this case—indirectly, of course, and never compromising the investigation. My mother was of the same opinion as my constables; Philip Brownley was a "dark horse," she said. "Once a heckler, twice an oppressor, and thrice a murderer," she added.

Diana Dray was another kettle of fish entirely. Brash, uber-confident, and out-spoken, she also made her mark on the minds of the police squad. "Ball-breaker," was the not-so-affectionate term my constables assigned to her. I'm sure I don't need to detail its meaning. Prepared for the interrogation, she confronted me with a dossier of critiques, all of them scathing and bone-chillingly insulting. As she pointed out, she certainly had not discriminated in her review of Professor Bari; Prudence had received the same discourtesy as everyone else. Proud and pompous, Dray took control of my men, and concluded the interrogation by storming out of police headquarters swearing at the top of her voice. I almost nabbed her for indecent language, but thought better of it. My mother said she was all talk, and no pork, and I had no idea what she meant. Consequently, I dismissed her as a suspect, although if ever a woman were capable of a heinous crime, it would be Diana Dray.

# OSWALD DANES

During my daughter's visit to England, Oswald telephoned frequently. "Is Prue back from London? When is she expected home? Do you hear from her? Why doesn't she contact me?" The succession of his sentences formed the same sequence in every telephone conversation during her absence. I had, therefore, equated his anxiety with a dependence upon my daughter. As Oswald's anxiety heightened, I equated it with love and, sometimes, with stupidity. I was, nevertheless, mindful not to raise expectations and aspirations that my daughter would reciprocate his feelings. To this end, I avoided answering his questions with any clarity of information whatsoever. I had a sense that disappointment was inevitable.

As a mathematician, I knew there were times when precise answers to calculations were not required and estimations would suffice. In those situations, I would round up or down the numbers in the computation: 50 instead of 47, 100 instead of 103, and so on. Very quickly I learned that estimation was also a useful tool in the English language. My solution to Oswald's quest for specific answers was to compose my conversation with words of estimation, such as "about," "generally," "usually" or "sometimes."

It was also, at these times, that I was thankful for the impersonal nature of the telephone, because I could excuse myself from Oswald's monologues with only a partial sense of guilt. The conclusion to the telephone conversation would invariably be: "I'm sure Prudence will contact you as soon as she returns home. She usually does, Oswald. Please excuse me. I must attend to my tomatoes because it's about to rain. I'll mention that you telephoned if Prudence calls. *Ciao*, Oswald." This strategy was difficult for me to employ without the medium of the telephone, and thus our levels of anxiety were mutually heightened when Oswald paid me an unexpected visit. A gentle tapping of the brass knocker roused me from my reading. I opened the door to Oswald.

"I'm sorry to bother you, Dr. Bari, but I was in the area and I needed to speak with you. I've been buying equipment for the farm." His large, apologetic frame loomed in the doorway. As he spoke, the fist of his right hand pummeled the palm of his left in a rhythmical motion, out of nervousness I thought. Simultaneously, he slowly rocked backward and forward on the heels of his size ten boots. His head stooped to peer into my face for I was not a tall man; he looked at me with a pleading frown.

"Come in, Oswald. Come into the living room." He was familiar with the house and strode ahead of me. "Would you like coffee, Oswald?"

"I'd like tea instead of coffee, thanks, and two teaspoons of sugars, and milk, sir. May I sit down?" He nervously jerked at his fingers.

"Please sit down, Oswald. I won't be long. There's a magazine or two on the table. Help yourself." Entering the kitchen, I raised my voice, "I think they're scientific magazines though. Sorry, I don't have any others, but I think *The Australian* is still there." I placed the porcelain teapot, two cups, and two saucers on a wooden tray with a small, cream-colored milk jug and matching sugar bowl. A sugar cube fell from the bowl, and I transferred it into the cup designated for my use.

Oswald was leafing through an edition of *Scientific American*, not focusing on anything in particular, when I positioned the tray onto the low, circular, mahogany table.

"Thank you so much, Dr. Bari. Sorry to trouble you. You see, I haven't heard from Prue at all and I've been a bit concerned." The magazine fell to the floor.

"She's only been gone for ten days—a fortnight maybe, Oswald. It's not long," I tried to reassure him. "She has some business in London." I returned the magazine to its lower shelf. The painting on the right-hand wall looked crooked, and I felt driven to straighten it.

"Yes, I know that Dr. Bari. Thank you for the tea. I know she's in London, but I thought she might have contacted me by now."

"I'll let you add your own milk and sugar. Excuse me while I get you a teaspoon. One minute." I returned with a teaspoon featuring the crest of Milan University, a memento from Prudence. "She mentioned to me that she'd contact you when she gets home. She didn't have time to see you before she went to London. She just had a few days to prepare for the public engagement, the lecture, remember? Then she had only a few days to get ready for England."

"I understand that. I do, but it's just that I thought she might be eager to speak with me." He placed two white sugar cubes and a dribble of milk in his cup. He spun the spoon anti-clockwise with his right hand while holding the saucer with his left. Fortissimo notes reverberated throughout the room as the metal spoon followed the circumference of the porcelain. Oswald balanced the cup and saucer on his closed knees as he sat precariously on the edge of the settee, stirring a dozen times before laying the teaspoon on the tray. When he settled into the comfort of the couch and widened the gap between his knees, he balanced the cup on his upper right thigh. "I don't know where to begin. I was hoping that—that Prudence would want to be mine. I, I mean that we've been together for a long time, and she's right for me. You know what I mean?" I nodded and let Oswald continue. "I know I've been slow to make her mine, officially, that is, but she's not here much and, what with the farm being a long way away, well, we don't see each other regularly. You know what I mean?"

"Yes, I know," I said empathetically. Periodically, he would comb his hair with his fingers, tucking a straying tuft behind his protruding ears. In my opinion, he needed a haircut. His glossy, thick brown hair was tousled, uncombed, and unwashed. Vertical furrows etched into his brow from frequent frowning and his eyebrows fused together to form one thick streak above his light brown eyes. Subtle dimples and dents pitted his cheeks and jawline from bouts of acne in his youth. Nevertheless, it did not detract too much from his looks. I had known Oswald for more than twenty years. He went to the same school as my daughter, but was two years her junior. After secondary school, he assumed farm duties at the request of his parents. They thought the life of a farmer was best suited to his capabilities, knowing Oswald was academically below average. Besides, he had a love of nature and the outdoors, with an instinctive understanding of the land. Though he was tall and broad with the appearance of being strong and capable, he was not a confident man.

"You know, I wanted to work hard to get the farm right, to have equipment, and to add value to the land." His hand stroked his hair again. Fleshy fingers coiled and uncoiled a strand of hair two or three times. His fingernails were partially chewed and soiled with the earth from his crops. The tapping of his foot turned my attention to his large solid boots. An attempt had been made to clean them. Dry earth clung to the sides of each boot, and some clumps fell intermittently onto the carpet. Inadvertently, he pulverized dirt into its fibers.

"I understand, Oswald," I said nodding my head to affirm my compassion. I was thinking of fetching the vacuum cleaner to sweep up the dirt. Instead, I looked at the painting. Had it shifted position? It looked lop-sided to me.

"Prue's so intelligent and so—she has money, lots of money now. I wanted to establish my farm so she could stop working in the university. We'd live on the farm together. She won't need to work, you understand?"

"Yes, Oswald," I said. In truth, I did not understand. Prudence's academic abilities were a gift. Why would an intelligent woman, like my daughter, want to be a farmer's wife? Nevertheless, at her late age, the possibility of marriage could not be dismissed lightly. A future with Oswald would be better for my daughter than a lonesome life. The farmer was not altogether unattractive but, indeed, he was not a matinee idol. He had an inelegant, lumbering manner, and disproportionately long limbs. Nonetheless, in all the time I had known him, he was a sincere and honest man. He was a man who had not shirked from physical labor: a man who had pursued a goal with persistence and determination. Surely they were virtuous traits? Indeed, in some respects, he was not dissimilar to my daughter. However, he lacked the great many other virtues that my daughter possessed. I rather liked him, and I felt sincerely empathetic with his concerns. I could not, however, voice the opinions of my daughter to Oswald. She was, indeed, capable of articulating her feelings and would find it inappropriate of me to intervene on her behalf. I maintained my sympathetic and non-committal position.

"I was wondering, sir, whether Prue had said anything to you? You know, about me, about us being together. I was just wondering. I feel it's time, you know, it's time to make her mine. I could look after her. Truly I could."

"You'll have to speak to Prudence, Oswald. We generally don't discuss relationships. She keeps those issues to herself. You understand. She's not likely to talk to me about men. I wouldn't know about these things."

He finished his cup of tea and placed it on the tray. "Thank you for the tea, Dr. Bari. I do appreciate you speaking with me."

"Would you like another one? I can make a fresh brew if you'd prefer."

"No, no, I can't stay any longer. I must get back to the farm." He fumbled with the buttons on his khaki shirt, reassuring himself that they were fastened. He smoothed the wrinkles in his shirt and folded the sleeves three times, exposing his bronzed arms. As he stood, he shook his legs slightly to regain circulation. He touched his brown leather belt, for security, and looked at his watch. "Thanks for your hospitality. Could you mention to Prue that I visited, please sir?"

I straightened the small picture of antique Roman urns. "It's my pleasure. I'll let my daughter know that you were here." I opened the front door to a lavender-scented breeze. I thought I should plant more lavender and made a note to myself to seek Franco's advice. My neighbor's yard was resplendent with purple flowers that I strived to emulate.

Oswald had one boot across the threshold when he turned abruptly. "I, I almost forgot. I meant to ask whether Prue is spending Christmas Day with me on the farm. Do you know?"

"It's best to ask Prudence when she gets back. We haven't talked about Christmas yet. *Ciao*, Oswald."

Prudence telephoned me on the evening of Oswald's visit. She spoke rapidly and excitedly about her lectures and presentations in England. "Listen to this, papa. I've been invited to the University of Arizona next week. I've—what was that?" she yelled. "I can't hear you."

I shouted into the telephone, "I said that's in America! Are you going to America? What are your plans?"

"Yes, it's in America. David, David McMurray, has invited me to the university's Lunar and Planetary Laboratory to see the telescope and to be a guest lecturer. David was in Manchester for the astronomy conference. He suggested that I might like to see his work, and I've decided to accept. There won't be much disruption to my schedule. I may stay there a week or so, but I'll be back in Adelaide during the first week of December. I've spoken to Fabian about going to America and he agrees with me. It's such a wonderful opportunity. I'll have a chance to talk to David about the planisphaerium that Innes is working on. Remember Innes? He's my student with— What?"

"I said I know Innes. He's the one that's designing the astronomical instrument." It was difficult to concentrate with the echo and time delay of the voice transmission. Although it was not a satisfactory connection, to hear Prudence's voice, intermittently, was the highlight of my day.

"Yes, he's the student with the planisphaerium—planisphaerium. Can you hear me? I'll call you from America on the eighteenth—your time. Can you hear me? I'll phone next week."

"Yes, yes, you do that. I'll wait for your call. I hope all goes well in America. Good luck! Just remember, you belong to me," I said, reciting the words of "our" song.

"And you belong to me, papa," she answered.

*"Ritorna a me."*

"I'll return, papa. Bye!" The call ended, and I had not mentioned Oswald's visit. It had been an inopportune moment.

When the telephone rang on November 18, Prudence was bursting with excitement. "Papa, papa. It's amazing here. I'm at the Lunar and Planetary Lab in Arizona."

The telephone connection was clear and stable, yet we continued to raise our voices in an attempt to overcome the distance between us. "What's it like there?"

"David and I have just seen the Leonid storm. It was incredible—much bigger and better than last year's. I've never seen anything like it. David took lots of photos. It lasted hours, it really did. The meteors streaked across Canis Major with Sirius in the center. It was beautiful. I wish you could be here."

"I'll be happy with a photograph if you could manage it," I yelled into the phone. *"Send me photographs and souvenirs, just remember that when a dream appears, you belong to me,"* I sang, imitating Dean Martin. We sang a few lines, trying to harmonize despite the time delay.

"You're getting croaky in your old age," she said. "I hope it's not a cold coming on. It shouldn't be a problem to get some photos for us. I'm going to stay an extra few days and the photos should be developed by then. I'll stay until the twentieth or twenty-first, then go back to London to see Michael. I'll ring you from London."

"You're so lucky to get a good view of the Leonids. Did you see lots of trails?" I couldn't hide my enthusiasm and excitement. It didn't occur to me to ask about Michael, though I suspected that she was emotionally fond of him and that he was not merely an occasional friend.

"Oh, yes. We even estimated that some were going over a 158,000 miles per hour."

"How many meteors were there?"

"One count was 1,200 every few minutes. But, so far, we've had reports of more than that. Some say 24,000 in ten minutes at the storm's peak. There were twenty-two fireballs as well. A brilliant green trail on one of the large meteors lasted long after the fireball had extinguished. It turned the whole sky blue-green. Fabulous! I hope it shows in the photos."

"Did you see the parent comet? What is it again—Comet Temple-Tuttle?"

"No, papa, we didn't, but we weren't specifically looking for it. I'd love to have the time to search for a comet, especially a new one. I'd better end the call now. There's lots of work to do here, and I'd like to collect some reports on the extent of the storm. I'll ring you again when I'm back in London. Must go! Bye, papa."

"*Ritorna a me.*"

"Of course." Again, I had not mentioned Oswald and the urgency with which he wanted to contact her. I surmised that Prudence was not interested in anything of a non-celestial nature at this point in time.

Prudence looked radiant and energized on her return to Australia as she related her astronomical and scientific experiences. She was blissfully happy, and I was blessed with her infectious enthusiasm for life. For all of her international experiences, she was always thrilled to be home, to return to some sense of normality. She always called our time together her "sea of tranquility." In time, I told her of Oswald's telephone calls. I did not, however, mention Oswald's unexpected visit and our conversation about his future plans. "Prudence, Oswald's been calling after you. He's wondering what you'll be doing at Christmas."

"Oh gosh! I haven't even thought of it. It's about three weeks away, isn't it? I'll be in Adelaide for the rest of this month and all of January. Isn't that wonderful? I'll give Oswald a call." She was rinsing the suds from her lingerie in the laundry sink. "I'll just peg these clothes on the line first. Back in a tick."

I watched her collect the basket of wooden pegs and neatly hang each item separately on the clothes line. The yellow daisies on her blue A-line frock appeared more vivid in the haze of the afternoon sun. It was hot, dry, and suffocating, but Prudence scarcely noticed the heat. Her bare legs and feet had not yet colored into the golden tones of previous summers, but it was early in the season. There was time enough for the long, scorching summer to tan her Italian skin. For me, it was an oppressive heat, but Prudence ignited in the fire of a summer day and glowed euphorically in the balminess of a summer evening. She tiptoed back to the house, her bare feet dancing sprightly on the scalding, concrete paving stones.

"It's lovely out there, so warm. The lawn needs mowing though. It's getting too long. There are some brown patches by the garage too. There, my washing is done. What are you looking at?" She followed my gaze to her exposed legs.

"Your legs and arms aren't as brown as usual," I said as she sat at the kitchen table and propped her legs on the opposite chair, stroking her faded dun-colored skin.

"Mmmm, a bit like creamy coffee, aren't they? I've had a few winters this year, it seems. It was freezing in America. I must ask Fabian to organize my travel itineraries more effectively so I can follow the sun. Wouldn't a sea of endless summers be fabulous? Oh, look at those veins near my ankles. I hadn't noticed them before. That reminds me, have you seen my toenail scissors?"

"The color of your skin has nothing to do with the weather. It's your clothes. You wear jeans all the time. You should wear dresses more often so your legs can see some sunshine."

"Oh, for Pete's sake. Everyone wears jeans these days. I bet you didn't know that last year was the first year the French women's clothing industry produced more trousers than skirts, did you? Trousers are much more comfortable than skirts and dresses, papa."

"Jeans are young people's wear. You should dress your age and not like the young people of today. I like you in dresses. You keep thinking you're twenty again, but you're not. Besides, you're an old maid because you're not married, so you should dress like an old maid," I smirked.

"Is that supposed to be funny? You like most of my clothes anyway, so stop being silly." She suddenly leapt out of the chair, scraping its legs against the linoleum tiles, and ran to the telephone. "I'd better ring Ossie." She stopped, turned full circle, and asked, "Hey, what are you doing for Christmas?" I merely shrugged for I had no idea.

Prudence announced we would both spend Christmas on Oswald's farm. I was not averse to the idea, but thought

Oswald's intentions were to entertain only her. Ninety-two minutes later, she finished her telephone call and joined me again in the kitchen. I was making cordial with lemons plucked from the tree in the back garden. "Is everything okay?" I asked. "How's Oswald?"

"Fine. Everything's fine. He's coming to town tomorrow, so I'll spend the day with him. We've sorted out Christmas arrangements. He'd love to have both of us at his property for Christmas. He's already ordered the seafood. I've got a list of things that I need to arrange."

"Are you sure it's all right? I don't want to be a nuisance for the both of you. Did he say anything?" I cut the lemons in half and manually squeezed the juice into a green glass bowl. I was surreptitiously probing for evidence of a romantic Christmas for Prudence and Oswald with the possibility of a marriage proposal. Tuned as low as I could manage in Prudence's presence, the radio crackled, *We're going to the chapel and we're going to get married, we're going to the chapel of love.*

"Don't be silly. He's fine about it. He likes you. He really does. It's going to be a relaxing time, so don't worry. Your job is to help me choose the wine, but we've got plenty of time to do that."

I sighed. "Yes, of course. The wine shop in North Adelaide has a sale at the moment. Where are you going tomorrow?"

"We've decided to go the beach. We'll have lunch there, and we may go to the cinema in the afternoon. I haven't seen *How to Steal a Million* yet with Audrey Hepburn. Or we might see *Torn Curtain*. Oswald likes Hitchcock movies. Anyway, don't expect me home until late unless I pop in to change clothes."

"You change clothes like a model in a fashion parade. When you get home from the beach, rinse your swimsuit in cold water straight away, and hang it up, but not in direct sun. Are you listening, Prudence?"

"Barely. You're the old maid, not me."

"Stop your teasing. I'll see Franco and Maria tomorrow then. We should get some of his fruit bottled, particularly the apricots. I've done mine. I dried some too. We'll make a start with Franco's apricots tomorrow." The pride of any Italian home was a varied and well-stocked larder, and it was the way of Italians to help each other to ensure that their friends and relatives had an adequate store of food.

Franco greeted me with a slap on the back, explaining that he had bottled and dried his apricots three days ago, but I could help him dry some mushrooms. When the last mushrooms were strung with twine and hung in the heat inside his galvanized iron shed, I returned home for an afternoon nap. My shoulders were tight and sore, and I was in need of a rest. Drying mushrooms was not an exhausting task; nevertheless, I felt languid and weary in the summer heat.

The house was cool and dark, and a haven from the intensity of the post-noon sun. Curtains were drawn and the windows were closed to prevent the searing heat from permeating inwards. I placed a towel across the leather armchair to absorb my perspiration. Thoughts of Prudence baking on beach sand accelerated the shallowness of my breathing. How can she like this heat? The older I became, the more the heat left me tired and lethargic. It wasn't always this way. In my youth, I would spend hours in the midday sun. My leathery skin is a legacy of those days. One of my earliest memories of Prudence was as a seven-year-old playing in the white sands of Henley Beach, clad only in a pink ruffled swimsuit with her creamy skin bare to the elements: the sun, the sea, and the sand. She'd gather shells, seaweed, pebbles, and fishy skeletal remains in her pink, plastic bucket. Washing the grit from her collectibles, she'd wallow in the rock pool for hours, resembling a mermaid from La Maddalena.

I taught my daughter to swim at an early age in the receding tide when school had finished for the day. The Australian coastline had legendary fine beach sand, but also turbulent rips, unlike the placid Mediterranean waters, and so I taught Prudence to swim between the flags on beaches patrolled by surf lifesavers. On isolated beaches, away from the summer crowds, I taught her how to handle the rips. It was useless to swim straight to the shore because strong rips would only tire the swimmer—even the strongest swimmer. I taught her to swim parallel to the beach until she was free from the rip. Even though I had labored the point of the dangers of the sea, and had instructed her to read the waves before she entered, I never let her out of my sight. She developed into a strong, sleek swimmer bathing in the invigorating waters of the southern ocean. But as a toddler, after the lessons, she'd bite through an ice-cream cone as I wiped sand from her wet body, then she'd climb onto the front seat of the car with a towel draped around her. I'd wind the windows down to let the sea air cool the car's hot interior.

Her mother disliked the heat and the inelegance of wet hair, sandy bodies, and musty perspiration, but she adored sunsets. In the evening, when we were courting, I'd drive to a parking bay overlooking the ocean and wait until the sun's last rays had fallen beyond the horizon before I returned her to her parent's house. So faded were my memories of my wife that I could not visualize her face; I could only see sunsets and Prudence. Whenever I closed my eyes, I saw Prudence as a baby, as a child, as a teenager, and as a young woman.

Prudence and I went everywhere together, and I watched her in the way that all doting, protective fathers watch their baby girls. There was a time, when Prudence was twelve-years-old, that I regretted not watching her closely enough. My daughter was roughhousing with a boy on the back lawn while I was busily sweeping lint from the laundry floor. When I glanced at the garden, she was lying on her back, on the grass, with her legs and arms flailing as the boy pinned her across the chest with his body, pulling her long, tightly-woven plaits. I dropped the broom, ran outside, grabbed the boy by the shoulders, and threw him viciously against the lemon tree. I was not a well-built man, but, had I not rationalized my actions, I would have ripped him apart. My daughter confessed that she had pinched the boy's arm with her long fingernails, explaining that they were just having fun. The boy, too, tried to explain the situation. "It's a game, sir," he said. I had gravely over-reacted. Ashamed and embarrassed, I retreated to the house, muttering in my defense, "Boys aren't supposed to wrestle with girls."

In my heart, I knew that Prudence had started the rough-housing. She had a competitive nature from birth and endeavored to keep up with the boys at school. I was not experienced in teaching her all the finer points of femininity. I knew about fashion, perfume, and color coordination. Cooking and fine food were my forté. I was clean and meticulous about the house, and I could darn socks and sew on buttons. Unfortunately, I was not a woman and, therefore, I could not teach her all there was to know about being a lady. During the occasional times when she was strong-willed and defiant, I found it difficult to discipline her. I did not want to harm her in any way, physically or emotionally. I did not want her to dislike me, and thus I was, for the most part, an accommodating and conciliatory father.

Believing in a sense of family, I had wanted her to be hearth-bound, but I also wanted her to be independently worldly. These were mutually exclusive aspirations, but I had to choose between them. I opted for Prudence to gain a universal education and career in mathematics, but it was with great sorrow and suffering when she left me to study in an Italian university. So fond of her company, I had become dependent on her love and adoration. It was difficult for me to lose her, even temporarily, but I was not unrewarded. It was fortunate that with her fame came remuneration, more than enough for long distance telephone calls and frequent visits home. Prudence and I maintained our mutual adoration and companionship throughout her post-teen years. We continued our special, loving connection and shared in each other's happiness. It seemed to me that it was a mutually dependent relationship.

# NEW YEAR 1967

Prudence saw much of Oswald in the summer of 1966, particularly during the festivities to mark the end of the year. Christmas Day was a relaxed occasion on Oswald's property, south of Adelaide.

We entered the property along a driveway of almond trees that directed us to the rear courtyard and disused stables. The long ranch-style house was nestled against a rise in the landscape with panoramic southerly views of the distant ocean. Rough plaster in sunny tints of yellow and buff splattered the internal walls. The stone chimney ended in a charred cavity that swallowed mallee tree roots. Log fires provided glowing warmth in winter. In summer, the house opened its many glass doors to the surrounding wooden veranda. The dining, kitchen, and living rooms were amalgamated into an expanse filled with light and diffused sun. It was an altogether different style of house compared to mine.

There were only the three of us that Christmas. We cooked, ate, washed the dishes, and played cards together during leisurely and languid days of indulgence, of *dolce far niente*: enjoyable idleness. Prudence playfully teased me for not wearing shorts in the summertime, but I was comfortable in my cotton trousers; they covered spidery veins and scaly skin that resembled the leathery hide of lizards. I avoided exposing the jagged scar on my right leg, below the knee. The three-inch, unsightly gash cut the flesh, leaving a zigzag legacy of foolish bravado. As a youngster, I dared to cross the creek near my village, on my bicycle, as flash floods increased its flow to a dangerous level. In a sweep of rushing water, I collided with hidden debris of glass and metal that gashed my skin open in a bloody, painful laceration. Occasionally, I would roll up my trouser hems to knee-length and allow the breezes to cool my limbs. This was one of those times as we sat casually together, free of restraint and restriction.

In the late afternoon, when the intensity of the sun was less fierce, Prudence and Oswald left me on the veranda to admire the view. They walked together along the row of lemon-scented eucalyptus trees parallel to the barbed-wire fence leading to cropped fields. A hedge of photinia formed a barrier below the mature gums. Jacarandas were in flower and their unique shade of blue was distinct against a cloudless sky. The faint breeze ruffled the hem of Prudence's pale-green cotton dress. A thin, green silk ribbon loosely held back her red curls. A few strands escaped and danced freely in the breeze. Oswald sauntered closely beside her in his navy cotton shorts and his trademark khaki shirt with the sleeves rolled up. His tan was darker than usual, almost matching his brown leather loafers. He was without socks and a strip of pale untanned skin was visible below the ankle line. They strolled together, loosely holding hands. In the twenty years that I had known Oswald, I had never seen him kiss Prudence. This moment was the closest that they had ever been. My eyes followed them to the end of the fields until I could no longer see Prudence's red hair.

Closing my eyes, I was transported to Italy. Side by side with my sister Blanca, we walked along the dusty roads clinging to the hands of our grandmother, listening to her whispering words as I listened now to the whispering wind. This was how a permanent bond was formed between children and their families, I thought. Her own father had died of pneumonia, and everyday my grandmother would murmur the words, "A little girl never forgives a father who abandons her," as she walked us to school. She was our constant companion, teaching us the values of life as my parents spent long days in the potato fields. One day she abandoned us to live with our grandfather and great grandparents in heaven. That was when my parents said we would eventually travel far away from the poverty of our little village. They had heard of an egalitarian place called Australia and had long held the dream to live there. It took many years to save enough money to journey to our dreamland because my parents first paid for my university education. Magazine cut-out pictures stuck to our bedroom walls reminded us every day to save for a better life. Every few months my mother would say, "In six months, life will be better." Eventually, it was. The week after my sister graduated, my father announced that our modest home was for sale. Our neighbor was happy to expand his property and use our home as a guesthouse for tourists. The quick sale meant a quick departure, and we were soon on our way to our dreamland.

We sailed to England first before embarking on our grand journey to Australia. The ship's passengers were like one enormous family, all dreaming of their own piece of Australian soil. My sister and I made many friends on the ship, and I had never seen our parents so happy. Each of us speculated on our new lives and how much better they would be than the ones we were leaving behind.

In our new land, my mother was forever busy at her sewing machine, contributing to the earnings of the household while my father worked in a scrap-metal yard. Life in our home was governed by a puritanical ethos in which hard work was prized above all else.

I added to my Italian qualifications by studying for my teaching diploma in Australia while Blanca studied nursing. Pleased that I married into my heritage, my parents never knew that it ended prematurely with the death of my wife. My parents died of heart conditions before my greatest moment—the birth of Prudence. My mother died in her bed; she never woke up. Then my father collapsed in his kitchen. My wife and I did not inherit the house because my parents rented it from the government. Like all Australians, they were saving to buy their own home, just like the government one: a rectangular house with its own yard bounded by a wire fence, with a gate and a driveway. At the end of the driveway, the garage would accommodate the new car they planned to buy. My father even planned to make a wooden mailbox. My mother even planned to plant white roses along the front fence. My parents had many plans. They even planned to help my wife and I raise our large family. My wife intended to have six children: all boys. My wife, with the assistance of my parents, had a name for each of them: Luigi, Dominic, Russo, Marco, Adolfo, and Mario.

Blanca helped me raise Prudence. My sister was older than me, by three years, and I sought her advice at every opportunity until her death from a car accident when I was in my forties. From that time on, Prudence and I were on our own. We had each other. We rarely saw her mother's family, and I rarely went, if ever, to the cemetery to tidy the vases of plastic funeral flowers on my family's graves. Instead of wallowing in self-pity, I wished only to live for the future: to bask in the limelight of my daughter's passion for life and in the glow of her success. Just as my parents had done, I put money aside each pay period to provide Prudence with the best education I could afford. Education was the path to a better life. That philosophy was my parent's, and I knew it to be fact. Before me now was Oswald's potato farm, similar to the one in my youth. Unlike the poverty I endured, these were indeed better times. The peace and serenity of a lucky country enveloped me, gifting me with longevity of life my parents never had.

New Year's Eve was an altogether contrasting occasion. The peace of Christmas was replaced with the raucous celebration of the death of the old year, and the birth of a new one. The revelry of the evening was exhausting and I sat, for much of the time, in a large upholstered chair placed obliquely in the corner of Oswald's living room. At regular intervals, Prudence introduced her friends to me, but I found it pointless to remember their names for there were so many of them. The numbers swelled, cumulatively. Oswald invited a small number of friends who had each invited their friends who had also invited their friends. The swell ebbed and waned during the course of the evening as people arrived and departed. It seemed to me that they left with different people than with whom they arrived. It was difficult for me to accurately grasp their comings and goings.

"You know Cyril, papa?" Prudence clutched Cyril firmly by the elbow. "Cyril, talk to my father," Prudence instructed.

"How are you, Leon?"

We shook hands, and Cyril sat upon the low rectangular coffee table beside my chair. Beer had overflowed a glass and left a smear of moisture where he was sitting, but he did not appear to notice. A pretty blond girl in a blue caftan beckoned Prudence to follow her, and they wandered off with their arms around each other.

"Are you still studying music, Cyril?" I was politely making conversation.

"I'm a music lecturer at Adelaide University now, Dr. Bari. Isn't Prudey a dear? Ossie is too. Is the music too loud for you?"

I listened to the simple lyrics and could discern the words, *Love me doooo, love, love me do, you know I love you, so pleeeeese love me dooooo.* The music was, indeed, too loud, but I did not venture to say so. It seemed to me that this was a generation of two main types of songs: those of love and those of hate. At least this song was about love. In my opinion, the music of the times was getting progressively more political, with an aggressively loud message of protest. I did not mind, too much, the harmonies of Simon and Garfunkel, but this was largely due to the words being correctly enunciated. It was useless to discern the lyrics of modern songs since most of them contained a great deal of screaming and wailing. Music appeared to be the ultimate expression of truth, as the younger generation knew it: creative, free-thinking, and liberal.

"It's all right. I'm deaf anyway," I said.

Cyril shared my joke, shaking my shoulder with his firm hand. He laughed boldly, and from the heart, as the words *shaking all over* reverberated powerfully from the record player. "I'll see if I can find some Frank Sinatra songs for you. I reckon we might just have Nancy though." He was a polite, young man in his early twenties. His brown hair was longer, greasier, and more unruly than Oswald's hair, and in contrast to Oswald's clean-shaven face, Cyril had a veil of dark stubble. His eyes were penetratingly blue with long eyelashes. A slightly chipped tooth was visible when he smiled broadly, which appeared to be quite often. He was an affable and gregarious man, and I enjoyed his

company. It appeared too that others found him equally agree-
able for his company was much in demand.

He rose when a baby-faced, pimply boy stood swaying next
to him. The youth's glazed eyes stared at something beyond my
armchair. "Leon, this is Darren. He's just finished university and
wants to play in a band. He plays the guitar and the piano too,
don't you, hey Darren? And he composes music, real groovy
riffs, don't you Darren?" Cyril put his arm around the young
man's shoulder. It was, I suspect, to keep him erect. "I'd better
get him some fresh air. Excuse us."

Cyril guided Darren through the glass doors that opened
onto the wooden veranda. His hand moved down Darren's purple
sleeve and rested on the top of his hipster jeans. The younger
man did not respond and kept his arms by his side. As Oswald
approached them, Cyril removed a cigarette packet and matches
from his back pocket and lit two cigarettes. He passed one to
Darren, and a screen of smoke shrouded their faces. They were in
good spirits, laughing and leaning on each other. Oswald was the
taller and older of the three, with the shortest hair. The armpits of
his khaki shirt were darkened with perspiration. It was a garment
epitomizing rustic conservatism in comparison with the swirling
orange-browns of Cyril's shirt that clung to his hairy chest. The
first three buttons were undone and a silver medallion glinted
under the veranda's colored lights. Darren's monochromatic shirt
had mostly dislodged from his trousers and he used the exposed
hem to wipe beer from his hands. Oswald embraced the pair
before loping into the crowded living room.

Passing me, Oswald said, "Are you okay, Dr. Bari? Would
you like another drink? I'll get you more wine. Where's Prue?"

I declined the offer, and Oswald left in pursuit of my daughter. I continued to watch Darren and Cyril embrace as they
shared a cigarette. They were joyous: laughing heartily in each
other's company. I was not wholly unsophisticated in the knowledge of the human spirit, and I knew, full well, that Cyril and
Darren were lovers. I turned my attention to the pretty blond
who was, in fact, quite beautiful. She darted about in a skittish,
febrile manner, and I lost sight of her.

My eyes were heavy from watching the surreal pageantry of the young crowd. Every movement appeared distorted and exaggerated. The raucous countdown marked a year's end and another's beginning. Oswald embraced Prudence and, as he towered over her, she tilted her head backward. His large hands held her head and he gently kissed her ears and neck. His right hand strayed down her back and playfully clutched her posterior. Her sheer dress had fine shoelace straps and a shallow V-shape in the middle of her breasts that exposed a hint of bra-less cleavage. Oswald's left hand moved forward, across her right shoulder, underneath the dress strap and toward her breasts.

I had the view that men and women should form relationships with their own kind, just as my grandparents had done, just as my parents had done, and just as I had done. Even though I lived in Australia, I married an Italian girl because she was of my own background and culture. That's how things were done in my day. It was expected. It was inevitable, and I never questioned this tradition. It was, to me, like mathematical mapping where the elements of one set complemented the elements of another. That's how it was with Prudence's mother: we balanced each other, mutually, exclusively. In these current times, it was more like a mathematical mapping of seemingly unlimited permutations. Cultures combined, and I could not see how these relationships could be permanently bonded.

Oswald was a good man, but he was not an Italian man. I closed my eyes and imagined Prudence in the arms of Fabian. As I napped, Prudence's manager, dark, handsome, and erect metamorphosed into a gleaming, hard projectile: a rocket of immense proportions. In the vast, black universe, Earth floated in the immensity of space. The familiar geometries of planets and stars swam in my head like blissful, celestial fish. And then, as if by divine intervention, I knew that life in the universe was not an accident. It was not based on random processes. This knowledge, which came intuitively, was not a matter of discursive reasoning or logical abstraction. It was deduced from information perceptible by the sensory organs: a subjective realization. It was that spark of inspiration Prudence often spoke about. Nevertheless, it was knowledge every bit as real and as compelling as the navigational lights on a spaceship traversing the blackness toward a far-off galaxy. Life in the universe was not an accident! Fabian shot across the heavens like a comet ejected from the womb of an ebony, steel cannon.

I was startled when a damp hand shook mine and a voice wished me a happy new year. One after another, the well-wishers grabbed my hand or wet-kissed my forehead. An electric blue caftan stood beside me, embracing males and females with equal enthusiasm. The angelic figure leaned over me and, as she kissed me on the cheek, the neckline of her transparent cotton caftan gaped open to reveal the whiteness of her breasts. A whiff of fruity freshness exuded from her chest. Minute beads of perspiration swam into one another to form a large droplet that followed a descending line to her cleavage. She whispered, "Dr. Bari, I'm Polly. Have a happy new year." Damp with sweat, the cotton caftan clung to the creases and crests of her body. I followed its lines from her breasts to the Y-shaped curve at the top of her legs. It was a momentary gaze. In a blink, she left my side to embrace a nubile figure in tight red shorts. I was visually and intoxicatingly sated; it was time to retire for the evening.

Several party guests, through insobriety, remained overnight at Oswald's place. I was accommodated in a small room at the rear of the house, a lengthy distance from the living room and its revelry. Excusing myself soon after midnight, I rinsed cigarette smoke from my face and hair. Tucking myself into bed, I covered my ears with the cotton sheet to veil the noise. This proved to be ineffective as the music shook the floorboards and thudded a regular beat around me. Gradually, the pulse soothed me to sleep although I awoke earlier than expected as a result of excess fluid that required expulsion. I slipped my dressing gown over my pajamas and walked bare-footed along the passageway to the bathroom, guided by the dawn's early light. The door of Prudence's room was ajar. The bedclothes remained unruffled on the large double bed with her overnight bag placed at its base. Her purple and yellow party dress was neatly draped over the bag. Streamers, confetti, paper hats, and other party paraphernalia littered the carpeted hallway as I continued toward the bathroom. Before I could widen the half-opened door, I heard the moans of frenzied passion. Perched on the toilet seat was a naked, hairy young man with an albescent-skinned girl astride him, moving rhythmically and rapidly up and down while his gaping mouth engorged her large breasts. Resembling a landed fish gasping for breath, he sought gratification from her brown erect nipples. His fingers dented the delicate flesh of the girl's buttocks as he heaved her onto his intromittent organ. As I looked for the exit to the garden, the moans reached a crescendo of pleasure and pain. I relieved myself in a bed of roses.

The full impact of the placement of Prudence's party dress and her vacant room did not register until I was settled back into bed. Still exhausted and heady from alcohol, I was unsure of my feelings. Initially it pleased me that Prudence was with Oswald but, in all honesty, my heart was troubled. Images of them together prevented further sleep. Restlessly I tossed and turned, conjuring scenarios of their marriage, my separation from my daughter, and her unfulfilled physical life on the farm. It suddenly occurred to me that perhaps she had not slept in the arms of Oswald during the night. Perhaps she was with Cyril. Was that better or worse? Infinitely worse, I thought. What silly thoughts I was having. She wouldn't be with Cyril in Oswald's house. Surely not! Where was Fabian? Why didn't Fabian come to the party? Was he invited? It appeared that Oswald and Prudence were very much in some sort of relationship and that, no matter how much I imagined otherwise, she was not likely to form a romantic alliance with Fabian. If Prudence did marry Oswald, would she want me to live with her? Would she want me to leave my home in St. Peters and live on the farm with them? No, I would be on my own in my own home. What was the lesser of the evils: home alone or living with her, watching a union that displeased me? To be truthful, I couldn't work out whether it displeased me or not. I wanted someone better for her, but any man, at her age, was not to be rejected. Second or third best would, it seemed, have to be acceptable. I tried, in my way, to be happy for her, but I could not.

# INNES CARTWRIGHT

It was not in my nature to discuss intimate relationship details with my daughter, so I never mentioned the night of the New Year's party at Oswald's place. Prudence saw Oswald regularly, but there was never any reference to marriage by either of them. I continued to wonder whether Oswald had revealed his intentions to her.

Prudence coerced Fabian to arrange more Australian engagements. He protested quietly, but firmly, saying that she would be more highly paid overseas. Prudence democratically and idealistically argued that her motivation was not enhanced by money. "Fame and success shouldn't be motivated by wealth," she would say. Prudence and Fabian would amicably debate, for hours, their priorities: fame, success, or wealth.

I opted for success. Success, for me, meant an accomplishment of one's abilities no matter how simple. Each person was tinged with success, however small, however short-lived, and however tangential. It was my belief that success could be chosen and measured. For example, when I had secured employment, I regarded that a success. I did not, therefore, necessarily equate success with wealth or fame. Fame, I regarded, was outside the control of the individual. It was controlled by the masses. Wealth, to me, presented a burden. I would have felt too much guilt to be excessively wealthier than my parents.

Fabian favored wealth, preferably without fame. He liked anonymity, being a quiet achiever whose abilities were to promote the qualities of others. Reveling in the nearby spotlight of his clients, he was never under its glare, being decidedly uncomfortable with attention and adulation. Wealth without fame, he said, allowed him freedom: freedom to be himself without succumbing to the expectations of others. He maintained that it allowed him more options.

Prudence preferred fame. She loved the limelight and the adoration of her colleagues, and students, with or without wealth. Although she had the ability to pursue wealth, it was not her desire. Fabian and Prudence agreed to compromise and balance her financial obligations with charitable and pleasurable pursuits. To tell the truth, we both benefited from my daughter's career accomplishments and prosperity, and we did not ask for more from her.

Prudence was generous with her time, particularly with her students, and they visited our home often. Innes, in particular, was a frequent visitor. He was quiet and nondescript: a totally inconspicuous individual. Even Prudence rarely mentioned him, except when she spoke of his astronomical inventions. By all accounts, he was a brilliant, intellectually-gifted student although socially retiring and withdrawn. Nevertheless, I did not have cause to think of him all that often.

I was aware that Innes had written to Prudence when she was overseas. She saved these letters, along with others, in her room in a colorful wooden box. I occasionally pondered why a young student would write to his teacher, but, other than that, I did not dwell on the occurrence. On the day I collected Prudence's overcoat from the dry-cleaners, I was confronted with his correspondence and their relationship.

The overcoat was originally her mother's. After my wife's death, I gave it to her sister, Antonia. On Prudence's departure to Europe to study, Antonia returned the coat to her niece as a parting gift. Prudence embraced it with sentimentality, for it was the one and only item of her mother's that she possessed. Even though Adelaide winters were not cold by European standards, Prudence felt the cold more than most people, and thus it was worn rather frequently. It was a classic 1920s overcoat of black boucle, with a silver lining. Despite its age and less than perfect condition, Prudence treated it as if it were Italian haute couture. Every year, I took it to the dry-cleaner. It was when I collected it, removed the dry-cleaner's protective plastic covering, and examined the coat for any further damage and fraying, that I saw the envelope in the pocket. It was addressed to my daughter at the Cabrini Mathematical Institute in Milan. The envelope was open.

It was not, in any way, in my nature to be intrusive. I'm not sure, to this day, why I removed the letter from its red, white, and blue airmail envelope. I draped the coat along the length of the settee and sat in my brown leather armchair. The letter was written on blue onion paper best suited for airmail letters, being thin and weightless. The pages were folded in half. As I opened them, the scent of vanilla escaped; it was a fresh and deliciously inviting fragrance. I adjusted my spectacles to read the scrawling cursive:

> *My dearest mother, sister, benefactress, and teacher,*
> *Professor, I miss you so terribly much. I cannot concentrate on my studies when you are not here to guide and encourage me. Professor Addicott is an unbearable bully and is making such horrible demands on me. It is too, too stressful, and I cannot cope. Nor can I cope with the dreadful noise of the protests at the university campus. Students protest at everything, mostly overseas issues that they know little about, such as wars, and feminism, and gay liberation, and animal rights. It's all second-hand news to them, and I find their protestations futile.*
>
> *I need you near me, my loved one. I need your loving care and soft voice to nurture me. Your superior intellect provides me with the inspiration I need to pursue my academic interests. You are far more intelligent than Addle-brain Addicott is, in both astronomy and in worldly events. You are a gift from God. No one else could have the love and care of a student so much in mind as you have. You are the only teacher and lecturer I want to listen to. Please hurry home so that I can continue my experiments in your watchful presence.*
>
> *I have attached a diagram of the light meter with my inane notes and suggestions. My brain stagnates*

*when you are not here, but I know that you will instantly recognize its flaws and guide me to make the necessary improvements. I work slowly when you are away. I sleep little and I'm tired and despondent. I contemplate suicide often and in the event that this occurs, I leave you my planisphaerium and other inventions, and hope that they remind you of me forever. I'm turning more and more to God to help me endure the loneliness without you. Please give me hope that my doctorate studies will be successful. Please, please respond soon. You have the power to lead others. I hope you always have that power and will use it for good, as I know you will. You are divine and I love you so much. I will pray that we will be together soon. I want to hear your sweet voice, breathe your air, and delight in your intellect, for without you I am nothing. You are my one and only love. Hurry home to me, dear Prudence. I love you and I know that you love me too.*

*PS: If you come across a hydrometer (see my diagram) in Europe, could you please bring one back to Australia? It will help me enormously with my experiment. Again, I love and cherish you,*

*I am your faithful, loving Innes.*

I removed my glasses and closed my eyes. What did this mean? Was it purely the writing of a doting student, enamored with my daughter as a lecturer, guardian, and mentor? Was it the ramblings of a retarded pubescent youth smitten with my daughter's beauty? Or was it something more sinister, more sexual, and more deviant? He must be twenty years younger than Prudence. This thought distressed me so much that a sharp pain pierced my heart. I sat motionless, pressing my hands to my chest, praying to Mary, mother of Christ, for divine wisdom and truth. The salty perspiration from my forehead furrowed its way along the lines of my face, dripping onto my cotton shirt. My neck tightened, my parched throat constricted, and I gasped for every breath. I reached a hand to the pile of books stacked beside my armchair and seized one. Resting it first on my lap, I eventually raised it to my eyes in slow motion. It was a book of poems by Kabir, both a Muslim and a Hindu, and I opened it at random, wincing at the pain advancing along my arm. With glasses perched on my nose, and distressed breathing, I read the following passage:

> *You sense that there is some sort of spirit that loves birds and animals and the ants—*
> *Perhaps the same one who gave radiance to you in your mother's womb.*
> *Is it logical you would be walking around entirely orphaned now?*
> *The truth is you turned away yourself,*
> *and decided to go into the dark alone.*
> *Now you are tangled up in others, and have forgotten what you once knew,*
> *and that's why everything you do has some weird failure in it.*

"Some weird failure in it—some weird failure in it"—the words hammered in my brain. "You decided to go into the dark alone—into the dark alone." I contemplated the loneliness of my personal journey. It began from a state of incompleteness and it continued because of the love of and for my daughter. Love was the most basic emotion of all. I was in the dark alone: unmarried, single, and alone. Had I failed to love? Was I destined to be forever alone? Was that not the fate of all elderly men? If life in the universe was no accident, then was this the extent of my existence? All I had to live for was my journey's final impact with death.

# POLLY SMITH

A woman's voice echoed in the hallway. The pain in my heart ceased immediately. It was a miracle. I wiped the sweat off my brow and face with my long, white shirtsleeves and arose from my sleepy state to investigate the location of the voice calling: "Cyril, are you here? Cyril! Cyril!" A young, angelic blond stood on the back veranda, calling through the latched fly-screen door. Her fine hair radiated outward in the dry heat, forming a statically charged halo around her transparent face. It was as though a veil of pearly chiffon had clouded my eyes, leaving me dumbstruck with disbelief.

"Can I help you, miss?" I asked eventually. I was bemused as to why she had not knocked on the front door.

"Oh, Leon! How are you? I'm Polly. Remember?"

Her left hand shielded her eyes as she pressed her face against the black wire of the screen. The blinding light of the exterior was eclipsed by her presence, and I could see her with more clarity. Her delicate forehead, nose, cheeks, and chin filled in the peripheral features to reveal the face of the girl in the electric blue caftan at Oswald's New Year's party. Endeavoring to maintain a level of decency, decorum, and respectability, I combed my hair with my fingers. "Would you like to come in?" I asked, hoping she wouldn't.

"That's swell of you, Leon." She entered, kissed me on the cheek with familiarity, and sat at the kitchen table. "I'm looking for Cyril. He had some music sheets for me. Where's Prue? Doesn't matter. I'm in love with Cyril. You know Cyril, don't you? Isn't he just so cool? A living doll." She had the palest pink lipstick to match her pink T-shirt. She wasn't wearing a bra and her small, pert breasts jiggled as she fidgeted in her chair. Her

69

tight, pink jeans creased at the crotch as she tucked her right leg underneath her buttocks. A white sandal slipped off her right foot, slapping noisily onto the linoleum floor. Her chest advertised a current protest in black print: *Revolutionary women are more beautiful*. Pinned to her cotton T-shirt was a round, plastic purple badge with pink writing: *Revolution, I love you*.

"I hadn't thought of him that way," I answered. "I'm putting the kettle on for coffee. Would you like some?"

"No thanks. Have you got some cola?" I didn't have cola, but she accepted a glass of homemade lemon cordial. I poured two glasses. Taking a loud gulp and banging the glass on the black and white gingham tablecloth, she said, "I know people say he's gay, but hey, I reckon he's really bisexual, you know. He's a dream. I don't think he'll be able to resist me. No guy is going to say no to sex, is he?" A piece of lemon pulp lodged in my throat. I coughed with my hand over my mouth, water welling into my eyes. She didn't appear to notice. She continued fidgeting on her seat and fiddling with the ends of her white blond hair. "Well, you know, that's what it's about, this women's liberation. It's about sexual freedom, isn't it?" Polly waited for an answer.

"I don't think I'm the best person to talk about liberation. Prudence knows all about that," I answered, avoiding the question.

"You brought her up to be strong and independent, to be a career woman, and all that. You must be a liberal thinker, real progressive for an old man. You're close to Prue, so you must talk about sex and stuff? Lots of men like her, but you know, I think they're too scared to ask her out because she's smarter than they are. I'm not smart like that. I've done university, but I'm not real brainy like Prue. I just did a three-year fine arts course because my parents paid for it, but you know, men ask me out all the time. They aren't scared of me, like they're scared of her. Not scared, but you know—intimidated, that's what I mean. I bet Cyril wouldn't be intimidated of her though. Prue likes Cyril heaps, and he likes her too. He's not bothered by her age, you know. He likes older women. Older people are supposed to be better lovers. Isn't that right? That's why I hang around older men. Cyril's only a bit older than me. Everyone wants to screw Cyril and he'd screw anyone. Prue could have Cyril if she wanted to, but maybe she likes someone else. I know people say Prue's a virgin and all, but she's so old, so I don't think she's one. But, hey, some even say that she sleeps around. With all those men at her feet, I reckon she's had lots of sex, especially when she's overseas. She isn't as pure as people think. She's probably got a man in Italy. I've heard about Italian men: real lovers, you know, good lovers, good at sex, and better than Australian men. Anyway, I was just checking to see if Cyril was here, you know, visiting Prue."

My only thought was of how to ask Polly, politely, to leave. It looked to me as though she had settled into a long conversation, albeit one-sided. I light-heartedly said, "Well, Polly, I'm an old man and past thinking about such things. I haven't thought about it as much as you have. I'm sorry, but I need to go to the market before it closes." I fidgeted in my chair in the hope that she would get up to leave, but she did not. She talked incessantly, pausing only to ask questions or to pat my arm to emphasize a point. Unemployed, she existed on payments from her wealthy parents. She worked in the bar, at a local hotel, and took singing lessons twice a week. On the whole, she had plenty of time on her hands. Her dream was to be a famous singer. I said very little and, fortunately, she could sense my discomfort and said she had to meet a friend in the city. The angelic form wafted out of the house with a kiss and a wave, trailing a scent of Orange Blossom behind her.

I was greatly relieved by her departure. Although Polly's manner was uninhibited, open, and honest, I was not accustomed to the topic of sex being spoken so overtly and candidly in my presence. Strands of her silky blond hair appeared on my dark shirt. I held a gossamer fiber in my hand, rolling it along my middle finger with my thumb. Baby fine and barely visible, it was a linear cashmere cobweb: the direct antithesis of my daughter's thick red twists. I imagined stroking and caressing a woman's hair, smelling its freshness and youthfulness, and I was overcome with a self-indulgent desire to revel in all the senses of a woman: the physical, seductive, feminine sensations against my skin. It was a desire for gratification that I had not felt in a long time.

# MICHAEL McSHANE

Prudence had spent summer in Paris with Michael for her 43rd birthday. She returned with art exhibition brochures and summer flowers pressed for eternity into the back pages of two poetry books. In the warmth of the living room, Prudence sat at the escritoire, writing letters. I placed two logs on the fire and was scooping the debris of loose bark and dirt into a dustpan when Prudence insisted that I view her photographs of Paris.

"Let me put this away first," I said, "and then I'll have a look at them. Shall we have some wine?"

"Good idea. I've nearly finished this letter. I'll be ready soon."

Prudence licked a stamp and pressed it onto an envelope. She handed me a folder of photographs and perched herself on the armrest of my chair. Her hair brushed the side of my face as I looked at a photograph of Michael. The Irishman resembled a provincial Frenchman with a shock of black hair, a thin black moustache, and a red cravat tied around his neck. The oversized white cotton shirt was partially covered by a dark brown, open waistcoat that matched the russet-brown, hessian trousers.

"Who's this? This isn't Michael is it?"

Prudence laughed. "Yes, it's Michael. That's not how he usually dresses. It's fancy dress. We all dressed up for my birthday. Michael and I were dressed as Parisians. Michael doesn't really have a moustache. I penciled it on with mascara. But he can speak French. He used to live in France. I don't have a photo of myself because I was too busy taking everyone else's photo. I wore a white beret. This is Jon and Stefan from England, and here's Andre and his partner Marie Claire," she said, pointing at a photograph of a group standing underneath a statue. The top of the statue was cut off, leaving me to wonder who it was. "They live in Paris. This is a good photo." She turned the pages of the folder back and forth, sometimes two pages ahead, and then four pages back. I found it rather annoying. "There's Rosie—she's from Milan—and Gilbert and Mario and that's Professor Zollo. I think you've spoken to him on the phone. Remember? He was my lecturer years ago. He was in Paris, so I invited him to my birthday dinner. Look at his hair; it's almost all white now. Professor Zollo remembered you and sends his regards. It was wonderful, papa. The restaurant played Edith Piaf songs, and we dined on escargot and lapin. Oh look, here's a photo of Michael and me. I forgot about this one. I can't remember who took it. Probably Gilbert."

We discussed the exquisite cuisine of Europe and the culinary flavors of snails and rabbits. I thought it unusual that Australians rarely ate rabbit. All over the Australian countryside rabbits ravaged and eroded farmlands in massive numbers. Farmers berated their presence and often took to shooting the pest, disposing of their carcasses. I saw them only as food, but this did not appear to be the Australian way. In Australia, rabbit hunting was not a game sport; instead, it was pest control.

I held the photograph of Prudence and Michael and examined it fastidiously and scrupulously, noting the expression on their faces and the closeness of their bodies. They were laughing: their fresh faces glowing with liveliness and happiness. Michael's body leaned into hers, his left arm around her back and his right arm across her chest, forming a complete circle. Her right arm clasped his waist, and her left hand was placed on top of Michael's hands. They were one. I could not discern whether the union was a result of the wine and the occasion, or whether they were a loving couple with a history of intimacy between them. Prudence's black, sheer lace jacket was provocative and sexy. Her white beret tilted to one side, and her red curls fell over her shoulder. It was the passionate, sultry attire of a romantic evening. I surreptitiously and carefully inserted the photograph into my deep trouser pocket. I did not want Oswald or Fabian to see it. It was a picture of intimacy that made me decidedly uncomfortable.

# THE GRADUATE

Prudence loved the cinema. It was not unusual for her to see two movies in succession. Nor was it unusual for her to see the same movie several times, or to go alone. Mostly she went to the cinema or drive-in with a group of friends. To cater for this popular pastime, cinemas and drive-ins seemed to be sprouting all over the city and suburbs. The Star Line Elizabeth drive-in was the most popular, but it was such a long way from our suburb that to get to it seemed more like an event than an outing. Typically, a car full of her friends would go to the Mainline Gepps Cross drive-in which was closer and also had seating for walk-in patrons. I liked the informality of drive-ins, but Prudence preferred to dress in formal clothes to attend the cinema. I would only dress up for the cinema if Brigitte Bardot, Sophia Loren, or Gina Lollobrigida, were starring in the movie: my favorite actresses of all time.

Two weeks after Prudence's return from Paris, she went to the afternoon session of *The Graduate* at a city cinema with Oswald, Cyril, Darren, Fabian, and Polly. It was an odd ensemble of friends, and I was surprised that Fabian had joined them. He was a prominent businessman, an agent to celebrities, and had little in common with my daughter's younger friends, none of whom were potentially successful artists. Polly was a part-time bar maid with aspirations to be a singer, but had yet to land a gig. Cyril was an unsuccessful musician, uninterested in pursuing a life on the road, so he lectured music at the local university. Darren had yet to find his niche, and Oswald was a farmer. They were hardly the type of people that Fabian would want to promote. I did not ask Fabian for the circumstances that led to this gathering. I merely glanced at him quizzically. He sensed this and raised his eyebrows with a smile.

After the cinema, the group returned to my house for a light supper. As they entered the living room, Polly greeted me with a kiss on the left cheek. The men shook my hand. Prudence hung her mother's black overcoat on a brass hook in the hallway.

They made themselves comfortable on the settees, the ottoman, or on the carpet in an eclectic splash of color. The universally popular colors of their apparel were red, white, and blue, representing what appeared to be an American theme. Polly's long-sleeved red T-shirt had an American eagle holding a fluttering flag with the words *Politics is in the streets* encircling the illustration. A crocheted, white cardigan hung loosely over her shoulders, barely keeping her warm in the chill of the late winter evening. Cyril and Darren resembled identical twins with blue hipster corduroy jeans and thick, maroon shirts. Cyril's attire was the brighter of the two, the tones being crisp and clear, whereas Darren's clothes took on dusty, muted tones. They both wore white T-shirts underneath their shirts. Both had exactly three top buttons undone. Fabian wore a tailored navy Bill Blass blazer with navy trousers, and Prudence was elegant in a navy, red, and white knitted jumper with a Yale University logo. Her red leather trousers and matching boots were stylishly expensive, contrasting with Oswald's practical khaki pants and shirt. He also wore a khaki-knitted, sleeveless vest for warmth, which he nervously tugged at as if to lengthen it.

I opened two bottles of Italian red wine, and Oswald collected a tray of glasses. Fabian stoked the firewood in the grate, and we settled into an evening of wine and antipasto. The aromas of bread, olives, cheese, anchovies, prosciutto, garlic salami, dried tomatoes, artichokes hearts, and chili-marinated octopus blended together with wine, fire, and the body scents of people in close proximity. It was heady and inviting.

"What did you think of *The Graduate*? I haven't seen it, but the newspaper critic said it was good. I quite like the songs of Simon and Garfunkel," I said, as I motioned for people to help themselves to food and wine.

"Cloyingly sweet," answered Cyril. "Fancy having *Sounds of Silence* in a seduction scene. Wrong, wrong, wrong! They should've had something more sexual, more overt." He waved his arms in the air and his silver bracelet shone in the firelight.

"Like Dylan's *I Want You*—'*I want you, yeah, I want you so bad'* it goes, with a great riff to it." Darren tapped the beat on his leg.

"Or, *The Time's They are A-changin*. That song says so much more about the film, you know, the changing sexual taboos, women's liberation, and free-expression, and all that stuff," Polly added. She wasn't sure where to put the olive stones. I placed a dark brown Bakelite dish in front of her.

"It was moral suicide, Polly," said Oswald. "Ben didn't have the moral or intellectual sense to realize that he was being exploited."

"Mrs. Robinson was neurotic. She was really just a neurotic seductress," explained Prudence. She sat close to Cyril, picking her loose, red hairs from his maroon shirt.

"No, she wasn't. It was about her being young again by having an affair with a student. It's about true liberation," said Polly sipping from her glass. "Can we smoke in here, Leon?"

"There's the veranda for that," said Prudence before I could answer. "What were you saying? Oh, yes—well no, the movie's more about alienation and the problems people have in their twenties and thirties. The main character, Ben, isn't a young boy; he's an adult. He's twenty-one."

"Yeah, and middle class," said Oswald, "but he doesn't understand adult rules. They don't make sense to him. That's why *Sounds of Silence* is the soundtrack. It mirrors his feelings of emptiness and alienation." Oswald placed chunks of cheese on two slices of bread.

"Too unreal," uttered Polly. "The best bit was the hotel scene where they have sex. Ben just does it to defend Mrs. Robinson's accusation that he's a virgin. I liked that bit." Polly sat on the floor next to Fabian's chair and fidgeted frequently in an effort to be comfortable. She never appeared to settle in one position for more than two minutes; it was vexing to watch her. Nevertheless, she caught my gaze often for her beauty bewitched me. It was celestial but common, saintly but sexual, and seraphic but heathenish.

"But it's empty and meaningless sex," said my daughter, "shown by the confusing montages. The best piece of cinematography was the reflection scene when Mrs. Robinson invited Ben upstairs, and she begins to undress. Her nudity is reflected in the glass of her daughter's picture, remember? It reflects their relationships: that of Ben with both the mother and her daughter Elaine." She placed an anchovy on her tongue and tilted her head back to swallow it. As she did so, Cyril played with her hair, grabbing it in his hands to form a large, bushy ponytail. Seeing her search for a napkin to wipe her oily fingers, he grabbed her right hand and licked her fingers clean, kissing her palm and sucking noisily against her skin. Prudence laughed as she leaned closer to his muscled body.

"Yes, I think the only genuine feeling of love or attraction Ben has in the entire movie is when he's with Elaine after the strip joint, you know, when he comforts her and then talks about his concern for his future," Oswald postulated.

"I think you're right there, Ossie," agreed Prudence, looking away from Cyril momentarily to answer Oswald.

Polly added, "Yeah, Elaine has true love for Ben, but she almost marries Carl. Silly ending, I reckon. To be a really powerful liberationist film, it should've had more sex in it. What's this green thing, Leon?" I whispered to Polly that "the green thing" was an artichoke heart, and I rose to make more antipasto. She grabbed my cotton trousers near the calf and asked, "Artichoke? What the hell is that?" I explained that it was a vegetable.

"But the film was made by a man, Polly," explained Cyril. "It's not a woman's lib film. It's made by a man with a man as the main character, for Pete's sake. It's not about Mrs. Robinson. What's her first name anyway? Mrs. Robinson is rejected because Ben is tired of her, tired of fucking her. He'd rather fuck her virginal daughter, Elaine. Get real, Polly!" Turning to Darren, he said, "You were going to say something, Darren?"

"Yeah, you're right," said Darren. "And fucking the mother who represents parenthood is Ben's way of saying fuck adulthood, fuck the parent's image of life, fuck the establishment, man."

"I liked the scuba scene. It was funny and bizarre," said Oswald highlighting the comic elements in the movie.

I returned with a full platter of antipasto and placed it in the center of the coffee table. Polly's artichoke heart was at the side of her plate, half-eaten. She looked at me and wrinkled her nose.

"I agree. It's basically just a romantic comedy," confirmed Prudence. "And in the end, Ben gets the woman that his parents wanted him to have. Remember, in the earlier scenes, his parents—and Mr. Robinson—were matchmaking Ben with Elaine? So, you see, Ben's outcome wasn't different from his parent's expectations. What he wanted and what they wanted were the same. He's not displeasing his parents. The only one who doesn't get what she wants is Mrs. Robinson, of course. She gets nothing in the end."

"You're right, I suppose," said Cyril. "But, hey, it's just a movie, and in the end it tries to make statements about contemporary views and stereotypes about sex and relationships, like you're not supposed to fuck your mum's best friend, and you're not supposed to fuck a married woman. In a sense, it does bring these issues out in the open, on film, and that's a good thing. Except that it tells us what not to do, and I don't like that. I like the fact that the movie openly discusses taboos. These issues have to be discussed more often in the public media. Oldies— no offense papa Leon—think that these behaviors are deviant, but they're not. The oldies—again, no offense Leon—think that a person who likes both sexes is perverse. We've got to break down those attitudes. They've got to be seen as just different, but acceptable, ways of living. Like there should be films about civil rights, and gay liberation, and other sexual taboos. Isn't that so, Darren?"

Darren nodded. Prudence finished her glass of wine and refilled it. Oswald took the bottle from her and topped up everyone's depleted glasses. "But we wouldn't want movies to condone permissive sex or sex without precautions, like the pill or condoms," Prudence said. "There wasn't any mention in the film of catching sexually transmitted diseases, although I think that if the main character was a woman there'd be an outcry about pregnancy and promiscuity, so in a way the movie condones Ben's actions."

"But his actions weren't wrong," said Cyril. "They were experimental and stupid because he wasn't in control, but they weren't wrong. Like a man having sex with another man isn't wrong. It's just different; it's a sexual preference, Prudey."

I avoided looking at my daughter, pretending instead to read the newspaper on my lap.

"I'm not saying it is wrong, Cyril. I don't care who you have sex with, male or female, if you take precautions and if you're aware of your actions, and not just having sex for the sake of it. I don't want you getting syphilis and die an unearthly death. Sex is about being intimate with someone you care for. Wasn't that another message of the movie too?" Prudence rubbed her hand along Cyril's sleeve. He seized it playfully, pretending to wrestle with her.

Polly intervened. "There's nothing wrong with sex for the sake of it either. There's nothing wrong with free love, love-ins, one-night stands, men-hopping, call it whatever you want. That's what Germaine Greer says, anyway. I read it in one of her articles."

Prudence pushed Cyril away and placed a hand on his thigh as she answered Polly. "But what would you do if you got syphilis and transmitted it to other people? That's what I'm talking about," she said, cutting the air with her beautiful hands. "Or what if you got pregnant by a person you didn't know. I mean, if you didn't even know the person's first name. What then? That's all I'm asking. And what's more, would you want a syphilitic child? Think about that. Think about the consequences of your actions, Polly." Prudence was calm but firm. The reflection of the fire danced in her green eyes, revealing her scorching, arrogant pride. It was not a look of self-effacing timidity. Oswald, sitting opposite her, nodded in support of her argument.

"Jesus, Prudey," said Cyril, his hands gesticulating wildly as he spoke. "You're a real prick downer. I don't think about diseases when I'm fucking someone. Who the hell does syphilis affect anyway? I've never heard of anyone actually getting it.

It's like people saying to be careful crossing the street because you'll be run over by a bus. Who the hell does that happen to? No one I know. Lighten up, Prudey." Cyril and Prudence were vying for center stage, competing with dramatic gestures, like two Italian actors.

"I'm not saying don't have sex with anyone. I'm just saying do it with a dick protector."

I had not heard Prudence talk this way before. My palms were sweating and the black print of the newspaper stained my hands. I tried even harder to ignore the conversation.

"That's not what you're thinking, Prue," said Darren rubbing against Cyril. "You're thinking that you don't want Cyril fucking men or Polly fucking women. You don't like the idea of Cyril and me fucking each other. You don't like us, Prue. You don't like any man," he said. Cyril sat between Prudence and Darren, sharing their attention.

Prudence didn't respond and Polly changed the focus of the dispute. "Well I liked Dustin Hoffman. He was naive and cute, wasn't he, and funny?"

"Apparently Robert Redford was auditioned for the part, but he refused it," said Cyril, also diffusing Darren's aspersions. "That would've been truer to the book. The book's description of Ben is of a tall, blond all-American boy, not a short geek like Hoffman." He was less animated, dowsing the argumentative fire of Prudence and Darren with cold calmness, like a tap of running water, turning hot and cold.

"But Hoffman can act though," said Polly, in the actor's defense. "Hey, you guys, I bet you've seen Brigitte Bardot in her hot scenes. Isn't she a babe? I wished I looked like her."

Cyril smirked, "She's so sexy, especially in her little swimming costume. Frank, the head music lecturer at university, sings Harry Belafonte's song *Zombie Jamboree* all the time because it mentions her. It goes something like this, '*I'm going to talk to Miss Brigitte Bardot and tell Miss Bardot to take it slow; all the men think they're Casanova when they see that she's bare foot all over!*' And there's a line about her at least wearing earrings part of the time. She's a hot honey! Her movie *Masculine,*

*Feminine* is supposed to be good too; I think it's about sex and politics—something to do with children of Marx and Coca Cola. It might come to Australia next year."

Darren yawned. Cyril said, "Hey guys, we'd better split. It's getting late and I've got lectures to prepare. Come on Darren; let's go home. Are you coming too, Polly?"

Fabian hadn't said a word all evening. He had been watching Prudence. His quiet demeanor masked his feelings, making it difficult for me to predict his intentions. Was there a fiery heart smoldering? I secretly hoped so.

"Fabian, are you going now? Can I cadge a lift home with you?" asked Polly. She retrieved pink lipstick from her cardigan pocket and smeared it on her pouting lips.

Fabian looked startled by the request, and responded with a stammer, "Sh—sh—sh—sure. Yeah, sure. I can take you home. Where do you live?" He looked at Prudence and she shrugged her shoulders ever so slightly, but enough for Fabian to detect. He was used to her nuances and movements, as if they had a secret sign language between them.

"It's two streets from your place. I'd appreciate a lift because it's out of Cyril's way to drive me home. Ossie, are you driving home tonight?" Suddenly shivering, Polly added, "It's getting cold, isn't it? I didn't bring a jacket."

"I was going to stay with Fabian. I usually stay at his place if I'm in town. It's close to Prue and he's got a spare room. Fabian, is it still okay with you?" Oswald appeared flushed from the wine, the heat of the room, and perhaps from embarrassment.

Fabian couldn't have been more relieved. "Absolutely," he said emphatically. "Ossie, follow us in your car. It's not much out of our way, so we'll drop Polly home, and then we'll go to my place."

"Thanks, mate," said Oswald. He stirred the group to action. There were offers to help clean up, but Prudence dismissed their polite gestures. Farewells were said, kisses were freely bestowed, and slaps on the back replaced formal handshakes.

"Thanks for the food, Leon," said Polly. "I liked most of it, except the anchovies and the artichoke hearts. It's just that I haven't eaten them before," she said apologetically.

"That's fine, Polly. I'm glad you tried them. I'll put more cheese on the plate next time."

"And more ham, but less octopus," added Cyril.

"The prosciutto, you mean?" I corrected.

"Yeah, that." Cyril flashed a smile, and his chipped tooth looked strangely appealing.

I withdrew to the kitchen, immersing myself in domesticity while Prudence walked to the front door with her friends. Everyone appeared to be content with the homing arrangements, except Polly. Polly had wanted more from Fabian, it seemed to me, and he wasn't obliging her in any way.

# COMMISSIONER'S COMMENTARY

By the time I interrogated Polly, I had already questioned several suspects. Fabian Rossi was sensible and sane. He deliberated over his answers, and I was impressed with his perceptive, organized mind, and his professionalism. If he weren't Italian, he would've reminded me very much of myself when I was in my forties. Naturally, I asked him whether he killed Prudence. It was a standard question, but he was one of three known suspects to have last seen her, other than her father and Michael McShane. The question did not disturb him and he responded carefully, so as not to leave out any detail. In each interrogation of him, of which there were four or five, he never deviated from his statement.

Prudence had visited him briefly, before picking up Michael from the hotel and driving him to the airport. I presented Fabian with this hypothesis: he met her after she left the airport, they had an argument, and he killed her in a passionate rage. He answered meticulously and without flinching. Throughout the interrogation, I found him to be credible, analytical, and a reasonable judge of character. He was also diplomatic and tactful. I did note his ambitious tendencies, quiet confidence, and his steadfast drive for power, status, and success with a definite desire for material possessions. However, there seemed to be nothing excessive or obsessive in his approach. Subsequently, a search warrant of his home revealed nothing. My mother knew of Fabian Rossi and she said if he were found to be the murderer, she'd eat two hats.

Oswald Danes had also been interrogated a number of times. Although he was in his forties, he reminded me of an excitable youngster: nervous, fidgety, and eager to please. He would answer, rephrase his response, and then clarify it, not so much for my benefit, but to get things right in his own mind. When asked about the marriage rejection, he appeared philosophical and resigned to his fate. He had half expected it, he said. In fact, he said his relationship with Prudence was like a big brother to a little sister, but he was actually a couple of years younger than her. Friendship was as important as love, if not more, in his way of thinking. He admitted a tendency to hide his feelings out of shyness and insecurity. There wasn't much in his demeanor to warrant overt attention; he came across as being honest to a fault, and not in the least driven by power and wealth. I'd describe him as sincere, conscientious, responsible, reliable, and practical. Others had used the word "meek," but I preferred the phrase "gentle giant." Of course, this type of character has been known to commit murder, so he remained a suspect along with everyone else until the crime was solved. The squad was laying bets on who killed Prudence, but Oswald wasn't the favorite. However, as one of my officers said, the race had not been run yet. My mother reminded me to watch out for the quiet ones.

Michael McShane was still in Sydney at the time, although he was aware of Prudence's demise through Fabian and the media. I requested that he travel to Adelaide to assist with our investigations and he agreed to cooperate. In the meantime, my squad interviewed hotel staff, searched the room that he occupied, and investigated theories pertaining to Michael and how he may have committed the atrocity before his flight. Everything turned out negative, no matter how preposterous or inventive our theories were. My mother said, "Poetry is the way to true love."

Polly Smith was an unusual character. I'm not sure that she was capable of sadness, as she shrugged off Prudence's death as "one of those things." Seeing my amazement, she explained her theory of life, in a rather round-about way, excessively and endlessly. At one point, I left the room and on my return some twenty minutes later, she was still talking to my police officers. They raised their eyes to heaven and were visibly relieved to see me. To put them out of their misery, I changed the flow of questioning. Everything people had said about Polly was true.

She was an incessant talker, with the "gift of the gab" as I'd never witnessed before. Polly herself, when questioned, said it was because she was nervous at the thought of meeting people and felt ill at ease in a crowd. To combat her anxiety, she talked.

Her theory on Prudence's murder was that it was a copycat case, an imitation of the Charles Manson carnage, six weeks earlier. It was in all the newspapers, and was such a heinous crime that she believed it had attracted the attention of demented souls. I thought it highly unlikely. Nonetheless, my officers and I listened to her hypothesis because it was obvious that she had familiarized herself with the events in Beverly Hills and the home of actress Sharon Tate and director Roman Polanski. On August 9, 1969, eight-month pregnant Tate was murdered. Two bodies were found on the lawn of Polanski's mansion: a man battered about the head with savage puncture wounds to his body and a young woman with multiple stab wounds. A male body was found slumped in a car in the driveway. Tate was dead on the couch inside, smeared with blood and with a rope around her neck that extended over a rafter in the ceiling. At the other end of the rope was a man, also saturated with blood. Scrawled in blood on the front door was the word: PIG. The current suspect was Charles Manson, whom police believed masterminded the murder although he was not present at the scene. Manson, a composer and musician, leader of a hippie commune, was reportedly enraged over the rejection of his plan to finance a musical film with someone connected to Polanski. Polly equated Cyril Silverman with Charles Manson. She was of the opinion that Cyril was jealous of Prudence's fame and fortune and had savagely brutalized her in a drug-induced, Manson-influenced rage. It was an interesting supposition. My mother said drugs were an unnecessary evil. My conclusion was that Polly danced to a different drum.

# PHILIP BROWNLEY

Almost a year after Prudence's encounter with the heckling journalist, he again came face to face with my daughter. Fabian arranged for him to interview Prudence, and she preferred the location to be our living room. It was September, two days before my 73rd birthday and three weeks after a raucous student protest at the University of Queensland. Students were objecting to newly-introduced government regulations requiring groups holding public meetings in the city to apply for a permit. By all accounts, 3,500 university students held their own public meeting, without a permit, that resulted in a brutal clash with police. Students all over the world were voicing their anger with government restrictions to free speech; Australian students were no exception.

As the heckler, Philip, stood on our welcoming mat, he adjusted his tie and brushed the lint from his immaculate, dark suit. His light brown hair was smoothly parted on the left and combed across his forehead. Large ears were visible below razor-thin strands of hair that formed a neat, straight line from the sides to the back of his head. The aroma of after-shave wafted about him. He held, in manicured hands, a notepad, pen, and tape-recorder. His well-rounded vowels, as he introduced himself, created a respectable impression of an uptight, self-conscious man. Wavering in his handshake, he exuded nervousness and apprehension.

Prudence and Philip sat on opposite sides of the settee in the living room. The porcelain lamp reflected a subdued aura. Philip was stiffly formal with knees together, and his upper body turned toward Prudence. She leaned against the settee's armrest, completely facing him. She was relaxed in a short-sleeved, knitted, royal-blue sweater, orange cotton trousers, and navy plim-solls. The geometric patterns on her sweater distorted with the elevation of each breath. I inconspicuously laid tea and biscuits on the table adjacent the settee, and settled in my armchair with a book and newspaper.

"It's been a long time since I've seen you, Philip. How are you?" Prudence began the conversation.

"I'm working as a feature writer with *The Advertiser* now," he smiled broadly. His straight, white teeth had no gaps, no flaws, and no stains; they were perfect in every way.

"Congratulations, Philip. Well done! So, this interview is for *The Advertiser*, is it?"

"Yes, Professor Bari. We'll have a large feature on you, with photographs, at the end of October. We have some in our files. Nice ones, too. I'll just ask questions and take notes. I'll put the tape-recorder on too, if you don't mind. If I may be so bold, professor, I'd like to explore something of your intellectual character, and the fact that you were raised by a sole parent, in light of new studies on the effects on children of a broken home. I'm so nervous, and I haven't eaten or slept for a whole day. I'm sorry. Let me think about the question." The tape-recorder clicked on. "Oh yes, I wonder whether you've read the American domestic studies on one parent families?"

"No, I haven't. Social science and domestic policy aren't my areas of expertise. Can you outline them for me?"

"Sure. I came across these studies recently, and I was quite intrigued by them. I thought I'd raise the issues with you since you don't come from a 'normal' home, so to speak, and yet you've become rich and famous. Lots of academic and social science researchers in America have demonstrated that the way to success is through the traditional family model, that is, complete school, get a job, get married, have children—all in that order. They say that children growing up in a stable, two-parent family have the best prospects for achieving success as adults. They say children of poor, migrant, or divorced parents are likely, themselves, to be poor and unsuccessful. With the new morality and the likeli-hood that women these days are having children out of wedlock, the number of poor children and families may increase. In 1950, the rate of divorce was lower amongst high-income groups, and by 1960 there was a convergence of rates amongst all socio-economic groups. I raise it because of your situation. Your parents weren't divorced, I know, but your situation may be described as a broken home. In America, in 1960, seventy-five percent more children lost a parent through divorce than through death. The researchers said that divorce appears to result in the reduction of children's educational accomplishments. It weakens their psychological and physical health, and it pre-disposes them to early sexual relationships and higher levels of marital instability. It also raises the probability that they'll never marry, especially boys."

"Philip, I can understand what you're saying, but I'm not sure how this relates to me. What's the question?" Her green eyes looked directly at him.

"Well, it's like this. These divorce statistics led me to thinking about you. Only one parent raised you and, in a way, the situation is similar to a divorce. And your father's an immigrant. Yet you seemed to have overcome the odds to achieve success, although you aren't married, so I guess that's a failure. There seems to be similarities and differences in your case. I was wondering how you viewed the studies."

"True, my dad is not from this country, and he raised me without a mother and so, statistically, I guess I shouldn't have done as well as I have. Is that what you're saying, Philip?"

"Yes, exactly! Children raised in a two-parent home are more likely to marry. Those that experience a disruption in their parent's marriage tend to marry or cohabit at earlier stages, or never marry. Maybe you haven't married because you're from a one-parent family? Do you think so?"

"Philip, I don't know, but I think it's just a coincidence. I haven't married for a number of reasons, but I don't think my father not marrying again is a factor. He raised me like a mother and a father would. I haven't really thought about all of this, to tell you the truth. It's actually never occurred to me."

"It was just something I was interested in," Philip said sheepishly. "Of course, if young people are having children out of wedlock, I think more researchers are going to be interested in the social impacts of this type of situation."

"But the introduction of the contraceptive pill may reduce the number of children born out of wedlock. We have to consider that too. Perhaps the pill will result in planned families where children have the unconditional love and support of their parents."

"Maybe, but don't you think you've missed out on a lot by never having a mother, professor, or never marrying, or never having children of your own?"

"Please, call me Prudence. Again, I haven't really thought about it. But, you know, you don't miss what you don't have. I don't know any different because I've never had a mother. And I've never compared myself to my friends. I didn't feel, or consider myself to be, inferior to anyone else, nor superior for that matter, but I definitely didn't consider my thoughts and ideas to be inconsequential or different from the norm. I think the overriding factor in all of this, of finding inner truth and dignity, is confidence. My confidence comes from my father who told me every day that I was intelligent. Confidence is the greatest gift that any parent can give a child. Perhaps the answer may be that if one parent gives a child the gift of confidence then it's better than not getting it from two parents."

"What about two parents giving a child the gift of confidence? You can't do better than that, surely?"

"In a perfect world, but I certainly can't complain about the gifts that my father gave me."

"But just imagine how much more you would have achieved, professor. Did you know that the vast majority of children who live with a single parent are in households in the bottom twenty percent of earnings? And children living with a single mother are six times more likely to live in poverty than are children with two parents? Let's be honest. With the feminist agenda, the gay lobby, and the destruction of family values in our society, we've ended up in a right mess. We've ended up with escalating youth crime, adolescent suicide, substance abuse, and illiteracy—all consistent with the devaluation of the nuclear family and the place of the father. The change of attitudes has blown the nuclear family to bits. It's quite the opposite of your 'planned family' scenario. I think science has a lot to answer for—what with the pill, abortions, and drugs—not to mention the atomic bomb and the nightmare of a nuclear war."

I thought Brownley was agitated in mind, yet his body remained stiffly formal. I was deeply fascinated in where he was headed with this interview, but I tried not to look too interested.

"I think, in my case," Prudence answered, "my father worked very hard at improving his employment opportunities. He studied English diligently every day, studied to be a teacher, and went on to be a university lecturer in mathematics. It was really his hard work that made my accomplishments easy. He provided me with the best education he could afford, and he also educated me himself on a range of subjects and social values. I think I was very lucky. Maybe in my case the law of averages played a large part? Perhaps a good father can overcome all other negative factors."

"Perhaps luck, but you ignored my comment on science," Philip said with a smile. "And do you think there is such a thing as a perfect mind?"

Prudence returned the smile. "Science has given society a lot of positive advances. Films like Kubrick's *Dr. Strangelove* have made people suspicious of science. The advent of the atomic bomb has also made people aware of the potential dangers of science. However, when you look at scientific history, there are many life-saving discoveries that we should be proud of, particularly in the field of medicine. As for me, I've never fancied that my mind is more perfect than anyone else's. On the contrary, I wish I had more creativity or imagination, and a more perfect memory. Other people have these abilities to a far greater extent than I do. So what qualities make a perfect mind? Who knows, Philip? I don't. My father certainly had enormous ambitions for me. I think he expected that I'd have a spectacularly successful life. Perhaps I've achieved it. I'm not sure that I've managed to truly please my father."

She spoke as if I was an invisible or an insignificant presence in the room. On the contrary, it was the inverse. I had high expectations of Prudence, but she had surpassed all of them. Had I not told her often?

"But you are at the top of your career. You're a brilliant woman," Philip said.

"Some people have achieved success at an earlier age than I did. Some achieved more success than I ever could. I look at people who are at the top of their field and think the difference between them and other people is not that they are gifted. It's not that they are talented. That's partially a factor maybe, but I believe that it's more about focus. You have to want something and not look back and not look sideways: just straight-ahead—no variance, no deviance—just straight-ahead. You have to devote your entire life to being focused on achieving a goal. I'm not sure that I've been that devoted and dedicated to my goal, to any goal. I think it just happened. Perhaps, in my case, it was a combination of preparation, education, confidence, and luck that has led me to this point."

I did not agree with Prudence that talent and a given gift were only partially involved in the recipe for success. Prudence had a talent, and all the beauty and grace to achieve success, but she had more than that. In my mind, she had will and the ability to be flexible and adaptable. But, above all, she had passion: a passion for mathematics, for work, for living. Could it be that I was too focused on a goal for Prudence's success and fame? It couldn't be so, because I didn't predict the consequences. The consequences happened entirely independently of my assistance. I never, in all my dreams, imagined that she would be so incredibly gifted. I did not plan the consequences. Nor I did not plan the destination, only the journey. Perhaps her success was pre-determined by God, or by divine providence.

Philip had gradually unstiffened. They talked for a considerable period of time about science and philosophy. It startled Philip when Prudence asked the inevitable question.

"Philip, tell me, why were you heckling me on the night of the lecture last year? What brought that about?" She was interested but non-committal, curious but non-judgmental.

"I, well, I, I had heard so much about you. Different things: some good, some bad. Some people were saying things about your sexuality. I was silly enough to believe them. I don't know why. I was going through some relationship troubles and financial problems, and alcoholism too."

"What sort of things were you hearing? Were they about me being masculine or androgynous?" Philip had aroused Prudence's curiosity.

"Well, yes, to tell you the truth. I heard a scientist talking about genes. I interviewed him actually. He talked about how fetuses with XY sex chromosomes develop into boys and those with XX sex chromosomes develop into girls. He was saying that, if a fetus is not sensitive to androgens, such as testosterone, then XY fetuses develop into girls and not boys. He was speculating it happened to you: that you had XY chromosomes, male chromosomes, but that you developed into a woman." The tape-recorder clicked off and Philip flipped the tape and re-inserted it.

"That's interesting. Tell me more," she smiled.

"Well, he said that if that happens, a person looks like a woman; she has breasts and she doesn't have a penis or excessive hair or anything like that, but she may look a bit manly."

"Really?"

"Well you've got to admit that you have strong masculine shoulders. You've got muscles and you're fit. And you don't have a big butt like most women have. Bottom, I mean. Sorry professor for being so rude." He covered his mouth with his hand as if to prevent further embarrassment.

Prudence laughed. "Big butt! So I don't have a big butt! That's good. Anything else?"

"He said, the scientist said, that outwardly you're female, but you might have smaller breasts than most women, have a high incidence of osteoporosis and other bone diseases, you might not menstruate, and therefore you might not be able to conceive children. That's why you don't have children. That's what he said. He said, basically, that you are really a man. He thinks that you have lots of men friends because you're actually a homosexual: a male homosexual inside a woman's body."

"But don't some people think that I'm a radical, lesbian feminist too?"

"Well yes, but that's because they think that you're a woman who hasn't married. Some think you see lots of men because you're hiding the fact that you're a lesbian. That's one theory. But the scientist doesn't think that. His theory is that you've got male chromosomes and that you like men, and you're gay. But you've got a vagina and stuff; you look like a woman but you're really a man. You've got the mind of a man. Your brain is like a man's brain. That's why you're good at mathematics and science. That's why the scientist thinks you're not really a woman and therefore not a lesbian. Do you see what I mean? He says if you are a man that likes women, you are therefore not a lesbian. But, if you are a man that likes men, then you are homosexual. He even said that it would be interesting doing psychological tests on you to assess your personality. He thinks it might prove that you have a man's brain. That's what he said."

I couldn't believe my ears. I was strongly tempted to say something, but dared not. My heart was beating arhythmically and rapidly from embarrassment, shame, confusion, and anger. Prudence, on the other hand, was laughing heartily. She thought it highly amusing. Philip joined in her laughter.

"He thinks I'm a man? Oh, how silly!" she laughed.

"See how silly it is? At the time, I believed it. I got myself so worked up that I wanted to harm you in some way because I thought you were a weirdo. When I knew that you would be giving a public speech, I thought I would go there and harm you in some way. But, of course, I'm not a physically fit man and, if you were a man, I thought you'd overpower me. That's why I had the idea to attack you mentally. I thought I'd humiliate you by heckling at you when you spoke. I feel so stupid now, of course. I never realized that the security guards would be there. They gave me a hell of a fright. And then everyone was staring at me. It was embarrassing. I was so humiliated, which is strange really because I wanted you to be humiliated, but you just looked at me. Right at me. I'm so glad it's all over."

Prudence was still laughing. "Sorry Philip, I can't stop laughing at how ridiculous this is. I'm so glad you told me. And it's all so confusing. So, am I a lesbian, a gay man in a woman's body, androgynous, or am I just an ordinary person? You tell me. This scientist believes that I'm a man. Who is this scientist? What's his name? I want to see his work and his analysis. Who is this scientist?" She was leaning forward, expecting an answer.

"But professor, if his theory is true for women, could it be true for men? Like, could some men have XX sex chromosomes and still look male, but have the qualities of a woman? It couldn't be true, could it?"

"I don't know. I'm not a doctor. What's the scientist's name and I'll ask him?"

"I shouldn't have mentioned it. I can't tell you his name. He said that his work is experimental and that people wouldn't believe him yet. I'm not even allowed to write about it. He said that if anything is printed and his name is mentioned, he'd sue me, or kill me: one or the other. He said that he'd make his work known sometime in the future, in the next couple of years, maybe. You don't seem upset by it though."

"No, I think people shouldn't pay too much mind to the opinions of others, or to theories. Theories are just that: only theories. It's not fact, at least not yet, and besides, you become toughened to adverse comments when you're in the public eye all the time. I try not to let negativity or jealousies detract me from my own worth, or my own truth."

"Your own truth? Isn't that the problem today? We're all trying to find our own truth, but no one knows exactly what we're looking for. Have you found it, professor?"

"Let me tell you a story: a story that will show you how to find your own truth. I don't know where this story came from. Maybe it's from an Eastern religion in which there are many gods. In the beginning, the gods created the universe. They began with the stars, the sun, and the moon. Then they made the seas, the mountains, the plants, and the clouds. On the last day, they created Truth. The gods wanted to hide Truth so that humans could have an adventure seeking it. One god suggested that they hide Truth on top of the highest mountain. Another wanted to hide it on the farthest star. Another god suggested the darkest and deepest abyss in the Earth, and yet another suggested putting it on the dark side of the moon. Eventually the wisest god said, 'We will hide Truth inside the very heart of every human being. They will look for it all over the universe without knowing that it is inside their own body.' We should listen to our hearts and have inner dialogue with our innermost beings. Then we'd find our own truth."

"It's a nice story, professor, but when I listen to myself, all I hear is a babble of mixed messages, contradictory comments, and confusing chatter. How do we know that the message we hear is not a self-deceiving fantasy or a lot of crock? Tell me that." Philip laughed.

"We can never be a hundred percent certain, but it'll feel right. It's hard to explain, but you'll feel that you've been led to an understanding. You'll feel calm and re-assured. You'll get a clearer perspective of the predicament or problem, and your action will be precise and without hesitation." She leaned forward and looked at Philip quizzically to see if he understood.

"Well, I must admit that I've felt times like that. When I met my wife, Julie, I knew instantly that she was right for me. Yes, that felt right. I certainly didn't dither about proposing. I can see what you mean. I hadn't thought of it that way before." He looked pensively at the lamplight.

"You must have listened to yourself, to your own thoughts. You knew in your heart that it was right." She leaned back against the armrest.

"Yes, but so did everyone else. Everyone was telling me to marry Julie, especially our parents. Now they're telling me to have children. They all seem to know what I should be doing. Perhaps I'm not listening to myself because I'm so bombarded by other people's opinions that I've come to accept their views as my own. I can't tell the difference anymore." Philip looked at his silver watch. "Goodness, I'm sorry to take so long. I didn't realize the time. Just one quick question before I go. What is a beautiful theory? You talked of Plato's vision of the good, the true, and the beautiful notions of science in your lecture last year. I was just wondering if there was such a thing as a beautiful theory."

"A quick answer is that there is such a thing as a beautiful theory, in my opinion. A beautiful theory is a presumption of truth that is elegant, economical, and general. It must simplify and unify. It must—" The ringing of the telephone interrupted Prudence.

"I'll get that," I said as I lurched toward the telephone.

Philip took the opportunity to make a departure. "I must leave you to your work, professor. Thanks for the interview and the tea. I'm just glad that I've had a chance to speak with you. I feel so privileged." Philip clicked the tape recorder off. He gathered his writing paraphernalia and fastidiously straightened the pages of his notebook.

"Keep in touch, Philip. I'd be happy to talk to you again, anytime." I believe Prudence actually meant it.

Prudence walked Philip to the wrought iron gate and returned with the day's mail. She sat at the escritoire in the living room, deftly opening the mail with her exotic letter opener, a memento from a tour to Africa. The prowling lion intricately carved into the smooth, ebony wood, sliced through the envelopes with neat precision. Letters and invitations, bills and brochures; some were discarded, some were answered immediately, and the remainder were bundled together and fastened with a paper clip to discuss with Fabian.

# FABIAN ROSSI

Fabian arrived with a posy of roses, fresh from his garden. He had one of the most glorious rose gardens in all of Adelaide, tendered with an expert and loving hand. Clever color combinations were a feature of his yard, an average suburban block in an affluent part of the city. In one section, the black-leafed perennial Corydalis *flexuosa* was teamed with lime-colored feverfew, enhanced with tripods of the golden climbing hop, Humulus *lupulus* "Aureus." In another corner, resting under the curious fossil of the gingko maidenhair tree, was a kingfisher-blue ceramic pot. The gold leaves of a maple, providing shade to the area, coordinated harmoniously with blue benches. Another part of his garden was edged with Euphorbia *dulcis* "Chameleon." Its bronzed leaves, which turned burgundy in spring, were superb against the colors of the roses: apricot hybrids and fragile coconut-ices. Separated from other roses, was his red collection: hues of cerise, blush, scarlet, crimson, cardinal, and magenta. Above all, his obsession was to cultivate the darkest, blackest rose of them all.

Fabian stooped in front of the dresser that held my collection of vases. He selected a low crystal vase for an elegant exhibition. Trimming the leaves of each cut rose artistically, and with an eye for presentation, he positioned each flower to complement the one next to it. He looked at the vase from every angle before adding water and placing it in the middle of the kitchen table. As he tidied the debris and wiped the kitchen sink, Prudence collected the papers for their discussion.

Fabian was organized, reliable, and astute. They developed a schedule of appointments that included travel to Europe for three months. Their thinking was on the same wavelength. I was certain they admired each other greatly.

Fabian was a handsome man, but I admit a bias toward the swarthy European countenance. Although not nearly as tall as Oswald, he was, nevertheless, a striking man of impeccable style, grooming, and manners. He rather reminded me of Dean Martin, my favorite singer: the thick, well-styled, short hair; the dark, well-groomed eyebrows; and the teeth as white as a row of Paspaley pearls. In Italy, Dean Martin was the image bachelors of my day aspired to: a carefree, martini-sipping, and nightclub-hopping ladies' man. I suspected that Fabian was equally as popular with the ladies, in a quieter way. It was rare for him to be seen with women except when he escorted celebrities and starlets to major functions. On these occasions, photographers would swoop to take a shot of his latest up-and-coming artiste. Fabian always looked debonair in these tabloid photographs, with never a hint of scandal, no matter how hard the press tried to conceive of one. He was, indeed, my idea of the perfect Italian man. He could sing too, although not as magnificently as Martin. My favorite Dean Martin songs were his chart-topping hits: *You Belong to Me* and *Memories are Made of This*. I would always finish the telephone calls when Prudence was overseas with *ritorna a me*—return to me—which was a line in a Dean Martin song. It was "our" song.

I cupped my hands around the rose-filled vase. Removing it from the kitchen table, I meandered around the house with it, looking for the perfect location to display the perennial beauty of the velvet and variegated petals. I settled on a diffused disposition in the living room, and as I placed the vase on a lace doily in the center of the mahogany table, a peachy petal landed upturned on the shiny surface.

Prudence had coerced Fabian into her bedroom to show him her new clothes. She never did this with Oswald. He would not understand her extravagant obsession with textiles. She was screaming with laughter as I entered her bedroom with a tray of tea and biscuits. Fabian's appearance startled me, and my grasp of the tray faltered. Prudence quickly removed it from my trembling hands and placed it in a safer location as I covered my face with my palms. They giggled as Fabian sashayed around the room in a yellow shawl draped around his shoulders and a matching leather clutch bag in his right hand.

"You should have seen him in my Pucci dress. He looked stunning in the wild pinks and purples," Prudence said. "And the pearl earrings with the navy dress; he looked just like Audrey Hepburn. Not really, papa, I'm just joking!"

"Not as svelte, though, such a pity," said Fabian as he removed the accessories, placing them on the pile on Prudence's bed. "I do love this jacket. It'd be great in Europe. It's so French," he said as he lifted a baby blue, satin jacket from the bed, holding it against his chest. "It matches my eyes." They both broke into fits of laughter.

We seated ourselves on vacant land, amid a sea of glamorous garments, tittering like juveniles in a capricious exhibition of unfettered emotions. It was a moment of serendipitous fun and merriment that was indelibly imprinted in my store of favorite memories.

# NEW YEAR 1968

I remember 1968 as being a tumultuous year. It began with heightened conflict in the Vietnam War. At Nui Dat, Viet Cong guerrillas continued their full-scale offensive in South Vietnam. Three Australian soldiers lost their lives.

Fabian and Prudence were in Europe and the United States for three months, and I fretted for them, particularly as they were visiting universities amid the most violent student demonstrations of the decade. The younger generation's spirit of inquiry and soul-searching begged them to question the decisions of their governments and of "The Establishment." A widespread social conscience began to develop. For some, guilt bred introspection. Others were hopeful that issues would be resolved and that truth would overcome hypocrisy and secrecy.

The Vietnam War was immensely unpopular in the United States, sparking student riots across the nation. However, there was more to the unrest than the Vietnam War. There was dissatisfaction and frustration with social and political inequality, as well as racial hatred fuelled by the assassination of Martin Luther King. Students barricading themselves in university offices and stoning the police were common occurrences. Protests weren't always violent. Hippies, concerned with love and peace, protested by "dropping acid" or dropping out of society and living in self-sufficient communes. Their "anti-everything" attitude led to anti-fashion, the trend to merge the clothes of the sexes together to create a uni-sex look. It became increasingly more difficult to distinguish men from women; they often looked the same to me.

My only solace when Prudence was in America, was that Fabian was with her. He had distinct and definite manly looks and qualities: strength, dependability, common sense, level-headedness, and a deep sense of responsibility. He would protect Prudence, not with violence and bravado, but with a firm hand, a vigilant eye, and a calming voice. Prudence, as always, telephoned me regularly, but I was not content until I had spoken to Fabian and heard his reassurance of my daughter's safety.

When they returned to Australia, I spoke to Fabian in his magnificent garden. I was pleased to notice that my asparagus was in a more advanced stage of growth than his, although his lettuces were deliciously leafy and insect-free. We compared notes on peas and agreed that it was not a good year for them. He was a tidy gardener, like me, and we both praised the therapy of gardening. Weeding was like meditation in its tranquil tediousness. However, whenever I visited his garden, and indeed, the garden of Franco, or of any other real gardener, I had an obsession to compare my labor with theirs. It provoked a feeling of self-justification, self-critique, and the compulsive desire for perfection. Obsessive comparison was the undoing of any therapy gained from the initial activity and, in many ways, I felt considerably lacking. Nevertheless, Fabian was most complimentary whenever he walked around my garden, being careful not to deflate my pride. In turn, I praised his gardening prowess.

"Your cousin Mario has done an excellent job while you've been away," I said as I eyed the perfectly straight edges of his manicured lawn.

"Yes he has, but there's still a lot of work to be done. A gardener's job is never done. Re-planting and re-designing. It's the obsession of us all, isn't it?"

"I was just thinking so. It's the beauty and the form that I'm constantly striving for. It eludes me most of the time. I talk to my plants, Fabian. I tell them to grow well, and to produce their finest color. I tell the vegetables to grow large and juicy, and I tell the flowers to bloom profusely. I talk to them, but mostly I just look at them in silence, thinking how wonderful nature is."

Fabian nodded and slapped me on the back. "Ah yes, me too. Luckily they don't answer back, hey?"

"I'm thankful that they don't tell Prudence what I say and think. I'm sure she thinks I'm getting too old and silly. I haven't thanked you for taking care of her while you were away. I'm glad she was safe with you. You did a fine job."

"You've thanked me a thousand times already! There really wasn't any danger in America. What you read in the newspapers happens in isolated parts in only a handful of cities, and it's a large country, like Australia. The Americans were wonderful to us and we had a very productive time there. Prue's got enough material to write a few books and to do a tour of Australia to promote science courses at universities. There was never any need to worry. You really do worry too much about her sometimes." He looked debonair in his navy trousers and tan, Italian-knit sweater. He was always well-attired, not succumbing to the psychedelic colored clothes of the younger generation. He had a style of his own. Placing his steady, firm hand over mine, he re-iterated, "There was never any need to worry. You'll get ulcers."

"Alas, I think I already have them, or perhaps I have indigestion." I held my free hand against my chest. "I had gastric reflux a lot when Prudence was away. It's gone now."

"Did you see a doctor?" He spoke with a comforting and compassionate voice.

I waved my arm in the air in a dismissive manner. "What do they know? They have you in hospital taking out parts of your body if you sneeze."

"You do exaggerate. When was the last time you had a check-up?"

"Check-up? What check-up? I'm fit and healthy. A small bout of gastric reflux won't harm me. There's nothing wrong with me except old age and feeble eyes."

"I'll make an appointment and take you to my doctor, Tony Barretto, a fine man. Just leave it to me. You must stop fretting about Prudence when she's away though. It does you no good." Again, he took my hand and patted it, as you would do to comfort a child. I did not take offence. It's what Italians do to show that they understand. It was our way of talking to each other. He was always the soul of generosity, forceful optimism, compassion, self-confidence, and social grace; I admired these virtues.

I knew Fabian through his Uncle Dino and Aunt Helena who were the first people I met when I moved into my new home in St. Peters. I'd been telling them of Prudence and her studies in Milan when they said that their nephew had just returned from a holiday in Italy. Fabian had heard a great deal about Prudence. When he completed his finance degree at university he approached me to ask whether he could be her agent. I had an instant attraction to him. Another favorable omen was his name because it was the same as my grandfather's. I attached great significance to this coincidence. The way I saw it, it was more than coincidence. It was destiny. Fabian was pre-destined to be with Prudence.

"I know I shouldn't have fretted. You always have her best interests in mind. I knew she would be safe with you. Did she see Michael in England?"

"Yes, she did. We all had dinner together one night. She enjoyed it, I think. He's very intellectual and creative. I'm more into finance and business, so I couldn't quite understand everything they were saying, but Prudence was pleased that we had time to see him. We didn't stay long as we had a flight to New York the next day."

I could not detect any jealousy or bitterness in his voice. Perhaps there was a touch of inadequacy, I thought. He did not display a lot of emotion. Where was the Italian passion? Had the Australian way of life sapped the passion from this Italian man? Was his interest in my daughter purely financial after all? And yet it was obvious that he cared for her deeply. He was always so idealistically sentimental with a tough business drive that I found it difficult to know where he drew the line between the two extremes.

"Did she see Michael only once? Were you were with her?" Was I probing too much?

"I believe so. We had much to do and there was so little free time."

"Did you visit David McMurray in America?"

He shook his head, "No, we didn't go to Arizona."

He knew whom I meant, and where he lived. "Oh, did you have time to go to the opera or any art exhibitions? You didn't work all the time, did you?"

He released my hand, picked out a weed from the rose bed, and tossed it under the shade of the Maple tree. "We didn't work twenty-four hours a day. I'm not an overbearing, domineering, demanding ogre, Leonardo. I made sure Prudence had rest days so that she didn't tire herself too much."

Fabian seldom became angry, but there were, on occasions, a brief shower of sparks that quickly extinguished due to his complete inability to sustain anger. He would apologize to his worst enemy rather than fuel a fire of hatred and spite.

"No, I wasn't implying that," I said. "Of course you didn't overwork her. Is there such a thing, anyway? I don't know where she gets her energy. I was merely asking about the culture and entertainment there. I just wondered if you managed to see some interesting theater. She loves the theater."

"I'm so sorry. You know I think of Prudence as my own, and I'm always sensible about her schedule. We did go to some shows. Prue told you about the Bob Dylan concert. And we saw a brilliant film when we were in England. It was called *2001: A Space Odyssey*. It was extremely futuristic, pure science fiction, not science fact at all. Not that it's going to come true, of course. It was interesting though. And we saw some university theater in the States. No big productions, just small in-house shows. Very experimental. Not quite my scene. I mainly prefer quiet dinners in small restaurants."

"Did you do that? Did you manage to have intimate dinners?" I glanced at him while pretending to de-head a dying rose.

"I don't know what you mean by intimate dinners. We had to eat. We often just had a meal in the hotel, although sometimes we went to a restaurant. Prudence knew of some good restaurants from her previous visits to America."

"Of course! That's what I meant. I meant to ask whether you had hotel meals or restaurant dinners." It was not what I meant at all. I could tell that nothing of any romantic consequence transpired between them, or perhaps Fabian wasn't the type to reveal the truth. Prudence, of course, had said nothing, as usual.

—⚏—

I was hemming the trouser legs of a new pair of black cotton pants. Prudence was stretched lengthways on the settee with a book, eating Swiss chocolates.

"Are you using black cotton?"

"Of course! This thimble has shrunk. I must get a new one. Fabian said that you went to the Bob Dylan concert in America."

"Mmm. I told you about it, remember when I rang you?" She selected a chocolate in a gold and red wrapper, carefully unfolding it to reveal the rich, dark treat.

"Yes, I know, but isn't Dylan a protest singer?"

"He's an incisive, intelligent songwriter."

"He can't sing though. His voice sounds terrible. You saw *2001: A Space Odyssey* in the cinema, Fabian said."

"Mmm. I told you about that too. Are you going senile? Perhaps I should put you in a home for the aged, or for the terminally insane." She continued reading her book, not looking at me when she spoke.

I ignored her comment. "So, tell me about the film. The reviews weren't very good." I wove the thread in and out, securing the hem in place.

"I've already told you. Poor Fabian, I don't think he fully understood it. He liked it, I think, but he asked an awful lot of questions about it. He wanted to see it twice to make more sense of it the second time. But, of course, we didn't have time to see it again. Apparently Rock Hudson walked out of the premier of the movie because he didn't understand it, so Fabian's not the only one. It's a bit surreal, I must admit. The special effects were good though." She nibbled at a chocolate, indifferent to my questions.

"I don't think the reviewers knew what it was about either. They wrote that it was a film inspired by either a mad man or a genius, but they weren't sure which one. It's got apes in it, hasn't it?"

"Mmm. It starts with a scene of prehistoric apes confronted by a mysterious, black monolith. To defend themselves, they throw bones at it. They realize that bones can be used as weapons, the first tools, I suspect. But that's just the beginning, papa. The story is then fast-forwarded dramatically in time. There's a moon sequence where man also confronts the monolith. The humans then employ their most elaborate tool: the spaceship Discovery. It's a partnership with the artificial intelligence of the onboard computer named HAL 9000 that's programmed never to lie to humans and to administer psychological tests. They do that to determine if the crew is in danger of jeopardizing the mission. The best part is when the men attempt to have a private conversation in a space pod and HAL reads their lips. It's visually very clever. The soundtrack and the star-gate sequence are brilliant too. It's a sound and light journey as an astronaut travels to another space, another dimension. It looks to me similar to the way one moves from life to death when you're dying."

"How would you know that?" I reached forward to the coffee table to select a chocolate.

"People who've had near death experiences mention a bright light and travelling toward it. It's like that in the movie too, but very psychedelic, apparently like an LSD drug trip. That's why young people in America have been flocking to see the movie. They think it's just a big trip."

"I heard that it was rubbish." The needle plied easily through the cotton.

"Well, there's not much dialogue. It does appear disjointed, and there's no clear narrative. Fabian couldn't understand the ending. It ends with the astronaut inexplicably finding himself in a bedroom somewhere beyond Jupiter. That really confused Fabian. He didn't realize that it was just a statement about man's place in the universe. But I guess most people found it confusing."

"Would I like it?"

"Yes, of course. And you'll understand it. I'll take you when it's released in Australia. That'll be ages yet." She continued to read her book while conversing with me.

"But what's it really about?"

"Simplistically, it's about a quest, a need. See the movie. Can I read my book now?" she asked in frustration.

"Fabian said that you went out to restaurants together." I probed a bit more.

"We had to eat," she said abruptly.

"That's what he said too. You two are conspiring against me to not tell me what happened in America." I had finished hemming the trousers and prepared to knot the cotton to secure the thread in place.

"Stop asking nosey questions then. He told me that you'd interrogated him. He said you were like a dog at a bone." The book remained steady in her left hand. She hadn't turned a page for more than five minutes.

"It wasn't an interrogation," I said indignantly as I cut the cotton thread, put the trousers aside, and placed the needle in its case. "I'm just putting the sewing box away," I said as I rose, picking up loose pieces of cotton thread. When I returned, I asked, "Well, did you stay in the same room as Fabian?"

"What is this, the Italian inquisition?" She didn't move from the settee.

"Spanish inquisition, don't you mean?" I muttered, correcting her.

"No, you're Italian, aren't you?" she answered. I ignored Prudence's sarcastic comment.

"So, you're not going to answer me?"

"What did Fabian say when you asked him where we slept?"

"I didn't ask him. I'm polite." I looked at her, but she continued to read her book.

"Good, then be polite to me. Let me read my book in peace and stop asking silly questions. You do go on and on sometimes," she said bluntly. "You're making something out of nothing. He was asking me questions too, so you can stop getting him to ask me questions that you want the answer to. I'm getting as angry with him as I am with you."

"I did no such thing! What are you getting angry with him about? What's going on between you?"

Prudence was quiet for a considerable time. I sighed and closed my eyes. I had hopes of Prudence and Fabian living together. I had hoped that the three months in Europe would ignite a passion between them, but it seemed that this was not so. Perhaps Fabian did not fancy Prudence in a sexual way at all. It seemed to me that they were both quiet about the European trip, and I could not work out whether they argued or whether they made love. More often I suspected that neither incident occurred, and that the two of them were merely respectful of each other and thus felt exasperated with my intrusion. I feared that my dream of Prudence and Fabian being eternally bound in matrimony would not eventuate.

# COMMISSIONER'S COMMENTARY

Bari was obsessive about his daughter marrying. When I read his journal I thought of my own children and, of course, I would wish that they marry one day too. It really came as no surprise that he mentioned it often. It occurs to me now that, as I interrogated him, he spoke contradictorily about his feelings. Simultaneously he spoke of wanting her to marry Fabian, or Oswald, but in summary I think he just wanted her to be married, and it had come to the point that it didn't really matter whom she married. I recall him saying that Prudence was the paragon of perfection, yet he let slip that her not marrying was a failure.

Concerning that matter, I was uncertain whether he meant that she was a failure, or that he regarded himself as a failure, and I forgot to ask. Nevertheless, he added that he was frustrated with her imperfections. By his own admission, he thought one of her faults was her inability to form a loving relationship with one person due to her indecisiveness, and work distractions. Strangely, he revealed that she was imbalanced in her life's activities, skewing her actions too much toward work, and too little toward relationships. It was then that I realized a level of disappointment in his voice. More startling to me, as I read about Fabian in Bari's journal, was that I recalled Fabian's view of marriage when I put the question to him.

Fabian appeared to be an unromantic man to me. He was evasive about past or present relationships, merely saying that he had "friends." With regard to Prudence, he was rather business-like, answering without emotion. Then, quite suddenly and unprovoked by me, he confessed that he was looking for a house to purchase with Prudence. I had heard that before in my first meeting with him at the identification of her body but, at the time, I didn't place a lot of meaning to it. On this occasion, I idly asked him what suburb they were interested in, and he floored me by saying that they were looking for a house in Italy. My interest was well and truly piqued, so I prodded him for more information, particularly about his relationship with Prudence. Openly, he admitted to a romantic relationship that had blossomed during the beginning of 1968 when they were overseas. He had proposed and she had accepted, so he said. Her father had not been told as they wanted to wait until they had purchased a house. Bari, I believe, went to his grave not knowing that his dream had come true.

# RICHARD SMYTHE

The year 1968 ended as it began: with an escalation of anti-war demonstrations. The youth of the day opposed conscription and the involvement of Australians in a war that was not their own. There were violent scenes in Melbourne and Sydney, the likes of which I had not seen before. It was made worse for me because, for the first time, I saw the images of war on television.

Prudence wanted to buy a television set. At the time, I could not possibly imagine what there could be on television to watch. Prudence said that there would be international and local news programs, but I could read the newspaper for that. She said that there would be entertainment programs with comedians, but I could not see the usefulness of that. She said that there would be sporting matches, and I was mildly interested in that. Eventually, I relented when Prudence announced that she was going to be interviewed on a television program. We thought that was exciting. So it came to be that Prudence bought a brand new television set. The first images were frustratingly flawed. Statically-charged blips and waves appeared which made me nauseous. My neighbor, Franco, came to our assistance. He affixed an aerial to the chimney and, after many adjustments, the image on the screen was perfect.

Prudence asked me to accompany her to the television interview in a Melbourne studio. I was scared of flying, but Prudence said she would be with me all the time and that airplanes were safer than cars. In any case, I remember the day well. It was one of those brittle summer days. The studio was hot and airless. A conglomeration of cables, lights, and fabricated set designs cluttered the room. Cameras rolled along the floor in search of the perfect angle for filming. I was seated, alone, in a corner of the studio in an uncomfortable, red plastic chair. The crew frequently collided with me as they maneuvered the cameras in place. I felt as if I did not belong and no one made me feel, in any way, welcome. The only person who looked at me was my daughter, perched upon an upholstered chair under a spotlight. A vacant chair was placed alongside her, then a side table, and finally a backdrop with books in a cabinet painted on it was strategically positioned behind her. When the confusion settled, Prudence was told not to look at me, but to keep her eyes on the interviewer and to act "naturally."

She was wearing a crisp, green, cotton pantsuit with dark green shoes. I could see the outline of her bra and was relieved that she was, indeed, wearing one. She sat cross-legged with her hands on her knees. The lights turned her hair a fiery red, matching the rouge painted on her cheeks. I was not permitted to style my daughter's hair as the studio had its own stylist and make-up artist. My daughter's make-up was, therefore, of a thicker consistency than usual so as to look natural on television. To me, Prudence resembled a flaming, masqueraded Medusa, a harridan, a harlot, or a comic clown. Prudence said that I was over-reacting and, in all probability, I may have been.

"Welcome Prudence," Richard said, as he seated himself. "We're taping the program, so it's not live. The audience will see it on television next Tuesday. If we make a mistake, we can re-tape it, but I'd like you to relax and pretend that it's just you and me, without the camera crew. Are you ready?"

A crew member yelled, "Lights—Camera—Action." Everyone was hushed. It was the quietest moment in an otherwise clamorous afternoon.

"Hello, I'm Richard Smythe. In the program this evening, we have the world-renowned mathematician, Professor Prudence Bari, talking to us about her career. Welcome to *A Moment of Your Time,* Prue."

"Thank you very much. It's good to be here." She blinked at the blazing spotlights and repositioned herself to avoid their glare.

"Tell us a bit about yourself. For a famous person, there appears to be a bit of mystery about you. Tell us something of your childhood."

"My father left Italy with his parents to start a new life in South Australia, as many people did at the time. I was born and raised in Adelaide. I went to the local primary school and to Adelaide High School before studying in Italy. It was a wonderful time for me, my university years."

"You're very close to your father?"

"Yes, of course. He's a retired mathematician. He also lectured at Adelaide University, where I now work in between overseas assignments. He was a great teacher of science, art, culture, philosophy, music, and physical training. And Italian, of course." She glanced at me, taking care not to make it look too obvious.

"Your mother died when you were born, didn't she?"

"She died soon after I was born, due to difficulties with the birth, so I don't know much about her. I do know that my parents met in Brompton, a suburb of Adelaide, where they both lived. She was also Italian."

"Is that why you have chosen not to have children? Are you afraid that you may suffer the same consequences?"

"No, Richard, absolutely not! With modern medicine there are fewer fatalities now, of the mother and of the child."

"Then why don't you have children? Why aren't you married? These are questions that I hear people ask."

Prudence did not seem at all perturbed by these questions. I, on the other hand, was shifting nervously in the red, plastic chair.

"I've been very busy with my career. I have students in Adelaide and in Milan, and I have many speaking and lecturing commitments. I also travel a great deal, as you know."

"So, you've made a choice? You prefer a career to marriage?"

"You can't have it all, Richard. That's been the hardest lesson in my life: learning that there are choices in life."

"Is it really about choice? Some people would suggest that you dislike men."

She did not take her emerald eyes off him as she said, "No, that's not the case, Richard."

"What then, is your view on women's liberation?"

"It's a complex issue, but briefly, I think women's liberation is changing the way women think about their choices in society. At first blush, women's liberation is a commitment to achieving gender equality by eradicating oppression, and providing real choices for all women: choices concerning relationships, marriage, career, and so forth. I think this is a period of discovery for women. And I hope, in the future, woman can have it all."

"Has it made women more promiscuous, do you think? Has contraception changed a woman's sense of morals?"

"I think it appears that some women have become more promiscuous because we're reading about promiscuous situations in magazines. It's become a prominent issue. However, I think that there are still many women who believe in monogamous relationships. There are also women who believe in platonic relationships with men, and support waiting for marriage to express their love for the person they are with."

"Virginity is an issue for you then?"

"I support celibacy, yes. Celibacy doesn't necessarily equate with disliking the opposite sex, nor is it equivalent to virginity. Celibacy is a virtue and is usually practiced for a period of time for a particular purpose. For me, it's also a cultural norm; it's the essence of my ethnicity and cultural upbringing. I practice Catholic values."

"Some would see it as a puritanical view to wait so long. You are in your forties, now, aren't you?"

"Some people would see it as being puritanical, particularly some youth of this generation, but others like you, Richard, may view it as taking a moral stance."

"Yes, of course." The interviewer straightened the pleats of his beige trousers and crossed his legs. He was a meticulous, conservative dresser, fastidious and exacting in his grooming.

"Also Richard, there's the issue of venereal diseases."

I was startled when someone yelled, "Cut! Cut! She can't say that. Richard—Richard, ask another question when I give the signal and we'll take it from there."

My daughter looked at me with a bemused smile and shrugged her shoulders. We repositioned ourselves in our seats. Hers looked considerably more comfortable than mine. It was an armchair of navy blue material with wooden legs. She sipped water from a small, plastic beaker and returned it to the table by her chair. Meanwhile, Richard primped and preened himself, straightened his brown and white striped tie, and fiddled with his gold cufflinks. He checked the sheen on his polished shoes and appeared visibly restless until a crew member shouted, "Get ready, Richard." He miraculously transformed into an image of stillness, calmness, and tranquility. "Richard, commence on the count of three. All quiet! One—Two—Three."

"Prudence, there is talk that you may marry your long-time friend, Oswald Danes. Can you comment on that?"

"We've been friends for a long time, but I can't speculate on any change in the relationship at this time."

"You spent some time overseas with Fabian Rossi, didn't you? Is there any chance of a romantic relationship with Fabian?"

"Fabian is my manager, Richard," she said forthrightly.

"Are you having a relationship with your manager, Professor Bari?" he persisted. Richard had astonishingly clear eyes reflecting his surroundings, as if they were mirrors of glass. There was a genuine intellect, a purity of expression exuding from those delicate eyes. They were mesmerizing in an intellectual way.

"Yes, of course. We have a working relationship. That's what you meant, isn't it, Richard?" She smiled.

"Let's move onto your work, shall we?" He returned the smile. "I understand that you'll be campaigning for more women to undertake science courses at university?"

"Yes, I've just returned from America where I researched the rise of women undertaking university science courses. I'll soon start a lecture tour to educate women on the importance of science in society and the choice of careers that may be available to them when they graduate. It's about raising their awareness. The English scientist, Ernest Rutherford's view is that no physics can be good unless it can be explained to a person working behind a bar. I'm hoping that future barmaids will be studying physics and science in the future, and that eventually they'll be explaining complex issues to the average beer drinker. Society's perception of women and science is changing, albeit slowly. The great preponderance of evidence indicates that there is no mathematics gene, as first thought. This means that males and females, equally, have the ability to undertake mathematical and scientific studies."

"Is the campaign really a campaign for feminism rather than a campaign for science education?"

"Feminist thinking is really just rethinking: rethinking the way certain assumptions about women have developed. For example, the assumption that males are more logical than females and that females are more intuitive than males requires rethinking. It's like science itself, and the discovery of scientific principles. Scientists are continually rethinking and that's why there are so many powerful achievements at the moment. An example is the American mission to put man—or I should say, a person—on the moon. Current thinking dictates that it can't be done. People say it can't be done because it hasn't yet been done, and it's a concept that's beyond most people's imagination. If it is achieved next year, then it will be a miracle of science. Scientists will have demonstrated their drive to achieve a solution despite the odds and negative criticism. To not pursue the mission would be to take the path of least resistance. Similarly, women have been positioned to view the world and their environment in one way, that is, from a patriarchal stance. They've been on the path of least resistance. It's time women looked at their world-view differently. It's not a question of what makes a career woman or a housewife. It's a question of womanhood in general. It's about independence and free-thinking, or rethinking, and to take strength in their independence to act in their world, in their society."

"So, rethinking can then lead to reaction?"

"It can lead to reaction or it can lead to pro-action, being pro-active about certain issues."

"But this appears to be causing great conflict for men because women appear to be blaming men for everything negative." Richard gave the distinct impression that there was a serious problem on his mind that he was struggling to resolve.

"With any new form of thinking, or revolutionary thinking, it will be a confusing time for all concerned. It's about challenging pre-existing thought and this makes some people uncomfortable. This new way of thinking will soon become accepted and become the norm, just as the conversion from pounds, shillings and pence to the new currency of dollars and cents is now the norm. It's been two years since the introduction of the new currency and there was a period of adjustment before acceptance. In time, people will forget about pounds and will always be thinking in terms of dollars. It'll be that way with feminism too, I believe. Women will begin to take an individual form in society, just as men do."

"But is it about individualism and independence, or is it about all women behaving in a specific way? For example, will all women be in the workforce taking jobs from men?"

"No, some women will not want to work; they will want to stay home and raise children. Some women will take on jobs that traditionally we see men undertaking, and they'll be better at it, but it will be about who is best for the job. More importantly, it will be about choice. There will be a choice: an independent choice. That is the ideal of feminist thinking. It will be that way for men too. Men will also have choices."

"At present, it appears to be a 'no-man's land,' and men don't get a say in this," he said. Crystalline eyes reflected a green hue as he fixated on Prudence.

"In what way, Richard?"

"Whatever men do, they can't win. They are frowned on for opening doors for women, yet it is the polite thing to do. I'm really interested in the confusion of genders. Men are growing their hair and look like women now at a time when a lot of women seem to want to be masculine or to be like men. It has even been said that you are, or want to be, masculine. There appears to be a gender identity crisis at the moment."

"I assure you I'm not masculine. For a while there will be some women who will have what some call 'feminine denial' or 'feminist denial.' Denial always runs the risk of merely shaping itself in the negative image of what it rejects. There may be initially an abyss between standpoints, but this abyss will close in time, I believe. I don't believe that there is anything untoward in a woman taking on preconceived male values; or a preconceived maleness, such as strength, seriousness, or independence; or logical thought; or even business and finance skills. Rethinking means that some values and attitudes that had been deemed to be predominantly male values may not merely be male values any more, but they may also be female values. What I'm stressing is that women can change some of their limitations, such as passive compliance. They'll be confident about thinking and acting for themselves."

"But, from a man's point of view, it appears that the women are now conforming to a new ideal, rather than expressing any individuality."

"Conformity can bring about power. By conforming to a group, there is power to change or to force a change. Without the support of other women, there will be no change. But I believe that from conformity there will emerge independence, equity and freedom, and individualism for all. The distinctive individual identity of a female, or male, for that matter, will be generated by defiance, by revolution, by changing the status quo, and by changing the way we think. Women's quest for independent selfhood can be achieved through feminist thought and action, as a group or as an individual."

"Thank you very much, Professor Bari. That's all we have time for on our program this evening." He turned from my daughter and looked into a camera. "We'll be back next week with Dr. Germaine Greer, English lecturer and eminent feminist. Goodnight, until then." The spotlights dimmed and the intensity of heat emanating from them diminished. Richard and Prudence remained seated and continued a casual conversation.

I was pleased that the interview was over because I was most uncomfortable with the entirety of the conversation. Raising Prudence in the best way I knew how, I had nurtured her to be an individual person, confident and competent in all the things she undertook, but I realized now that many of the choices in her life were not hers. I had chosen a life of a mathematician for her. Had I taken the path of least resistance because mathematics was familiar to me? Or was her destiny irrevocably and inexorably ordained when I changed her name? Could there be credence in numerology after all? Could divination be based on assigning meaning to numbers? Surely numerology could not be more powerful than God? Who or what dictates one's destiny? Is it God, is it numerology, is it parents, or is it individuals? Perhaps I had taken the easy path, a path of inaction, or of least action. It had occurred to me that perhaps Prudence was not living the life she wanted. I felt decidedly uncomfortable.

My back ached, so I stood and stretched. In the studio, I realized that there were a whole set of associated dichotomies between Prudence and the way I had raised her. She was female, like all others, but she had been educated in a universe of masculinity more than any other woman because I had thrust her into the powerful and ubiquitous patriarchal world of mathematics. Had she become the androgynous form that people were talking about, and had I, in all ignorance, created it? And had my life of celibacy, since her birth, had an altogether negative impact on her relationships with males? It was too much for me to consider.

Richard and Prudence stood and shook hands. He departed with a slight limp as though a pebble had lodged in his left shoe. Prudence took my arm and led me out of the studio. She followed a young man. "Here's the room, Professor Bari. There's tea, coffee, and sandwiches for you and your father. If you need a taxi to the airport, Melinda at the reception desk will arrange it for you. It's a pleasure seeing you." As my daughter autographed the notepad he had given her, he said, "Stephen's the name, Dr. Bari."

As we entered the room, I noticed the kitchenette and began making Prudence and myself a cup of coffee. Prudence walked toward the armchairs arranged in a semi-circle around a low, rectangular, laminated table. A young woman had just switched off the television set in the corner of the room. She slumped into an armchair, her cigarette trailing streaks of smoke behind her. Her denim jeans were old, frayed, and stained.

"I'm Prudence Bari, Miss Greer. How are you?" Prudence extended her hand to greet the sultry woman.

The woman ignored the gesture. Thick, dark curls protruded from a multi-striped, knitted cap of rainbow colors. She picked up a glass of white wine from the table, spilling some contents on her misshapen, tattered T-shirt. "Oh fuck!" She made two wiping motions on her T-shirt, and then gave up. "So, you're the famous Miss Prudence Bari, the great fucking mathematician. Except that you don't fuck, do you? I've heard about you, Miss Prude."

Prudence camouflaged herself on the green chair next to Miss Greer. I fumbled over the powdered coffee and it spilled onto the green, marbled, laminated bench. "I've read your articles. You're a very articulate writer, Miss Greer. I saw you on British television recently too, on a talk show. You were lecturing on Elizabethan and Jacobean drama. And I've seen your photograph in the Dutch magazine."

The woman seemed disinterested. "The nude photo, hey? I co-founded the magazine, you know. *Suck,* we called it. Great name! When are you going to do a nude centerfold? Pornography is not just for men. Sure it's designed to achieve a particular purpose. Masturbatory orgasm, that is. But that's not how I look at it. I regard a general state of sexual arousal or erotic interest as sort of normal. Not that I really understand the connection between the eye and the cock, but there's something highly visual in pornography. It's a visual phenomenon, no doubt." She blew the cigarette smoke in the direction of my daughter.

"I don't think nude centerfolds are my scene. I'm not as young as you, remember."

"Gawd. I'm fucking twenty-eight. Yeah, what are you now? Forty-something? Perhaps your visuals aren't that perfect looking any more. Pass me the cigarette packet. Take one."

"No thank you," said Prudence as she slid the cigarette packet across the table. "You would never have chosen pornography as a career, would you?"

"Good heavens, no!" exclaimed Greer. "I'm not a performer in that sense!"

"Yes, you are. Talking of performances, are you still lecturing English literature in England?"

"Still lecturing? Yeah, but above all, I try to remain true to who I am. Ernest Hemingway, when his cock wouldn't stand up, blew his head off. He sold himself a line of bullshit and bought it." She continued drinking wine, jumping from one thought to another. "Musicians know their worst shit makes them famous. Jim'd be playing *Hey Joe*, which he didn't like that much to start with, and he was so freaked out of his head that his E-string would be out of tune, and he couldn't fix it. The audience wouldn't know or care. It was just another mass masturbation scene for them all."

I didn't know who or what she was talking about. Stephen, the young crew member, burst into the room. "Miss Greer, will you be able to wait awhile longer? Mr. Smythe is running a bit late changing. I'll call you as soon as he's ready, and then we can get your interview taped for the program that airs in a couple of weeks. It's the one after Prudence Bari's. Is that okay?" He waited politely for an answer. She nodded acceptance. "Thanks so much, Miss Greer." Content with the answer, he shut the door quietly behind him as he left.

"Fuckin' hell," Greer complained. "I'll need more wine if I have to wait too much longer." Focusing again on my daughter, she said, "So you're into logical shit. I am too, in a way. I've been told that my articles are very logical. My literary agent has asked me to put my thoughts and articles on paper and he'll find a publisher. My book will be on feminism and women's liberation. It'll be a logical exposition, a scholarly piece on the emancipation of women as total people. What do you think of that? I know exactly what I want to write, but I have no idea what to call it. Something like: *Love Your Breasts*, or *Female Sexlessness*, or *Women Without Features*, *The Female Eunuch*, or *Eunuchs All*. I don't know. It'll be something that expresses this trap that women are in whereby they don't love their own bodies; women are ashamed of their own sexuality. What I want to say is that it's okay to be sexual, it's okay to be naked, it's okay to enjoy sex, and it's okay to demystify sex. As I said, it'll be a rational, logical text on emancipation from all forms of sexual repression."

"I'm sure your book will do well. Women need a strong woman, like you, to identify with."

"You're right. And I'm the one to do it." Her slurring worsened. "They'll probably give me a shit load of money for it. What am I supposed to do? I won't give that money to England's taxes. I tried to form a foundation for women, a center where they could maybe get a bed if their husband's beat them, or where they could just drop-in if they need help. The British tax office called it a tax dodge. I tried to incorporate myself. No good. My agent decided that I should spend a year out of the country, out of England that is. That's why I'm back in Australia." She shook her head, tugged at a curl, closed her eyes, and said in a quieter tone, "But there'll be more money waiting for me when I return to England. Not that I have real problems with money."

"There's always charity, Miss Greer."

"Call me fucking Germaine, for fuck's sake! Did you say charity or chastity? Chastity isn't my middle name. It'd be yours, of course: Prudence Chastity Bari." She laughed to herself. Suddenly serious, she said, "You know, Prue, in America the female liberation movement has two distinct facets. There are women who work on committees and make statements that are read into the Congressional Record. They work within the system, a system that oppresses the people. Then there are the more radical women who band into all-female groups and learn karate and violence. That's their trip, isn't it? They'll crush us at it. I dig the Redstockings. I think they're into something, real dialogue, allowing women to be true women. I don't dig women being violent. I'm going to write a book because words are my thing. What we need, and I'm being serious now, is for each woman to find their true thing, their true purpose—what works for them. Do you know what I mean?" She was leaning forward, looking straight at Prudence. "What we really need is an all-girl rock and roll band that can lay down a riff no one will be able to forget. That's what we women need, not women in men's clothes, not aggro women, just a bloody great female band." Still in her chair, she pantomimed strumming an imaginary guitar.

Greer stubbed out her cigarette and stood up. She had the longest legs I'd ever seen. With lengthy strides, she was at the door. She turned to my daughter and said, "Prue, I despise your Miss Prissy ways and your neater-than-thou clothes, and holier-than-thou attitude, but you've got a fucking good brain—the best—and you speak well. You've just got to be more direct, more forceful. Drop the fucking façade. You've got to accept your own sexuality. Celibacy and monogamy aren't the way to liberation. In fact, they are the opposite. They are nothing but repressive sexual stereotypes. You need to know what real liberation is. Even burning your bra is not liberation. Fuck, it's just subjecting you to another form of repression if it becomes a rule of feminism, that is. I oppose all rules. Think about it, Prudence. Just think about it. Nice meeting you. By the way, I was watching the monitor while you were being interviewed. I don't agree with a lot of your beliefs, but the best thing you said was 'at first blush' and I love that phrase so much I'm going to use it in my book. But for now, I'm going to hurry their butts up out there and—" She was out of the doorway before she finished the sentence.

Prudence looked at me for the first time since entering the room. "The coffee must be cold by now. Let's go. We'll get a taxi to the airport." There were many things I wanted to say to her, but I knew that this was her way of asking me to wait until we were in the comfort of our own home.

# THE DINNER PARTY

Prudence was unusually silent during the flight from Melbourne to Adelaide. When we arrived home, she turned the television on and sat in silence watching the news of the Olympic Games from Mexico City. We sat together in communal contemplation for I dared not disturb her.

Prudence remained in a listless, uncommunicative state for two days. I suggested that we play chess. Winning would stimulate the mind, I thought. Prudence was an excellent chess opponent, winning many chess tournaments in Italy. I had not beaten her since she was in her teens, and I, myself, had won a number of prestigious tournaments in my youth.

Positioning the marble figures on the chessboard, I placed it on top of a portable card table in the living room. I made the environment appealing, with a tray of tea and chocolates close by, and the lamplight casting a spotlight over the chess arena. This would be a mental contest between two strategic minds. We sat hunched over the board on a Sunday afternoon, and while I was keen to commence, Prudence contemplated her first move for many minutes.

"What are you doing? You don't need to think so much about your first move, surely?"

"I'm trying to focus, papa. Leave me be."

Prudence began tentatively, hesitantly, rubbing her brow, scratching her head, and twirling her hair. All afternoon she touched a piece, released her fingers, and touched the same piece, contemplating a move then changing her mind. She fiddled nervously and distractedly with the figures. I had not seen her play like this before. She played like a junior, dithering and delaying her moves by pacing the floor and running her hands along the

126

covers of the books on the mahogany bookshelf. Her concentration was poor, her strategies were inconsistent, and her heart and soul were not in the contest. Aggression and determination were missing. She was not the strategic terrorist of previous games. What had undermined her spirit? She left me no option but to play a winning hand. Her aura of invincibility was shattered when I made my attacking move and she conceded defeat.

"I guess I'm not match-fit," was her justification for the loss. "It's like playing the piano, isn't it? I haven't exercised my fingers."

Chess was an art, not a science. I had beaten her at an artistic pursuit: that can be forgiven. It was a game of strategy, of ideas, of dynamic and aggressive play, but more importantly, it was a game of preparation. Prudence was not prepared mentally for the game and I had taken advantage of her vulnerability and carelessness. I had penetrated her cerebral profundity. However, it was not as I had intended. I was certain that her mental agility would defeat me with swift deference. But it was not so.

"The best of three, then? We'll have a tournament," I offered. Usually I aspired to win, but I was uncomfortable with this victory.

"No thanks. Are you sure you weren't named after the great Giovanni Leonardo di Bona da Cutri, the genius of the game?" she teased.

"Ah, I would love to be as great as the master Leonardo: he who shifted the balance of chess power from Spain to Italy and was rewarded handsomely for it. And what is my reward today—a smile from my beautiful daughter?"

She stood and tousled my hair. "I'm okay. It's just a virus, or swollen glands. I'm just tired, that's all. No great drama. I'll make some more tea. I don't feel like chess. What about scrabble? I'm sure to win that!"

"Let's play in Italian then," I said, as I packed away the chess pieces. "I'll get the almond biscuits. I made them from Oswald's almonds."

She had not quite emerged from her apathy when she half-heartedly invited Darren, Polly and Oswald to dinner for Cyril's

30th birthday. I did the majority of the cooking, although this did not perturb me as I rather fancied myself as having culinary expertise. I was more concerned with the state of my daughter's health, but I was sure that an evening with fine cuisine and wine would improve her spirits.

Dinner was well received. After considerable consumption of wine, tongues were glib, inhibitions were relaxed, and arguments were irrational. Polly flirted outrageously with Cyril, Darren was progressively angered, Oswald was disgusted with Polly's coquetry, and Prudence was tired of the petty squabbling.

"Come on, Cyril. Let me give you a kiss for your birthday. If you're lucky tonight, I'll give you more than a kiss." Polly's sheer, red blouse was unbuttoned beyond her cleavage and her minute brassiere barely covered her pert, pale breasts. Her exquisite prettiness was masqueraded under provocative make-up that emphasized her iridescent, blue eyes. Habitually, she applied lipstick to her pouting, blood-red lips to enhance their sexual sheen: irresistible for any man, I would have thought. "Come on, Cyril, sexy Cyril." Leaning into him, she stroked his exposed chest hairs, and said, "Cyril, come on. Take me to your place tonight."

Cyril silently sipped his wine, letting her caress his body, but not acknowledging her with an answer.

Darren, sitting on Cyril's right, was incensed. "Get off, you tart. Leave him alone. You can't keep your hands to yourself, can you?"

"Calm down, Darren," placated Oswald. "Polly, leave Cyril alone. Stop teasing him. You're embarrassing yourself."

"Leave her alone. I like it," answered Cyril without looking at Polly. She continued to move her hand down Cyril's chest to his navel and below to the top of his jeans. She toyed with his leather belt, pretending to unfasten it. Cyril smiled like Lewis Carroll's Cheshire cat, although he behaved more like the hookah-smoking caterpillar, in a very unpleasant state of mind, taking not the slightest notice of Polly or anyone else.

Darren leaned across Cyril's body to shift Polly's hand from his lover's swollen crotch and push her away. "Get off, you sex maniac. Get off." In what was intended to be a dominant display of aggression, he folded the sleeves of his thin jumper, which only served to reveal his scrawny, sallow arms, bruised and pockmarked.

"Cut it out both of you. Cyril, put a stop to it," said Prudence who was annoyed with his acquiescence. She bunched her hair together in a ponytail and released it. "Cyril, come into the kitchen and help me with the food." Prudence held his hand to help him stand, but he didn't move.

"I'd love to princess, but Darren doesn't like me being alone with you. I'd have my hands all over you and you know it. If I can't have you, and if I play my cards right, I can have both Darren and Polly tonight," Cyril smirked.

"Get fucking lost! I'm not screwing you if Polly has touched you. Get off, Polly, he's mine. Cyril, tell her to get off. And you're not going anywhere near Prudence. You stay away from Prue! Do you hear me? Keep your hands off her."

"Come on guys, not in front of Dr. Bari," said Oswald. "Have some respect. Darren, Cyril's just goading you. He doesn't mean it. Cyril, how can you be so rude? You've had enough to drink."

I cleared the dirty crockery from the table and ran hot water in the kitchen sink, squeezing a dollop of dishwashing detergent into the basin. In the reflection of the kettle, I saw my distorted face and the furrowed frown lining my olive skin. My eyes were small and faded; the drooping rolls of skin made me appear more advanced than my years. Rolling on rubber gloves, I looked at my prominent age spots and spidery veins: the cruel artwork of age.

"For the love of whatever, you're old fashioned, Ossie," said Cyril as I entered the living room. "You and Prudey wouldn't know how to have a fucking good time, would you? Or perhaps you're jealous? Let's make it a threesome," he goaded.

Polly purred and, with licking motions, flicked her tongue around Cyril's ear. Her ubiquitous flirting irritated Prudence. Cyril was aware of Polly's transparency, but enjoyed the attention. To Darren and Oswald, she was a leech, a barnacle, a parasite, or an adhesive limpet. It seemed to me that she simultaneously attracted and repelled people in equal portions. Polly was totally oblivious to the reactions she caused.

"That's enough, Cyril," Prudence said. "You've had too much to drink. Why don't we call it a night?"

The tension constricted my chest, and my breathing became shallow and painful. I excused myself, kissed Prudence on the forehead, and retired to my bedroom, straightening the rectangular mirror in the hallway.

"You fucking bitch," I heard Darren scream amid the noise of chairs scraping across the linoleum.

"Hey, hey, hey, settle down." It was Oswald. "Settle down. For Pete's sake Polly, give it up. You sort out who you're having sex with tonight, but not here, not in front of me, and not in front of Prue. Get out. You three are all the same. You'd screw anything that moved. Haven't you got any sense of decency? You're disgusting, all of you. Get out! Go on!"

I almost cheered. I loved Oswald's authoritarian tone. I wanted to go back to the living room to watch him in action. Bravo! Bravo! I was bursting to know what was happening. The voices subsided and there was movement along the passageway as I unbuttoned my shirt and sat on the bed. It was not my place to intervene. In a contest for power and authority with inebriated, impassioned men, I would never win. I heard Prudence telephone for a taxi. She was cut short.

"I can drive! I can drive! I'm not that inebriated. Fuck off. I'm okay to drive. I'll take these guys home. I said I'll drive Prue! Don't ring a fucking taxi. I'll take Darren and Polly home, I tell you. Let go of me, bitch. Come on Darren, let's split this place."

"Let Cyril drive then, Prue. Let him go." Oswald's boots kicked against the front door.

"Yeah, you fucking homophobes!" I heard Darren shout. "Leave us alone, you old fashioned prudes. We're going home. Don't touch me, Polly. Keep your fucking hands to yourself. As for you Prudence, don't go near Cyril again. Stay clear or I'll kill you." Darren's vitriolic language lingered in the hallway long after he was gone. I could hear Polly giggling in the street, car doors slamming, and the screech of tires as Cyril left the driveway.

When it was quiet, I opened my bedroom door and peered along the hallway. Prudence had her hand across her forehead, sighing and shaking her head. Oswald's hand lay on her shoulder consolingly. I quietly shut the door, changed into my nightwear, and slipped into bed. I rested in bed reading Aristotle's *Poetics* by lamplight, but I could not concentrate. My eyes ached with tiredness, but my mind was cluttered with impressions of angry, young men. Surely men were never that angry in my youth. Their hostility was like corrosive acid eating them away. It seemed unnecessary to me. I sucked in deep breaths to relieve the constriction in my chest, repeating the phrase: "Close, tired eyes, close, tired eyes." Bach's lullaby soothed me to sleep: *Schummert ein ihr mueden Augen. Mueden Augen. Mueden Augen.*

An exquisite, nubile maiden appeared at the doorway of my room, dressed in a sheer trace of ivory voile. Barefoot, she tiptoed toward my bed, the voile clinging to the mounds of her naked breasts and the coils of her pubic hair. Her long, fair hair brushed against my face as she whispered seductively in my ear. I reached out to her to grasp her small breasts. "Leon, Leon," she murmured, her hot breath skimming my outer ear. "Polly, come to me," I replied, my lips stroking the softness of her nose. Her image vanished into the gossamer curtain moving on a waft of warm air through the open window. The curtain trailed between my fingers. "Polly, come back to me." Pressing the ephemeral cloth against the naked flesh of my gaping nightwear, I prolonged her presence, urging her close to me. I needed her near me. I needed her. I panted rhythmically and lustfully as the friction of voile engorged my useless appendage. I slept fitfully, dreaming of a sensual desire that would never be fulfilled.

# OSWALD DANES

In the morning, I was surprised to see Oswald sweeping the kitchen floor.

"Good morning, Dr. Bari. I'm just tidying up after last night. Sorry about the mess. What are you having for breakfast? Prue's in the shower."

I was embarrassed by my shabby nightwear, without my dressing gown. "Oh, Oswald, I, I didn't expect to see you. I'll get my dressing gown. I, I'll wait for Prudence. No, hang on, I'll get breakfast. No, no, let me put something on first." I couldn't decide what to do. Flustered and annoyed with myself, I was sure my prurient night was reflected in my appearance.

"Sure, Dr. Bari, no worries, you take as long as you like. I'll set the table." He was bright-eyed, energetic, and clear-headed: void of any evidence of a hangover. "You can stay in those clothes, Dr. B. It doesn't bother me. It's your home."

Without my dressing gown I felt less than respectable in front of Oswald, so I donned my robe and tidied my disheveled hair. We prepared breakfast together, politely maneuvering ourselves around each other. Prudence collected empty wine bottles and tossed them in the garbage bin on the back veranda. She was casually dressed in navy plimsolls, denim jeans, and a crisp, white T-shirt.

"Aren't you going to be hot in those jeans?" I asked.

"No, I'm fine. I'll put shorts on in the afternoon if it gets too hot. And you should wear some shorts today too, papa. It's going to hit the century mark today. I'm sorry about last night. It got out of hand." She sounded weary. Her hair, darkened with dampness, was held off her forehead with a white, elastic headband.

"I'll serve the eggs now. Do you want bacon, Dr. B? Two slices? Heck, that was embarrassing last night. I can't apologize enough. I'll ring Cyril later today to see if he's okay."

Prudence buttered her toast and said, "Ossie, just leave it be. They just had too much to drink."

"I know that. That's why I want to check that Cyril's okay. If you don't want me to phone him, why don't you ring him?"

"No, I'd better not. Darren gets too nasty when Cyril and I talk to each other."

"But you've been friends for years, long before Darren came on the scene. Tell Darren not to be so defensive."

"That's easier said than done. Let it be. I think Arlene's coming to Adelaide soon and I'd like to spend time with her. We can go out with Fabian too. He could do with some company, I'm sure. You know, I think Fabian may even have a woman friend, so we can all go out together."

"How do you know he's got a woman friend?" asked Oswald, although I was about to ask the same question.

"Well, he's been wearing new after-shave, he's styled his hair differently, and he's bought new clothes. Haven't you noticed that he's even been wearing colored shirts instead of white ones? He had a light, denim-blue shirt on the other day with his navy blazer. It looked very smart too. I wouldn't be surprised if he's seeing someone." She finished eating her poached eggs. "Does anyone want more tea?"

I looked at her damp hair. "No thanks," I answered. You should dry your hair in the sun. Do you want me to comb it for you?" She shook her head. "I don't think he's seeing a woman. Surely he would've mentioned it," I commented.

"No tea for me," said Oswald. "I agree with your father. The media hasn't photographed him with anyone. I think it's a safe bet that he doesn't have a woman friend. Maybe he's going through a midlife crisis. Has he bought himself a new car? I'd better get going. I have to fix the tractor, the blue one, it's playing up. Thanks for breakfast, Dr. Bari."

It was a pleasure to hear Oswald's manners. Where were the manners of the younger generation these days? We weren't rude in my day. I was beginning to like Oswald more and Cyril less. In the eighteen months since the New Year's Eve party of 1966, Cyril's behavior had altered significantly from a charming, gregarious socialite to a smug and surly young man.

# COMMISSIONER'S COMMENTARY

Reading Leon Bari's journal about Prudence and Oswald had me completely baffled. Oswald staying the night at their home puzzled me, for a start. Secondly, I couldn't fathom why Prudence would think that Fabian had a woman friend. It was, you see, anomalous with what Fabian told me when I interrogated him.

Fabian Rossi had said, quite clearly to me, that he had proposed to Prudence, and she had accepted. That would've been early in 1968, yet by the end of that year, Prudence appeared to be with Oswald, if Leon Bari's journal is accurate. Had Fabian lied to me? Or is Bari telling untruths in his journal? Naturally, I had not further investigated whether Fabian had actually proposed because I was only aware of the discrepancy when I read Bari's journal. Neither did I question Fabian about his feelings for Oswald. Had I known previously that Oswald had stayed the night I would have probed this further too. I hate to admit that my investigative approach may have been flawed, but maybe I had not been as thorough as I should have been. I swear I questioned the major suspects several times. It just goes to show that if you don't ask the right questions, you don't get the true response. Or, people are just so damned good at lying these days. No one had mentioned any bitterness between the two men, but that didn't mean that there wasn't any hidden resentment. Were Fabian and Oswald together? My mind boggles at the thought. My gut tells me, even now, that Oswald was not gay, Fabian was not gay, and they didn't have those feelings for each other. But was there resentment toward each other because they both liked Prudence? I hate to admit this, and thankfully this is not an official police record, but I surely should have interrogated these two guys even more than I did. How many interviews should I have conducted? I must have had them both in police headquarters half a dozen times.

All was not as I had been told. Was Prudence playing games so as not to reveal the truth to her father? I couldn't sense the point of it because surely she would have been aware of her father's strong affection for Fabian Rossi.

I did, however, question Fabian about his feelings for Michael McShane. Certainly I thought that if Fabian had committed the murder, it would be out of jealousy. Prudence had visited Michael in England and Fabian knew about it. Then Michael had come to Australia to see Prudence. And Prudence had gone to Fabian's place first, before taking Michael to the airport. So these two guys may well have been the last two men Prudence had seen. My theory was that Fabian was jealous and had confronted Prudence after she had driven Michael to the airport. I'm saying that I thought Fabian had followed Prudence to the airport, waited until she had dropped Michael off, and followed her home. He intercepted her and killed her in a fit of Italian rage. I had heard how hot-headed some of these Latin lovers could be, especially in cases of unrequited or jealous love.

However, my interrogations of Rossi did not expose any weaknesses in his character, or he was a bloody good actor and liar. I can't believe that he could have pretended to be anything other than he was. I concluded that jealousy was not a motive. Now I wonder whether Fabian was jealous of Michael or Oswald or both and, in defense, told me a fabrication about his marriage proposal and Prudence's acceptance.

Strange what you read in people's journals.

# PRUDENCE 1969

Prudence commenced a public campaign to promote university science courses for women amid a heightened campaign for their emancipation and the right to free speech.

"Thank you for inviting me here today to talk to you on the gender perspective of mathematics," she began to a roomful of university students. She was confident and relaxed in a charcoal-colored pantsuit. It was a classic cut of feminine, but stylish comfort. Her hair was loosely held with an onyx clasp that matched the delicate drop earrings. They were gifts from her Irish friend, Michael. She smiled at me and continued.

"I strongly believe, through many years as a mathematician, that females can accomplish a great deal in this educational endeavor. I don't believe that it's purely a matter of ability that there are more males than females undertaking mathematics at university. I believe that there are two factors that have largely been overlooked by educators. One factor is the perceived usefulness of mathematics, and the second factor is the confidence by which males and females approach the study of mathematics. Males, in general, believe that mathematics is, and will be, more useful to them, and therefore they do well in it. Females, on the other hand, may believe that there is no usefulness in learning mathematics, believing it to be something that 'boys do.' The issue of gender, learning, and mathematics is an emerging and developing area of study. There have, to date, been no definitive studies on the topic, so I'm not stating this as fact; it is purely my belief. I also don't hold the view that teacher treatment and different teacher interactions with males and females are significant contributing factors to the development of mathematical skills. Nor do I believe that male teachers, and the majority of mathematics teachers are male, have a direct positive impact on males learning mathematics and a negative impact on females learning mathematics. At least, I don't believe that it's a significant factor in the gender debate. I learned the majority of my mathematical skills firstly from my father, Dr. Leo Bari, and later from a series of male lecturers in European universities. And I certainly feel that I have not been treated differently by my male teachers and lecturers."

My mind had a habit of drifting to other worlds, and on this occasion, it was no different. I tired easily, and I wanted the lecture to finish. Prudence smiled at me as if to reassure me that she knew what I was thinking. With a nod of her head, she indicated that she would not be long. I stepped out of the room to breathe fresh air instead of the musty smell of students. When I returned, Prudence was summarizing her presentation.

"I also believe that factors affecting a person's ability to study mathematics may vary with individual males and females, and these factors may include available choices, individual interests, mental maturity, socio-economic status, ethnicity, the nurturing environment of the school, and it may also include the individual teacher and a student's interaction with the teacher to some degree. I'd like to say, in conclusion, that we need research to document the status of gender differences in mathematics as they exist, but, more importantly, we need to educate males and females on the importance and usefulness of mathematics in society. Thank you."

After the presentation, Prudence tutored a group of students while I read the foreign newspapers in the university library. I liked to keep informed of the political events in Europe but, above all, I preferred the sports pages and the soccer results. Never had I been a competitive sportsman but, in my youth, I remained fit with bouts of soccer, cycling, and swimming. I knew the benefits of an active life, a philosophy I imparted to Prudence throughout her childhood. Soccer was in my Italian blood and, in my early years, so was gambling. My Lebanese friend, Alto, and I would bet on the soccer results in our university days in Rome, and I convinced myself that I was engaging in rigorous mathematical calculations. In reality, it was mostly luck and the law of averages that enabled me to add to my winnings. I was, therefore, blissfully content in the university library with the foreign newspapers spread before me with a cornucopia of world news.

After the tutorial, Prudence and I walked the short distance along Plane Tree Avenue to the Adelaide Botanic Garden, our arms entwined. It was a glorious day of dappled, spring sunlight. Young girls in floral blouses with a skip in their step passed us on their way to lectures. The air smelled of cut flowers and freshly mown grass. Prudence's confidence seeped under my skin, making me feel twenty years younger. Boldly I asked, "Have you ever regretted taking up a career in mathematics?"

"No!" We entered Friends Gate, a spring-coiled, iron gateway to the Botanic Garden. The shaded avenue of Moreton Bay fig trees filtered the sun's rays as we admired the northern European style of the garden, a grand and historic place that felt comforting and homely to me. Native and exotic plants grew side by side and thrived in the dry, Mediterranean climate and alkaline soil: the lush greenery of palms, cycads, and bromeliads bloomed among the dusty foliage of the indigenous trees and shrubs of Australia.

"Prudence, I'm serious. I need to know. Do you resent me for mapping out your career? You know I only meant well, don't you? Mathematics was all I knew, and you were so gifted at it from a very young age. I didn't mean to push you into something you didn't want to do."

"Don't be silly, papa. I love mathematics. For years I didn't even realize that 'girls don't do science.' I did it because I enjoyed solving puzzles and then everything seemed to hang together and make sense to me. Just look at this garden. Mathematics is everywhere: it's ubiquitous. It's in these Moreton Bay fig trees and in those cycads over there. And look at the rotunda. It's a perfect mathematical structure. Everything has a pattern in its structure. The pattern of the leaves, the flowers, the seeds, and the way the bees dance around the blossoms. See how aesthetic mathematics is."

"You're preaching to the converted, remember! That's what I like too. The laws of nature are concerned with regularities. I like that. If something is proven to be mathematically true, then it's always true. Regularities are independent of so many conditions, so are principles. It doesn't matter whether it rains or not, or whether the mathematician is a man or a woman, or even whether the mathematician is English or Italian. A principle is true wherever you are in the world. That's what I like about mathematics."

"True. Different mathematicians living in different countries, in different cultures, and in different circumstances have invariably come up with the same calculations. Marvelous, isn't it?" she said as we walked. "It's truly a universal language. That's what I found so interesting in Italy. When I was learning Italian and not sure of the words, mathematical symbols were the same. My colleagues and I knew exactly what we were talking about. It was such a bond for us. No one misunderstood my computational sentences even though my Italian wasn't perfect. Do you remember when your school students taunted you sometimes, papa, when you were learning English? They laughed at you a lot. They thought you were stupid because you didn't know all the nuances of the English language or because you mispronounced some words. This was not the case with me in Italy. Everyone respected me. They knew I was intelligent simply because they could understand the complex mathematical concepts that I was solving. You know, no one thought it was odd that I was a woman. It seemed that only later, when I was in England and America, when people began to tell me that I was different. I'm so thankful that I studied in Italy. Those years were the best years of my life."

"I'm glad," I said wistfully. "I remember when I was teaching. Lots of people thought I was stupid. I know that feeling. It wasn't nice at times. That's why I studied English 'like crazy,' as Australians say. I carried my dictionary with me everywhere. It took years to learn English, but once my English improved, students didn't laugh so much. For a long time, I didn't even know that 'wog teacher' was a derogatory term!" We laughed together at those early and difficult years. "And I even wrote a couple of mathematics books in English. Not bad for a simple man, was it? It didn't take long for me to fit into the Australian way of life really. And there were many Italian families in the same situation, all making a go of their new country. Australia's a good country. It's been good to us." She kissed me on the cheek and I rubbed away the stain of her lipstick.

"I love coming home to Australia, but I love the culture and history of Europe too," she said. "I guess I have the best of both worlds living in two hemispheres. I wouldn't give up living in Australia though. So you were right in what you did. You made the right decision." She embraced me firmly. Her perfumed scent of *L'Air du Temps* mingled with the sweetness of pear blossoms and camellias in the garden beds. "Let's sit on the lawn near the museum for a while."

"Do you really think I made the right decision, or are you just being kind to your old father?"

"I mean it. How else would I have been able to travel overseas? How else would I have met so many interesting and famous people? How else would I be able to afford the glorious European fashions? But if truth were known, I wouldn't have minded being a singer, but I yawn every time I try to sing. I'd fall asleep on stage," she said as she brushed away a persistent fly attempting to settle in her hair.

"That fly likes your hairspray, I think. You must've put too much on. So, you wanted to be a singer, hey? Yawning is supposed to be a good sign; it's something to do with opening the vocal chords, I think. A good singing coach would've trained you properly, I'm sure. Perhaps you should've been a singer, or an actress like Sophia Loren."

"Me, a singer or an actress? Never! You're obsessed with Sophia Loren. She's far too young for you anyway. I don't need a good singing coach. You're a good coach in mathematics. Remember when you got your first lecturing job at university? Your English had improved so much and you were so confident and raring to start work. You loved it. Your university students loved you too. I think you are mathematics incarnate. You're never wrong."

I'm never wrong! I would like to believe my daughter was right. I, however, displayed the folly of an aged man when I thought I could add to the theories of mathematics in my late sixties. Well past my prime, I wanted to be useful in my old age, and I hankered for another chance to work in the university. Always wanting to be a geometer, I offered to be of assistance to the geometry program at Adelaide University. Professor Chemsley suggested that I study a recent paper by Louis Nirenberg on closed surfaces. I scurried to learn topics such as Poincare-Bendixson theorems as well as existence and uniqueness results for hyperbolic partial differential equations. I tried hard to recast the definitions used by Nirenberg in a way that would apply equally well to polyhedra. The result was a surprising simplification of the notion of minimal total absolute curvature. Nirenberg proved theorems for smooth surfaces that satisfied technical hypotheses necessitated by his differential equation techniques. He used a definition that stated that any local support tangent plane to the surface, intersecting the surface locally at one point, must be a global support plane, meeting the surface at no further point. I observed that this definition was sufficiently geometric to apply to polyhedral surfaces as well. So determined was I to prove a polyhedral rigidity theorem and apply approximation techniques in the case of convex surfaces that I worked day and night. Unfortunately, the approach failed completely.

In another project, Professor Chemsley noted that the theory of total absolute curvature could be reworked in the language of critical point theory. He had exploited this fact in the case of smooth surfaces to show that if a smooth surface was embedded in an $n$-dimensional Euclidean space so that no height function had more than one local maximum, then the surface had to be contained in a five dimensional affine subspace. Moreover, if it did not lie in a four dimensional space, then it had to be a very specific surface, the Veronese embedding of the real projective plane. I set out to establish the analog of this result in the case of polyhedral surfaces in higher dimensional space. The project failed in a rather spectacular fashion. I desisted from offering further assistance in the geometry program. Another failure would have devastated me. In any case, I had not mentioned these endeavors to Prudence and, as far as I was aware, only Professor Chemsley knew of my failures. Dispirited, I returned to tendering my garden.

"You're teasing me," I said to her. I shifted position on the grass to avoid an angry ants' nest. "You forget that being right in mathematics just means being logically consistent. Perhaps I've just been consistent. Or does consistency mean that I was regimented or boring? I don't know. You keep telling me I'm boring."

"Maybe, but you have been consistent. You don't like to change much, do you papa? But you know consistency can be a wonderful thing. You were never critical of me, and you supported me unconditionally. Oh, I forgot to tell you. We must go to a camera shop this afternoon. I've got David McMurray's photographs with me of the 1966 Leonid storm. I want to get them enlarged and use them for my lectures. It was years ago and I haven't had time to get them developed. They'd look fabulous for lectures, wouldn't they?"

"Let me see them again," I said. Prudence rummaged through her black leather tote bag and retrieved a folder of photographs. "I like this one," I said pointing to a photograph of green streaks across a blackened sky like the phosphorescence of glow-worms. "I love comets. They're incredible inventions of nature."

"They're fabulous to watch. Look at this one." Prudence pointed to a massive fireball of iridescent green.

"Look at the trail on that one," I said. "The 'snows of yesteryear' they've been called. Snowballs of gas, dust, and ice moving toward the Sun, orbiting it in a pre-determined path, they are. But alas, if comets get too close to the Sun they burn off and disappear into the cavernous darkness. Have I recited the comet poem to you lately?"

"Lots of times, but you can say it again. You're going to anyway, aren't you?"

It was my favorite poem. Gerard Manley Hopkins certainly had a way with words and a way with science. I recited the words slowly and deliberately, savoring every syllable:

143

*I am like a slip of comet,*
*Scarce worth discovery, in some corner seen*
*Bridging the slender difference of two stars,*
*Come out of space, or suddenly engender'd*
*By heady elements, for no man knows;*
*But when she sights the sun she grows and sizes*
*And spins her skirts out, while her central star*
*Shakes its cocooning mists; and so she comes*
*To fields of light; millions of travelling rays*
*Pierce her; she hangs upon the flame-cased sun,*
*And sucks the light as full as Gideon's fleece:*
*But then her tether calls her; she falls off,*
*And as she dwindles shreds her smock of gold*
*Between the sistering planets, till she comes*
*To single Saturn, last and solitary;*
*And then she goes out into the cavernous dark.*
*So I go out: my little sweet is done:*
*I have drawn heat from this contagious sun:*
*To not ungentle death now forth I run.*

"Your memory is still good." Prudence squeezed my hand. "You're not suffering dementia yet."

"I love that poem. Why is it that comets are both good and bad omens, I wonder?"

"What do you mean?" asked Prudence as she returned the photographs to her bag.

"When Halley's Comet appeared in 1066 during the Battle of Hastings it was a bad omen for the Saxons and a good omen for William the Conqueror. 'A new star, a new king,' he said. When it appeared again in 1456, the Christians and Turks were at war, and Pope Calixtus III condemned the comet as an agent of the devil."

"Yes, Christians won the battle, not the Turks, so it was a good omen for the Christians. But then, it was a bad omen for the Turks. Men will fight for a superstition as quickly as for a living truth, often more so. But the fact is that comets, to a large extent, have devastated Earth. They've caused major environmental damage and mass extinction and they've distorted weather patterns and altered geography, so they're bad omens after all. There's no reason to assume that the threat of a large meteorite impact on Earth is any less now than it was in the past. We could be blasted out of the Milky Way by a wayward comet any year now. Let's enjoy the day while we can," she smiled as she exaggerated an explosion with her wayward arms.

"You're teasing me again. It won't happen in my lifetime anyway, and I'm too old now to care. I like the way Hopkins invented words in the comet poem. The poem is like the comet, not entirely random, but moving in an orbit until it heads for the Sun. We should have brought a blanket with us; this grass seems damp to me."

"You like everything to be regular and symmetrical and orderly including the uniform syllabic counts of a poem," she teased, grabbing my arm. "Don't you?"

"Don't laugh at your father. I can only tolerate a few degrees off center and I'm too old to change that now." I clasped my hand around hers to hold still her Italian gesturing arms.

"That's another reason why I like mathematics; it's in poetry too," Prudence mused.

"Is there anything you don't like about it?"

"It can't predict the future. Not with any certainty at least. We can monitor patterns, such as weather patterns, and we can predict that there may be more precipitation from one year to the next, but there isn't enough accuracy in it. But that's the weather. Human behavior and the future are too unpredictable. We can't predict what will happen to us. I wish we could."

"Yes we can, to a certain degree," I said. "We know that if something is born, it will inevitably die. That's predictable."

Prudence eyed me as though I were an imbecile, playfully rolling her eyes and puckering her lips to show disdain. "But what happens in our lives between birth and death, papa? No one truly knows what will happen."

"Except God," I answered. "And what if people did know? The truth might not live up to people's expectations of their lives. Then what would they do? Not live out their lives because they don't like their fate, their destiny, and the consequences of their pre-destined path? It's best that we don't know. Then we can always live with the hope that tomorrow will be a better day and that our lives will have an impact on society somehow. We can live with the hope that we are here for a purpose, Prudence. Only God should know what's to become of us."

"Okay, except God then. He knows all, but he's a mathematician." She beamed at me, her eyes mischievously glinting in the sun. Pointing ahead of her, she said, "Look at the old woman over there. Will I look like that when I get old?" A stooped, frail woman stopped to admire petunias near a row of hothouses. The tattered, dusty-pink dress swinging against her ankles would once have been expensive. Her dirty-white handbag matched her shoes, her floppy hat, and crocheted shawl. She had worn her Sunday best on a weekday for a walk through the Botanic Garden. "Perhaps she's been to a christening. Perhaps she's been shopping in the city. I hope she's had a good life. But will anyone remember her after her death? Maybe that's one good thing about fame. We measure our lives by the death of influentially famous people. We know exactly where we were and what we were doing when the person died. It's a pivotal moment in the life of a celebrated person that becomes inextricably entwined in the memories of others."

"That's true," I said. "I remember what I was doing when I heard about Marilyn Monroe's death. It was August 7, 1962, two days after she died. I read it the newspaper. I surely remember that day. People will remember the day you die too, when you are old. Marilyn was only thirty-six years old when she died, but you, you will be old and famous, my beautiful Prudence."

"I'm not that famous. I'm only famous in Adelaide! I guess I have to be happy that I may leave a slight impression, an indefinable dent, in a handful of people's lives." She played with a handful of grass, pulled from the luscious verdant lawn, impressive in its vastness as it swept up the mound in a wavering pattern. It wasn't a rectangular lawn like that of the regimented houses in my street but a rambling carpet that linked the beds of botanical themes.

"Of course you will! You'll touch lots of people's lives. What if Innes becomes the next Leonard da Vinci? It'll be because of you. You'll be remembered forever, on your own merits and as his mentor. I'm glad I haven't ruined your life," I said.

"Ruined my life? What do you mean? Are you still harping on? How can you or mathematics ruin my life?"

"I mean that I may have ruined your life by choosing your career. I feel guilty that you didn't have more choices. And I feel guilty that I brought you up without a mother. Perhaps I should've married again? I worry about my inertia sometimes. I feel guilty that you're not married with children of your own. People are saying terrible things about your sexuality, so I feel guilty about that too. There are lots more things that I feel guilty about, like taking the easy way out, the path of least resistance. What if you'd wanted to be a nurse? What if you didn't want a career at all, but a life of marriage and motherhood? How could I have helped you become a nurse or a mother when it was something not familiar to me? I would have failed. But I've failed after all, haven't I? I've failed."

"What are you rambling on about?" Prudence tossed clumps of grass into the air and let the breeze scatter them on top of her, allowing the blades to land on her clothes. She didn't brush them away.

"I haven't listened to the myths of the past. They warned me, but I didn't listen," I said. "It's all about Phaethon. He was taunted at school, and he was hurt and angry. He asked his father, Helios, the God of the Sun, if he could drive his chariot for a day, the chariot that bore the fiery Sun across the sky. His father agreed, thereby sealing his son's fate. The horses pulled the chariot higher and higher through space. Phaethon felt triumphant, victorious, powerful, and majestic. But then the horses realized that it was not Helios driving them. They knew that there were different hands at the reins. They left their usual path and flew at random, flying too close to Earth. The fields burst into flames from the searing heat of the Sun. Rivers dried up. The fiery sphere would have devastated Earth if the chariot wasn't stopped. Zeus, the king of the gods, to avoid catastrophe,

147

shot Phaethon down with a thunderbolt. A meteor flew through space to its death; that meteor was Phaethon, a poor, unhappy boy who believed that he could conquer the infinite by driving the chariot, the important chariot of the Sun. He tried to compensate for his feelings of inferiority. He thought he had increased his status in the eyes of others. But alas, his triumph was short-lived. It resulted in disaster. Disaster! Was his father, Helios, to blame for giving him the chariot? Was his father to blame for failing to protect him? He failed in his duty as a father. Perhaps I am like Helios. Perhaps it was in the numbers? I changed your destiny when I changed your name. The letters in a birth name each have a numerical value, and I changed the letters. Numbers hold the meaning of our lives. I altered your numbers, and I've changed your destiny, your life. Was it for better or for worse? I just don't know. All I know is that I'm Helios. I'm ultimately responsible."

"The sun's got to you, papa. I don't know what you're rambling about. What disaster are you talking about? Even if you didn't know anything about nursing you would've still given me the confidence to be a nurse. The same applies with motherhood or whatever. Stop being silly! What's got into you?" Her exasperation with me was beginning to show.

"But Germaine Greer's remarks about your sexuality were not very flattering, and it's my fault."

"For heaven's sake! I know what Germaine said. I admire her immensely. I've been thinking a lot about her. I've even read more of her articles. Germaine has extremely clear ideas about feminism, and she knows her own mind. She's a very intelligent woman—and incredibly perceptive. But I don't think that I can change my past. No one, no one on Earth could state categorically that I would've made a different career choice. Or that I would've stayed home to look after a husband. No one knows what one decision can lead to. One decision! And then another. No one can say whether something is meant to happen, that a decision is irrevocable. As for numerology, it's not a science. Mathematics and numbers don't hold answers to our individual destinies in the way that you think they do. They can't predict someone's life. Not in terms of our destiny anyway. *Che sara, sara*: what will be, will be. That's life. Are you listening to me? But Germaine is right in many of her presentations and articles. She wrote that people need extreme polarities in order to move ideas forward. She's right. I must move some things forward. I've been so self-centered that I haven't done enough to move science forward. There are many undertakings I haven't done in my life. What are you looking at?"

Prudence prodded my arm, but I didn't respond. It was true. She was stubborn and forthright, and I had not changed that in all the years of her life. Selfish at times, but I had let her have her way at every opportunity simply because I wanted her to love me, above all else, above any other man. But now that is not what I want. Had my dreams of perfection made her aspire to be a perfectionist, looking for the perfect man? There is no such creature. Her expectations were unrealistic and extreme; if the man is not perfect, she will have no man. Perfection should never have been my goal. It was my downfall and would be my daughter's also.

# POLLY SMITH

"Oh, no, there's Polly," I said, closing my eyes. "I wish I could hide. She overwhelms me when she talks about sex. She never stops. Oh no, she's seen us."

"She means well and you're probably a grandfather figure for her." Prudence returned Polly's wave, though less enthusiastically.

"Hello!" She sat infinitesimally close to me that she was almost sitting on my lap. "I'm on my way to university to see the live band *Hunks of Spunk*. Do you want to come along?"

"No thanks. Prudence and I haven't had lunch yet, and we've some shopping to do. We've been lazing about in the botanical gardens and now we must move on." I wanted to be definitive and defiant, and I was pleased with my quick-thinking response.

"What a shame. Cyril's going to be there." Polly's long, thin, alabaster legs were stretched out before her on the grass. Her denim shorts covered only the barest amount of flesh, and the blue, cotton singlet covered even less. Her nipples stood erect, leaving nothing to the imagination, and I was unsure where to look. "I'm not chasing Cyril for sex anymore. I like his friend John. And Jeremy's cute too. Hey! Hey, isn't that Raphael over there? He's with Julia. Raphael's gorgeous, isn't he? He's not interested in me though. He's been seeing Julia for ages. Practically engaged they are. Besides, he's too straight for me, you know. He's not into experimentation when it comes to sex, so I've been told. I suspect he's Catholic." Prudence was watching him intently. She shaded her eyes from the sun with her hands. She wasn't listening to Polly. "I reckon Julia must be Catholic too. She looks Italian. She's not though. She's from England. Look how brown her skin is. She's got big tits like an Italian.

150

Catholic girls don't have sex though. Raffy's got his hands all over her though. Look at that! It looks like he's lost something in her bust. Oh, it's okay. He's just getting a leaf or something out of her blouse. I wonder what size bra she has. I'm lucky in a way because I don't need to wear one. She must have the genes of her mother. What do you reckon?"

"Polly, I reckon you talk too much. You'd make a great companion for Karl Kraus," said Prudence.

I roared with laughter, but Polly had no idea of the joke.

"What's so funny about Karl? Is he a bit of a goober?"

In between a fit of the giggles, Prudence explained that the Austrian satirist once quipped that he couldn't think of a thing to say about Adolf Hitler, then proceeded to write a hundred pages on the subject.

"But I'm not talking about Hitler," said Polly. "I don't understand what's so funny."

"Nothing, Polly. You'll be late for the band if you don't go soon. Besides, the band will take your mind off sex," said Prudence, still looking at Raphael.

"No, it won't. Have you seen the guys in the band? I like Randy. Wow, is he gorgeous? Bilge is okay too. He's so tall with incredibly white hair. Real white it is; it's not bleached. Yeah, I think I like Bilge best. I wonder if he's got a girlfriend. I'll ask him."

"I'd take Prudence's advice if I were you. We don't want you to be late to see Andy and Bill."

"Oh, you're so funny, Leon. It's Randy and Bilge. I can't remember the names of the other guys. I suppose I'd better go. I'll walk with you and Prue to the North Terrace gate."

We stood up, brushed the grass from our clothes, and made our way to the southern end of the Botanic Garden and to the east of the city. Frustrated at Polly's excitable intrusion and sexual verbosity, I was glad to see her leave.

# CYRIL SILVERMAN

Espousing his views on the university's role in promoting equal rights for homosexuals, Cyril seemed like a different person. It was the commencement of the university year. He was standing atop a temporary stage on an oval of grass where trestles and tables were placed around the perimeter. In the communal area, students were touting for enrollment into sporting and recreational clubs. Two nubile nymphets sat cross-legged on the lawn, naked from the waist up, holding wooden placards denouncing the Vietnam War. It was a silent, effective protest. Ruby red lipstick messages of peace were printed across their ample breasts. Love, sex, and revolution were inseparably entangled in the consciousness of the youth of today.

I was like a fish out of water among the young faces, yet they did not appear to notice. I was as much a fixture of the university as the aged buildings.

"Hey Leon, old mate, how are ya? Waiting for Prusey? I haven't seen her about," said Dr. Gorrie from the physics department.

"I'm fine thanks, Stewart. I'm early, I think. Are you still working with Professors Garland and Chemsley? What are you doing now?"

"I haven't retired yet, like you, you lucky duck. I'll be here for years yet, more's the pity because students are getting more difficult to handle each year. You're lucky you retired when you did. I'd better go. I'll catch up with you for lunch sometime, at the usual place, yeah?" His unruly, wiry fair hair stood up in the breeze, and he smoothed it against his head. He looked older than his fifty-eight years; his ruddy face was threaded with fiery veins and stained with sunspots. His double chin mirrored the

152

twofold rolls of stomach protruding against his tight, striped cotton shirt, buttons yawning to reveal hairy, white flesh. The Scot enjoyed his meals and wine, but he relished them more in the company of others. I waved goodbye to Stewart and turned my attention to the voice puttering into a megaphone.

"Per, per, per, testing one, two, and three—per, per, testing."

Cyril strutted along the makeshift platform. He wore the tightest jeans I'd ever seen. I wondered how he managed to compress his buttocks and thighs into them. Surely he could not bend his torso, yet he appeared to be comfortable. His black, high-heeled boots elevated him to almost Oswald's stature, although Cyril was lean and sinewy compared to Oswald's stocky frame. His orange and yellow shirt was, as usual, opened almost to his navel, revealing his hirsute chest. He wore a black, cotton cravat around his neck, supposedly to absorb perspiration. The stage was open to the midday sun. I expected to see Darren nearby, but I couldn't detect his presence anywhere.

Cyril bellowed into the yellow megaphone, "The fabulous fashion designer, Mary Quant, said 'Good taste is death; vulgarity is life' and what do I know about fashion? Nothing! I just wished I'd said it first. What am I doing here? I'm not espousing a chess club, or a sporting club, or a drama club, or even a music club. My aim is to agitate and disturb you people: awaken your consciousness. Conservatism and morality are synonyms for rottenness and ugliness. My desire for reality is the reality of my desire, and my desire is for gay sex. While the conservative right is continually pushing the idea of maintaining morals, we should believe that no matter what we do, everything we do matters. We need to participate in overpowering the conservative morality; we need to participate in liberation. Liberation of oppressive sex, liberation of sexual stereotypes, liberation to have sex with whomever we want, in the privacy of our own homes, without vilification and reprisals. And what is the university doing about equality, equality for gays and lesbians? We have the right to be employed here under the same conditions as heterosexuals. We have the chance to reform oppression, discrimination, and prudish policies. Down with prudish views! Down with Prudence

Bari and her puritanical views and her discrimination of gays and lesbians. She doesn't believe in same sex relationships, she doesn't believe in relationships at all! We can discard the prudish morals of the oldies and forge ahead with sexual liberation for all. But you must know your enemy. Know your enemy is the first lesson in the survival handbook and the enemy is Professor Prudence Bari." His voice rose and he punched the air with his fist. "The fight for liberation is an undeclared war that has been raging worldwide for a long time, and it will rage and roar with increasing ferocity for a number of years to come for we will not relent. It's a war for freedom, freedom of sexual choice. It is, in a very real sense, a war of liberation against the evils of an unjust morality, an old-fashioned morality, and a morality stagnating in its reluctance to change with the times. And it is war. I can think of few acts more evil than to discriminate against employment, housing, and lifestyle because of sexual preference. And it's a war that we're in danger of losing if we don't fight the establishment and the conservative right. The old morality has failed us. We have opened our eyes to moralist bigots: the degradation, the humiliation, the beatings, and the deaths of people for no other reason than because they are gay. That cannot and must not continue. Is the university council going to perpetuate this persecution, the persecution of its staff and students? What on earth is a democratic government and a democratic university for if it is not to educate, protect, and provide study and employment opportunities for all its academic citizens. It's not an immutable policy. It's not an immutable law. We can change it. Down with bureaucratic euphemisms! Make no mistake, universities are the place to begin the reformation because they are the hearts of progress. Universities are not the product of yesterday; their solutions are solutions for the future. Liberation is happening everywhere. It's happening overseas and it's madness for the island nation of Australia to pursue a course of non-action. Negotiations within universities and state governments at the highest level must not fail," he shouted. More forcefully, he screamed, "Must not fail! It's reform or die. The future of liberation, if it is to have a future, lies in the completion of the reform process. I hope I've convinced you fellow staff and students that no matter how hard it may be to do so, we must continue the reform process. If you are not convinced then reform will fail, and gays and lesbians will continue to be harassed, discriminated against, beaten, and humiliated. You cannot stay quiet and do nothing. Stand up and speak out, because if you do not, then it may be your turn next; your turn to be discriminated against, your turn to be vilified and abused. We must stand united. As Edmund Burke said, 'All that is necessary for the triumph of evil is for good men to do nothing.' Fellow staff and students, you are good and intelligent men and women and on these evils you have been silent and done nothing for too long. My fellow comrades will take your names. Come to the table now and sign up to support the negotiation process. Get your free badges and change the university. Do it now! DO IT NOW!" He emitted an almighty yell.

Cyril jumped from the stage next to a table draped with rolls of overlapping white paper where he embraced a group of girls. The sexual Svengali rallied support amongst the queuing students using his charming and persuasive manner. He captivated young females with every sensual movement of his thrusting torso. They loved it and he loved their attention. He gyrated gracefully as they eyed his bulging crotch. He would have no trouble in gaining support for his cause, I thought. Even I could not take my eyes off him, or at least, parts of him.

"Great work, Cyril. Che Guevara would be proud. Power to Che!" A wild-haired, rough-cut youth raised his fist in the air. "Power to Che! Power to Marxism! Power to Silverman!" With every phrase, he punched his fist upwards, moving among the crowd for mutual support.

Whenever I met Prudence at the university, we would meet on these lawns, a central gathering place. She seized my arm, pushing me through the throng of students. "Hey, Prudence, what are you doing? Aren't we having lunch here? Where are we going?"

She didn't answer me. We sheltered underneath concrete stairs to the physics laboratories. The ground, littered with cigarette stubs, emitted an odor of stale smoke. In thick, red splashes of paint on the concrete stairwell wall were the words: PRUDISH PRUDENCE and, in smaller black print: PROFESSOR BARI DOESN'T SUCK (COCKS). Scrawled below it in different handwriting was: SHE SUCKED MINE.

I was on the verge of making a comment to Prudence about the graffiti, but she motioned me to hurry along. She placed her hand at the base of my back and pushed me into the crowd opposite the parking lot. The crowd wasn't unruly, merely dense and enthusiastically friendly toward each other. We entered the darkness of the concrete underground parking lot, walking briskly toward her yellow Fiat. Egg yolk oozed down the front glass onto the windscreen wiper. She dismissed it as a student's idea of a joke. As she turned the key in the ignition, an intolerable clanging noise reverberated throughout the car. Instinctively I closed my eyes and covered my ears. When I dared to look, I saw two youths wielding the lids of metal rubbish bins, beating them fiercely against the car.

"Hold on, papa," said Prudence as she backed out of the parking space and sped up the ramp. A youth hurled a lid toward the car and it crashed into the windscreen, splitting it with a piercing noise, right in front of my face.

"What's going on? What's going on?" I was frightened and upset, but more so, I was angry and confused.

"Don't worry. It's just students. It was getting too crowded and noisy on the grassed area. I was worried about your safety. I'll take you home," she said as we exited the parking lot into the light of the university grounds. Prudence veered left into the main traffic and headed for home. "It's okay now."

"Look at the windscreen! It's cracked." The spidery web of splintered glass radiated outward. The fragmented pieces held together precariously. "What did they want? What's going on? Who were they? Prudence? Answer me!"

"I said they're just students. They're probably playing a joke. It's only a small crack. Stop worrying; it's nothing. I'll drop you home then I'll take the car to the crash repairer. I'll walk or take a taxi home."

Her indifference was infuriating me. "You can't do that! Go to the police station! Go straight to the police! Do you hear me? Do as I say! Now! *Fermo! Fermo!*"

"Don't be silly. It was just students." She ignored my demands.

"They could've killed you. They could've killed us!" I yelled. My heart was still beating rapidly with anxiety and fear.

"Stop exaggerating. The students in the parking lot are okay. I was more concerned about the crowd on the lawn. You could have been crushed accidently. Have a good rest when you get home. I'll have to get these dents fixed. What a nuisance."

"What a nuisance! Is that all you're going to say? What a nuisance! It's more than that. It's vandalism. It's assault. It's attempted murder! And the students on the lawn weren't the problem; they were just a bit boisterous. The ones with the weapons are the problem; they were after you, not me!" My temples pounded and, with every thundering pulse, my anger rose.

"Stop being silly," she yelled back. "Rubbish bin lids aren't weapons. Calm down. You'll give yourself a heart attack." She stopped the car outside the house, forcing me out. "I'll be back soon. Put the kettle on. Make us some tea and some lunch, that's what we need. Go on!"

I was still shaking from fear and outrage as I fumbled for the house keys. The key ring jangled as I repeatedly jammed the key into its cavity. Had the students meant to kill us or was it some childish university prank? What had Prudence done to deserve this? I could not understand the motives of the younger generation.

I disliked being ordered about by my daughter, yet I dutifully obeyed her commands. Throughout lunch I tried, in vain, to persuade Prudence to contact the police. She obstinately refused until the telephone interrupted our argument.

"Oswald, slow down." I could hear her frustrated tone. "I can't hear what you're saying. What? What do you mean? A stone—what happened? What's happening? What's that noise? Ossie? Speak to me. What's that racket?—What!—Oh, no! Are you all right?—Oh no! I'll get off the phone now, so you can let the police in. Call me as soon as you can." Prudence was visibly distressed.

"What's happening? Is everything okay?"

With tears streaming down her reddened face, she explained that Oswald's house and car had been pelted with rocks, and two rear bedroom windows were broken.

I embraced her tightly. "He'll be fine. The police are there now. All we can do is to wait for him to phone back."

"I know he'll be okay. I just worry for him," she said as she gulped breaths amid the tears.

"Just as I worry for you! It's natural. You didn't tell him about your incident. You should have! Please, Prudence, phone the police."

"Okay, but after I hear from Ossie."

Prudence did not telephone the police. Not on that day, nor on any other day. She never mentioned the incident to Oswald and this distressed and angered me immensely. In the weeks that followed, I suspected further disturbances, although Prudence remained silent and introspective. She had also taken to whispering when she spoke on the telephone. When I questioned her, she said that my ears were as feeble as my eyes, but I knew this not to be true.

# COMMISSIONER'S COMMENTARY

Oswald commented on the disturbances at his house. He never mentioned Prudence's situation. After I read about this in Leon's journal, I asked my officers to check the records. As expected, she never reported the incident to the police. Oswald, on the other hand, delivered a carefully-worded statement: detailed and thorough. No further incidences occurred at Oswald's property. No arrests were ever made. We struck a dead end.

# THE LUNAR LANDING

I remember well the eight days, three hours, eighteen minutes and thirty-five seconds of Apollo 11's journey to the moon and back. Prudence welcomed the event with excitement, explaining to me that it would change the world forever by liberating society's thinking. From the launch of the rocket on July 16, to the landing on the moon on July 20, and to the splashdown on July 24, in American time, I watched, listened, and read everything about the first manned space mission to the moon.

Prudence made a special effort to be with me at this historic time, embracing me like a schoolgirl given permission to attend a class excursion. She said we'd always remember where we were, and whom we were with, on this auspicious occasion. She was right.

She was sitting on the carpet in front of my legs as I sat in my brown leather armchair. Her arms were locked around the raised knees of her green, paisley-patterned, straight-legged trousers. Her feet were comfortable in white socks and black cowhide loafers. I combed my fingers through her copper-red, silky-smooth hair, identical in color to her long-sleeved shirt. I layered her curls across the thighs of my black cotton trousers, stroking and caressing the ends. Together we watched the television screen's flickering black and white images of the descent of the lunar module onto the surface of the moon. It was 5:47a.m., Adelaide time, on Wednesday July 21, 1969.

"Five hundred and forty feet, down at 30—down at 15—400 feet down—forward—350, down at four—300 feet, down three and a half—47 forward—down." A fine mist of lunar dust spread across the base of the shuttle, called the Eagle, as a white

160

horizontal line inched down the television screen, slowly and repeatedly. It irritated me. Prudence said we shouldn't complain about the quality of the image, but thank our lucky stars we were watching it on our very own television in our very own house. She was right; I stopped complaining.

"Thirteen forward—11 forward—coming down nicely, 200 feet, four and a half down—five and a half down—five percent—75 feet—six forward—lights on—down two and a half—40 feet—down two and a half—kicking up some dust—30 feet, two and a half down—faint shadow—four forward—four forward—drifting to the right a little—okay."

"Thirty seconds," a voice from Houston called out, indicating the amount of fuel remaining.

"They've got problems, Prudence. They can't guide it down with only thirty seconds of fuel. You can't park a car with thirty seconds of fuel, let alone a spaceship! No, no, they won't make it. Oh, no!" The chilling prospect of failure began to take hold, strangling me by the throat.

"Hush, papa! They may have miscalculated a bit because we don't know enough about the moon's gravity yet," Prudence explained. "There might be irregularities in the lunar gravitational field that's influencing the speed of the shuttle. It's called the perilune wiggle. They look okay though. Keep still!"

"Contact light. Okay. Engine stop—descent engine command override on," continued the announcement from Tranquility Base.

"We copy you down, Eagle."

"Houston, Tranquility Base here. The Eagle has landed."

"Roger, Tranquility," said a Houston control officer. "We copy you on the ground. You've got a bunch of guys about to turn blue. We're breathing again. Thanks a lot."

"Thank you," said someone aboard Eagle. "That may have seemed like a very long final phase. The auto targeting was taking us right into a football-field-sized crater with a large number of big boulders and rocks with about one or two crater diameters around it. It required flying manually over the rock field to find a reasonably good area."

"Roger, we copy. It was beautiful from here, Tranquility. Over."

The time from the shuttle landing to the time men actually walked on the moon seemed an eternity to me. In reality the moonwalk occurred a little less than seven hours after the lunar touchdown. Prudence anxiously flitted about the house until Neil Armstrong climbed down the shuttle ladder backwards. She watched him push himself off the last step down to the moon's surface, where he uttered the words: "That's one small step for man, one giant leap for mankind."

The incredibility of the momentous event never ceased to amaze us. We experienced every second through the eyes of three men, pioneering a masterminded scheme of ingenuity and fortitude, determination and fate. For me, it was a calculation of chance and inspiration so extreme as to defy derivation. The minds of brilliant men produced a seminal seed of fundamental desire and germinated it with a fervid energy until it matured into inevitability and eventuality. For me, it was, indeed, a supreme miracle.

It was the ultimate achievement of the ultimate dream. But, sadly, I could never view the moon in the same way ever again. I wondered how long it would be before people would colonize the moon, just as we had colonized our own planet. Ten years, twenty years, certainly by the turn of the century, I thought. The space race between the Americans and the Russians had not ended. This was not the finishing line, but merely the inspiration to dream another dream. Surely, the space race would advance in earnest. The Russians would be the next to land on the moon, and the intense competition between countries would inevitably lead to mass settlement. In a way, this held both excitement and loathing to me because the moon was no longer a virginal paradise. Man had violated the pristine lady, the moon goddess. She had been sullied and stained with the flag and footsteps of development, of advancement, and of progress. She was an unblossomed female open to further desecration and brutality. The moon was no longer a romantic light in the sky, but another world, another frontier ripe for exploration. But what if the moon was just a stepping stone to the universe? Would humans exploit her, changing her irrevocably, or will they leave her to bleed in silence, of no further interest, and, instead, set their sights on Mars?

The next morning, Prudence tapped on my bedroom door. "I've got the papers. We can read all about the landing. I'll put the kettle on."

When I entered the kitchen, she had *The Australian* spread across the kitchen table, skimming the sentences with her index finger. "Why pay five cents for a newspaper? The local one's cheaper and it'll have the same information," I said. "Two! You bought two of the same edition?" I could not understand her extravagance.

"It's history. The ladder was gold-plated. Listen to this about Armstrong." Prudence read the printed words: "*That's one small step for man. One giant leap for mankind. He spoke after he had inched his way down the gold-plated ladder in the cold shadow of the lunar module and stopped a million hearts when he had trouble with stretching the last dramatic step—a step that put the first man on another world and mankind into the universe. This was the high drama of this most dramatic day in which the world saw a man skipping like a light-footed ballet dancer in the ghostly setting of Tranquility Base, a place which Aldrin called magnificent desolation.*

"It's so amazing, papa. Come and read it. Here, take your newspaper," she said placing it in front of me.

Prudence was flushed with excitement, as if with the afterglow of an exhilarating experience. "Oh, this whole event is so incredibly important, papa. I can't believe the magnitude of it. I'm going to be excited for months. I can just feel it. I'll be watching the next mission too, in September, I think. To think that this happened in our lifetime is unbelievable. It began in our lifetime! We're so privileged!" She stopped and listened. "I thought I heard something. Someone's at the door. Are you expecting someone? I'll get it."

"It might be Franco with some eggs."

It was not Franco. It was Oswald. Prudence returned to the kitchen holding a magnificent bunch of delicate poppies redolent with a powerfully fertile fragrance. "Aren't the flowers glorious? I'll put them in a vase straight away." She deftly arranged them in a tall vase that reflected the reds, pinks, oranges, and yellows of the blossoms, their spindly legs finding their place against the cold crystal, sucking up the freshness of the cool water. I drew my breath in awe at the floral spectacle, looking up at Prudence dressed in warm, poppy colors. Oswald watched her silently.

"And what occasion are the flowers for?" I asked Oswald. Prudence grabbed his hand, stained with the dirt of his land and led him into the living room.

"Because I saw them and they reminded me of Prudence," he said as his words trailed to a whisper as they left the kitchen. "I've got something to show you, Prue."

I remained in the kitchen with the newspapers although I was not concentrating on reading; I was alert to their conversation, straining to hear Oswald's hushed and gentle voice.

"Here, this is for you, Prudence. I've had it for a long time and I never knew when I should give it to you. We've known each other for ages and I like being with you. I want you to have this engagement ring. Will you marry me, Prue?"

I gagged on the cold coffee in my mouth, spewing it forth onto my shirt and the newspaper photographs of the lunar landing. Hastily, I reached for a cloth to wipe the newspaper hoping that the visions of Prudence's dream would not be tainted and spoiled with coffee marks. My ears labored to hear her response. She was silent for an agonizingly long time. What was she doing?

"Ossie, I like you too, enormously. I really do. But the answer is not now. Perhaps we should talk about this properly before we make a commitment."

How much more time did she need? They had known each other for twenty years: an eternity to an impatient, expectant father.

"I thought you wanted a commitment, Prudence. You told me that you wanted to be married. Remember? After you met Dr. Greer, we talked about marriage. Prue, we can marry in the registry office in King William Street and then have a short honeymoon. You could move onto the farm, of course. Then you can stop lecturing and you won't have to go overseas so often. We can work together on the farm."

Oh dear, I thought. I ought to have told Oswald that Prudence was not likely to give up her career. Instead of remaining silent, I should have spoken out. My stomach turned. I had done the wrong thing and I knew it. My inaction had made the situation worse. I should have warned him years ago. I should have spoken candidly to Prudence too, to determine her romantic and marital intentions. Twenty years ago I should have interfered and guided her friendships toward more favorable outcomes. I was frustrated and angry with myself for leaving the choices to Prudence whom, it seemed, had made none. Why had she not previously made a choice of suitors? Or was her inaction hereditary? I waited for the inevitable as I controlled my rage.

"Live on the farm? Give up my career? Ossie, how can I tell you that I can't give up my career? Not now. I can make a difference in the world of science. I wouldn't know what to do on a farm. A life in the fields and farmyards is not for me. I wouldn't be very good at it, like you are. Ossie, you do understand, don't you? I'm sorry to lead you on about marriage. I meant that maybe one day I'd get married. Not now. I meant with the right person. I'm not sure that we are right for each other. I know we've been friends for ever, but marriage is a big step. I can't take that step with you right now."

"You want marriage, but not with me. Is that what you're saying? What about the times we've been together? I thought you wanted intimacy. I thought you wanted commitment. Prudence, what do you want?"

"Let's not talk about it now." She was undeniably her father's daughter.

"But Prudence, I, I, we, we've been together so long. I just thought that you'd be mine. I wanted to make you mine when I got the farm sorted out. It's making a bit of money now and I can support the two of us. I, I thought you'd want to spend more time with me."

"It's not about property. You say it like I'll be part of your property. I need independence."

She was trying to let him down gently, but I could detect a lump in his throat. Tears streamed down my cheeks and I wiped them away with my coffee-soaked cloth.

"I can't wait any longer," he sighed. "I want someone to be my wife. I want someone to be home all the time like a traditional wife. I know you're not homely like that, but I thought you'd change. I need a wife, Prue. I hope I haven't embarrassed you. I shouldn't have asked until I knew for certain that you'd live with me. I didn't mean, I didn't mean to embarrass you. Please forgive me." It was the voice of a submissive man.

"I admire you a lot, Ossie. You've worked hard on the farm. Can't we continue being wonderful friends? I need to be close to papa too. He's old and frail. I know he can look after himself, but I don't want to leave him alone. He'll only deteriorate if I left him, and he won't leave this house. He loves this house."

"I understand how you feel. Let's just forget that I asked. Please? I don't want to spoil what we have. Can we just pretend that I came around and brought you flowers? I feel silly. Please don't say anything to anyone. Don't tell your father. I'll go around and see Fabian now. He wants to borrow the truck to pick up an antique dresser he bought from a farmer near me. I'll help him with it. Don't tell Fabian what happened today. He doesn't need to know, does he? Hey, why don't you and Fabian come up to the farm next weekend? I'll ask him. He works too hard and he might want some country air, mightn't he?"

"I'll come with you and help you with the dresser. Let's see Fabian and organize something. He'll love it on your property. We can get some work done and go for walks and have some wine in the evening. Let's go."

"Okay, I'll drop you back home later. Don't tell your father. I don't want him to think I'm silly. I like your father. Don't tell him about the proposal, will you?"

Was that it? Was that the proposal I had waited years for? One proposal, one setback, and then total acquiescence; what kind of a man was he? Where was the passion? Where was the fight for love and the hand in marriage? An Italian man would not acquiesce so readily, would he? If I had only planted the seed of desire in Fabian years ago, Prudence wouldn't be in this lonely, barren predicament. Had something happened in Europe between Fabian and Prudence? Had he proposed to her? Had she rejected him?

"Let's go," she said quietly to Oswald. Raising her voice, she said, "Papa! Ossie and I are going to Fabian's place. Don't give the newspaper to Franco until I've finished reading it. I want to save the pages on the lunar landing." They were walking down the dark passageway to the front door.

"Sure. See you later. *Ciao,* Oswald." The day's events may have been for the best. My only desire was to see my daughter eventually with a man she loved. My only concern was that, if she did not marry Oswald, the prospect of marriage would be a long time coming, if at all. Was it not better to accept the opportunity when it presented itself than to wait an eternity for fulfillment? Or was she waiting for perfection? I thought she had burnt her bridges, sealing her single fate, just like her father.

# ARLENE BERNIE

The week Arlene Bernie, the famous Australian actress, arrived in town was a week to remember. It marked a major disturbance in our lives: a rising tide in our "sea of tranquility." It was nothing less than a tsunami of the greatest proportions, as if a heaving rush of seawater had been sucked up, exposing coastlines and beaching ships, before a giant wave crashed onto the shore, obliterating life as we once knew it.

Prudence, Arlene, and I were dining in a fine restaurant situated in the theater district. The extrovert owners were gay men from Sydney who, in two years, began to turn the conservative tastes of the locals toward a culturally diverse eating regime. Imaginative chefs skillfully combined flavors of the east with traditional tastes of the west. It was unlike the provincial fare of my youth, but I was envious of their experimental flair for taste, color, and texture.

Not only did the food awaken the senses, but so too did the décor. Lime green and hot pink taffeta curtains penetrated my eyes with extreme garishness. Cotton, eggplant tablecloths, fuchsia placemats, and olive napkins replaced conservative crisp, white linen. The restaurant was opulent and lush, creative and carefree, and brimming with an eclectic combination of gregarious characters and extroverted luminaries.

Arlene's life was the antithesis of conservatism. It was outrageous and extreme with every moment photographed and recorded. Over prawn cocktails, we discussed the demise of her recent relationship: a very public affair. Her lover, Gloria, had jilted her for another woman and a singing career.

"Tell us all about it, Arlene. I've read so much in the papers," I pleaded as Prudence nudged my side, hoping I wouldn't ask.

"Poor Arlene has been through a lot. She may not want to talk about it," said Prudence, protective of Arlene's fragile emotions.

"Nonsense! I can talk to you about it. You're my dear, dear friends. Besides, I just have to talk to someone or I'll burst. Well, the break up was so public. Everyone in Australia, probably everyone in the world, knew about Gloria and me. Everyone. I tried so hard to silence the rumors about me being gay, you know. I had to say that Gloria was a special friend, but I don't think the public bought it. Keeping scandal from my door was so difficult and painful. I feared that my fans would be horrified if they knew my secrets. Can you imagine the old biddies having coronaries because I'm a lesbian? Never mind. I'm over it now. But I learned that you can't live your life on half-truths and hype. It takes so much away from what you're meant to accomplish. It startled me. It was like walking in and seeing your lover in an embrace with your best friend. The resentment builds up inside you. I was ready to strangle someone, snap their neck, and break every bone in their body. I really was. It was a horrid time. Horrid, horrid, horrid!"

"That's terrible, dear Arlie. What happened to Gloria? Did she really jilt you for Maxine?" Prudence touched her gently on the arm, the white chiffon sleeve crumpling under the weight. Arlene's openness was an indication that privacy was the least of her concerns, and it paved the way for further interrogation.

"Not straight away like the press said. She left because she said I was holding her back. Can you believe it? She said I was stifling her singing career, so she left to join a band and that's when she met Maxine. What really hurt though was thinking that I had allowed it to happen." Arlene pushed a cigarette into a tapered, ivory holder, puffing vigorously as she lit a match to the frayed end. Swirls of smoke veiled her face and blended with her chiffon blouse.

"What do you mean, Arlene?" I asked.

"Well, Leonardo, I said to myself, how many times are you going to allow yourself to play second fiddle emotionally? You see, she said that she was playing second fiddle to me in terms of her career, but emotionally I was definitely the second fiddle. I was there for her through everything, through all of her acting stints, both the successful ones and the flops. I put my career on hold. It's been years since I won that film industry award for best actress. It hardly guaranteed employment, let alone fame. But Gloria said that she felt obliged to continue striving for acting success. She thought I wanted her to act so we could do scenes together. She put her singing career on hold to do what she thought I expected. Acting would re-define her, and me, and she wanted to please me. Of course it wasn't true. That was just her perception. In reality, I was putting her life and career ahead of mine. How could she not have been loyal to me? Well, you can't play second fiddle to anyone, whether it's for love, friend-ship, or work. That's what I told myself. Then she left me. I was depleted. Shattered. Oh, it was awful."

"You didn't take to drink and drugs, did you?" I ventured.

Arlene touched me on the hand with her thin white fingers dipped in red-black lacquer, and exhaled a jet of smoke. She was famously fearless and infamously strident, known by the media as a "man-eater." She gave me a look that lingered between seduction and terrorism.

"Almost, darling. But no one and nothing gets the better of me. I wasn't on the seat of my pants. I was at rock bottom emo-tionally, but I wasn't suicidal, darling. I didn't want to wallow in drugs and alcohol. I didn't want to die in a bed full of vomit. Not me. I didn't want to kill myself. I wanted to fucking-well kill her and everyone associated with her. Not me. I love myself, darling. I hated her. I hated everyone who loved her." She was the moody manic person I had spoken to many times on the tele-phone. In real life, she was no different. "We've never met, have we Leonardo? But if you ever treated me the way Gloria did, I'd have your guts for garters. I have my mother's temper and I can see myself becoming just like her. My father and I never really got on. There was something wrong with the chemistry of my parents' marriage and I was the victim of it. An only child too, I was. I don't blame him anymore. I did initially. I regret some of the things I've said to my father in the past, but I wasn't old

170

enough to understand how relationships worked. I'd wear outrageous clothes to draw attention to the body I hated. It was my
armor. I had a lot of fun with clothes. You should have seen my
'bare foot and flimsy dress' period. What a fright that was to
people! I thought I was Isadora Duncan. Still do sometimes. I
love all that free-form dancing in the name of art and expression
with next to nothing on."

She laughed with her head tilted back, a loud hearty laugh
that attracted the attention of restaurant diners. Prudence joined
in the laughter and even I raised a subdued laugh. I dared not
laugh too much for fear that she would rip my stomach open
with her huge white teeth and leave my intestines in my lap. She
was a formidable woman.

"Do go on, I'm enjoying this," said Prudence.

Arlene focused her attention on me. "Leonardo, let me tell
you about my father. I'm telling you this because I envy Prudence's relationship with you. I would have wanted the same
relationship with my father. I've told that to Prue many times,
haven't I?" Her elbow rested on the table as she waved her cigarette freely and expressively.

"Many, many times Arlie." Prudence rubbed my arm as
Arlene launched into her memoirs as we began our entrees. My
entree of kidneys in Madeira gave me visions of Arlene devour-
ing raw kidneys soaked in blood.

"Oh, don't get me wrong, Leonardo, I had a great deal of
admiration for my father. I never loved him, but I admired him.
I admit his profession embarrassed me. I was teased at school
if I mentioned his real profession, so I made up one, a romantic
one. He designed feminine hygiene products. Can you believe
it? It's funny now, of course, but when I was a teenager it was
hell. Can you imagine telling your school friends that your
father designed tampons and sanitary napkins? I just couldn't.
Look at me, I'm a geek. I'm tall and thin and lanky, just as I
was back then, but I was so clumsy. Nobody at school liked
me. And it would've been worse for me if I'd told everyone my
father's real profession. So I fabricated the truth. I lied. I told
everyone that my father designed lingerie. Some people still

teased me, but not as much. It was a more romantic profession. It was to me anyway." Her large lips mouthed every word with a rubbery movement that fascinated me. I revered those huge projections coated in thick, red lipstick that thrust them further into prominence.

"It makes a mathematics lecturer for a profession appear boring," I smiled.

Prudence looked at me. "At least you could teach me algebra and we could have a conversation about it at the dinner table. But who talks about feminine hygiene products at the dinner table?" Prudence said. "Goodness, poor Arlene!"

My face reddened with embarrassment at the mention of that secretive subject, remembering the ordeal I endured when Prudence became a woman. I watched Arlene's steel blue eyes, darkly lined around the perimeters, their lashes thick with mascara.

"Yes, what was I to say to my father? What new model of tampon have you designed today, father? Does it absorb more blood? Can you leave it in three times longer? Really! What could we talk about? What could I talk about at the dinner table in front of my friends? Not that I brought any friends home, mind you. I was too embarrassed. I didn't have any friends anyway. I always made excuses. I was good at lying. So I wasn't very popular. In fact, I was the least popular girl in the class. So, to compensate for not being popular, I slept around to get attention. I thought that if I could be good at sex, then at least the boys would like me. Ha! That backfired because I had to have an abortion at twenty. I was sleeping with lots of men, usually only once. Then I got herpes and vowed never again to have sex with a stranger. A few years after that I decided never again to have sex with a man. I felt that they would betray me. And I'd lie about them. If he were a football player, I'd tell everyone that he was a brain surgeon. If he were a nuclear physicist, I'd tell everyone that he was a washing machine mechanic. I couldn't stop lying about their profession. I always wanted them to be something else and not what they really were. I hated it so I vowed never to have men as partners, only as friends because women weren't my friends. Gradually women thought I was okay, especially when I started acting because I had lots of make-up and dresses. Women liked me then. I fell in love with a lot of straight women and I thought I could change them, like a girl trying to change a gay guy. But I was fooling myself. Perhaps I was trying to change myself. I was living a lie. I'm a gay woman. What can I tell you? For a while I did go back to straight men, but in the end I was just living a lie. I've been with women ever since. I don't have to lie to them, well, not all the time anyway, and I don't lie about their professions. Odd, isn't it? I think it's because they usually don't have one. Gloria wasn't working when I first met her. I asked a friend to rustle up six people to have dinner with me one evening. Gloria was one of those people. She was the shyest of the lot. I hadn't met anyone like that before."

Arlene paused to suck in huge quantities of wine and pasta in between deep puffs of nicotine. She had an enormous appetite for a thin, gangly woman.

"Have some parmesan cheese with the pasta. It adds flavor," I advised.

She sprinkled layers of cheese on top of her asparagus and bean pasta. "That's a good idea. I've heard about your cooking skills from Prue. You're a real connoisseur of fine food. More wine? Leonardo, do the pouring, mate. Keep it topped up. Don't wait for the waiters to do it. It's too crowded and they can't keep up with us." I dutifully did as I was instructed. "Anyway," Arlene continued. "I'm thirty-eight now, and none the wiser, so it seems. I thought Gloria was going to stay with me forever. What a joke! But I do have another lover, I can say. We only met a few weeks ago, but everything is going well with Jade. She's a hoofer, a dancer. Anyway, as I was saying, I grew up in a male dominated family, but I couldn't relate to men, not like Prudence can. I learned to understand men emotionally, but not sexually. I'm good friends with men now—especially gay men—but I can't sleep with them. For all of that, my worst reviews have all come from women. Perhaps they're jealous. I'm not sure whether they're jealous of my success, or jealous of my lovers, or whether they disapprove of my sexuality. Anyway I prefer women to be women. I love the powder, the lipstick, the false eyelashes, and all that girly stuff. I just love it. That's why I love acting, I suppose. Have you seen these fabulous shoes?" she said as she raised one leg in the air. The shiny, red, stiletto ankle-strapped shoes extended her long frame another eight inches. My eyes darted along her naked, pale legs, up to the hem of her red and black mini skirt, and further to a hint of white underwear. Her leg lowered with a thud on the plush, pink carpet. Her knees formed a knobbly right angle, parallel to the chair legs. Prudence's voice distracted me.

"Tell us about the new play you're doing," Prudence asked as she ate small mouthfuls of grilled fish.

"It's wonderful, darling. I'm not in it. Now that's something new, isn't it?" She laughed. "I wrote it, dears. One of my gay male friends is directing it, and we've started rehearsing already. We're doing it in Melbourne, not Sydney, because the director lives there. It just works out better that way. Besides, I can stay at his place."

"What's it about? What's it called?" I asked, appearing interested, but I was thinking of her long thin legs. Prudence covered her legs in psychedelic orange and yellow stockings that didn't appear to coordinate with the long, red hippie dress, split to her thigh.

"It's called *Boys in the Band* and it's a high-spirited, high-camp play about a homosexual's birthday party. It's a real hoot, so outrageous and funny. You two must come and see it. It opens in the middle of September. You don't mind a few swear words do you? Lots of fuck words in it, but it is so funny. I know you'll love it."

"I'll get papa there. He doesn't like flying, but he'll fly if I go with him. As soon as we hear about it, we'll book two tickets. It'll be great to catch up with you again too."

"Done, darlings."

Cyril stealthily entered the restaurant and stood by Prudence's side. "Hello, my favorite, my pet, my most gorgeous love. How are you?" Before Prudence could answer, he had his lips locked onto her with such passion that it startled me. He embraced her with fervor and placed his hand at the base of her left breast, cupping it sexually. "Sorry I haven't seen you for so long. Darren's forbidden me to see you. He's so jealous. But he's out with some other people tonight. Fancy seeing you here though; I didn't expect to see you here. I was only going to have a quick conversation with the owners, but then I saw you with Arlene. I've missed you so much. Hug me darling."

Prudence draped her arms around Cyril's neck, magnetized by his hypnotic attraction. She pulled his head toward her and kissed his earlobe, oblivious of their surroundings.

Arlene shrieked with delight, turning the attention of diners in her direction. With a raucous clash of chairs, a man lunged at Arlene. It was Darren.

"You can't hide from me, Arlene," Darren yelled. "I heard you were in town. How dare you write a play about something you don't understand! You treat gay guys as if they are something to laugh about. You know shit, Arlene. Go back to Sydney." His lips distorted with anger and rage as he spat out the words with an infantile insistence on revenge. It was then that he saw Cyril and Prudence together. A fire was fuelled and he exploded with rage. He grabbed a wineglass and smashed it on the table, shattering it over the remains of the food. A waiter rushed forward and grabbed Darren by the shoulder, wrestling him, but Darren forced himself free and lunged at Prudence.

"What the fuck are you doing here?" Cyril yelled as he attempted to hold Darren back by the elbow. His actions were futile.

Darren seized a chunk of Prudence's hair and tugged it savagely. She screamed in pain and fright, and I instinctively stood to place myself protectively in front of her. The waiter wielded his large forearm against Darren's throat, forcing him to release her hair. His back arched against the waiter's barreled chest. He writhed free, pushing the waiter's arm from his jugular and twisting his body to face his restrainer. Darren struck the waiter in the nose, bloodying his face. Squirts of blood splashed over Arlene's white blouse and onto the white plates. Cyril tried in vain to restrain his friend while the waiter moved forward again with fierce determination. Darren was strengthened with rage, broke free and struck the waiter, for the second time, in the jaw. An audible crack left both of them shocked and motionless. Restaurant patrons froze momentarily. Arlene and Prudence held each other tightly.

"He didn't mean it. He didn't mean it," said Cyril in his defense. "I'll take him home."

An ambulance and a police car arrived as Cyril tried desperately to negotiate a settlement. It was too late. Two policemen seized Darren and took him into custody, charging him with assault and property damage.

Cyril dejectedly flopped into a chair as he watched the police escort Darren to their vehicle. I caught Cyril's eye. He was distraught. There was a genuine sense of sadness and despair that I had not seen before. He shook himself to action and approached the waiters to offer assistance. I could not hear the conversation, but it appeared to me that his offer was rejected. Cyril left the restaurant, turning to glance at me as he closed the door. I cannot be certain, but I believe that Cyril's piercing blue eyes were wet with tears.

# COMMISSIONER'S COMMENTARY

Arlene Bernie was exactly as Bari had described. She was in her Sydney house when Constable Hallett and I interviewed her. Larger than life, her red lipstick made her lips the focal point on her pale face. Rubbery with exaggerated actions, her lips never stopped. She admitted to loving the social life, extravagant parties, and the limelight. As we were trying to interview the actress, her telephone rang non-stop until she eventually unplugged it.

Thinking that Prudence had confided in her, I hoped to gain a great deal of information. On the contrary, Arlene knew little. It was all speculation. Names that she had heard Prudence mention included Michael, Fabian, Cyril and Oswald, but none with any romanticism, merely great affection. Prudence had neither talked more about one person than another, nor had she expressed any sexual desire for these men or any other. Arlene concluded that, on the surface, Prudence loved everyone equally in accordance with their role in her life. Secretly, internally, Arlene wasn't sure. She knew of Oswald's marriage proposal, but had heard of no future plans. Boldly, I asked her whether Prudence had any lesbian tendencies. The response was a long, loud guffaw that startled me. Preposterous was the exact word that she used: preposterous.

Constable Hallett asked the last question and one I had not thought to solicit. Did Prudence, in her opinion, have any negative characteristics or habits? Swiftly, the answer was: Prudence was stubborn. It was Miss Bernie's belief that her friend was rigid, stubborn, too exacting of herself and others, materialistic, ambitious, and driven towards status and power. Never was there a waver in Arlene's voice, nor a pause. The answer was definitive and authoritative, spoken with a hundred percent certainty.

Arlene's interrogation necessitated that we question Cyril Silverman again as she had given her account of the restaurant incident. She put the blame, fairly and squarely, on Darren. Alcohol was the cause, she said, mixed with a dangerous combination of jealousy, hatred, paranoia, self-persecution, and insecurity. Or drugs, she added. Not knowing either Darren or Cyril, she conjectured that Cyril controlled others with his charm while Darren manipulated Cyril through aggression. What was clear was that Arlene knew that Prudence liked Cyril, no question about it.

# INNES CARTWRIGHT

The day that Innes announced his decision to renounce science for the ministry I had been tending to my vegetables and was removing my soiled boots on the back veranda. Prudence was sitting on the concrete step leading from the veranda to the expanse of garden, drying her hair in the sun, with a distant, melancholic look in her eyes.

"What's up, princess? Is it Cyril? He'll contact you again when he's ready," I said as I lifted her wet hair to avoid it dripping down her back onto her floral cotton top. I tried to bundle it on top of her head, but it slipped down, flicking drops of water onto the concrete.

"No. It's not Cyril. It's Innes. He rang. He'll be here soon. He just told me that he's giving up science. He wants to be a priest." She draped the towel over her knees and put her head in her hands, pulling back her damp hair. "He could've been one of the best scientists in Australia, in the world, if he wanted to. Have I failed him, papa?" She covered her eyes with her hands and sat in silence.

I took the towel and dabbed her hair dry. Picking up her comb, I sat next to her and untangled her hair. With my hand on her shoulder, I drew her close to me. "Listen to what he's got to say. He must have a reason for such a big decision. I'll clean the outdoor table and get some drinks ready. You can sit there in the shade and talk to him. It's his decision, princess. Let me dry your hair first. It needs another trim, but I'll do that another time, hey?" She sat listlessly as I manipulated her hair into a long loose plait. "Hold the end while I get a ribbon." She had not shifted position when I returned. I wound the black ribbon around the plait's fish tail and tied it tightly. "Come on, get ready. I'll have the table spick and span when you get back. Take off that old skirt. You can't be seen in that. Why don't you wear the yellow skirt and your new blue knitted sweater? Not the skirt with the spots, the one with the blue stripes, the one that flares out. Are you listening to me? You know which one I mean don't you?" Eventually Prudence moved slowly to her room. She had taken my advice, and with a pink sheen on her lips and cheeks, appeared healthy and energized. "That's better. I think that's Innes coming down the driveway now. I'll meet him and bring him to the back yard."

Innes looked particularly pale that day, wearing light gray trousers and an un-ironed, white long-sleeved shirt. He resembled a disheveled, sickly, undernourished schoolboy with the weight of the world on his shoulders. I guided him to the back garden where Prudence was sitting on the veranda in the shade. The garden was at its best for it was spring, and I had trimmed and weeded in readiness for last week's birthday celebrations. Prudence's 45th birthday was in August and my 75th was on September 25, so we opted for a garden party to announce the advent of spring and our combined birthdays. It was an intimate affair amid the lilac and lavender, poppies and primula, wattle and waxflower. The lawn was lush and the bougainvillea flourished in a brilliant array of purple-blue flowers that obscured the steel-gray cylindrical water tank. It was a glorious time of the year. The sole telltale signs of the festivities were the sporadic divots from heels and chair legs: all else looked like a picture postcard.

I was proud of my back garden. It was a storybook yard, with a stylish European garden. There was a harmonious flow of foliage and flowers from the wooden back fence to the iron front gate. A sweep of old camellias graced the southern aspect, those closest to the fence producing an abundance of pink and white flowers, straying to a bed of hydrangeas, ferns, fuchsias, and Japanese anemones among the dappled shade. Fragrant honeysuckle smothered an old tree stump and a wisteria refused the limitations of the over-reaching veranda as it clambered to reach the light. A mellow, old urn lay among the flowers. A corner of the yard comprised a white patch that conceded to a spring invasion of blue foxgloves. As the seasons changed, the monochrome combination of Viburnum *mariesii*, Magnolia *stellata*, Iceberg roses, Solomon's seals, and shasta daisies would be in bloom. In another corner grew a feast of herbal plants that blended into an impressive vegetable garden. Citrus trees and the sensual fruit of the persimmon added to the edible section of the garden. Although proud of my garden, its constant nurturing frustrated me.

Prudence embraced Innes's thin, pathetic frame and positioned him on a cushioned cane chair facing the garden. "Innes, do tell me your plans. Talk to me," she said, squinting against the late morning sun.

"You know I haven't been happy for a long time, professor," he sighed. "I just can't live up to the expectations of others. I want to be a priest. I want to eventually be a bishop. I want to serve the Lord forever and to do that I must forsake the inadequacies of science. Science can't provide the immortality and perpetuity of God's calling. I must serve God and not science." He fixated his gaze on Prudence, searching her face for affirmation.

"Dear Innes, you can do both. You can serve God by being an eminent scientist and working for the welfare of society and civilization. You're immensely intelligent. You can achieve anything in science that you put your mind to. Science needs you," she implored. Responsibility for the weak and helpless appealed to Prudence, but not for long. She couldn't sustain the presence of a weak man.

"Please understand how I feel." He held out his frail arms and clutched her hand. Her pearl white nail polish was a few days old and needed a re-touch. I was glad that it was only Innes in her company, although he would hardly notice such detail. "It's this new morality. I can't come to terms with it. Women's liberation, gay liberation; the world is being turned upside down. The essential pluralism of the new morality is unscientific. Science can refine and synthesize new concepts, but it can't immerse the central concepts in subjective experience or introduce contradictory concepts and still remain science. Do you see my dilemma?

The new morality is incurably unscientific because it has a pluralism of contradictory ideas at its very core. It's schizoid and I can't rationalize these contradictions." His pale face contorted with anxiety and he tightened his grip on her hand.

"But morality is as changing as science," said Prudence. "Nothing can remain static. We need growth and change: that's part of the essence of science." She gently stroked his cheek. "I know these are turbulent times, but, like scientific principles, you can distill this new information and find what's important to you." In an attempt to lighten the tone of the conversation, Prudence jovially pressed her point. "Innes, you can metamorphose like a caterpillar pupating over winter to emerge in spring transformed into a magnificent butterfly."

He wasn't convinced. "Please don't be frivolous with me, professor."

Biology is full of miracles, but nothing I've seen is as miraculous as the metamorphosis of the caterpillar into a butterfly. Butterflies have minute brains, about a million times smaller than the brain of humans, and with this clump of nerve cells butterflies know instinctively how to fly and how to navigate over thousands of miles to a common breeding ground. It seemed to me that although Innes had a larger brain than the butterfly, most suitably applied to scientific matters, he did not have the wherewithal to face the reality of a changing society.

Prudence continued soberly, "We're all going through these times. We can help you. God can help you. You can find your truth in science. Life is not easy for any of us. We must have perseverance and, above all, confidence in ourselves. We must believe that we are gifted for something, and that this thing, at whatever personal cost, must be attained. Your gift is astronomy." She glanced at me, but her green pleading eyes darted quickly back to his pale face.

Innes was on a one-track mode to his truth. "God has placed me face to face with a choice between good and evil. The scientist and the common-sense individual are in their essential rationality face to face with truth. Union with God is an ideal and the knowledge of truth is an ideal, but both are ideals to be realized. The real fundamental option is whether to live by the spiritual or by the sensual; the concupiscence of the flesh over chaste self-control and humble submission to the commandments of God." He coughed pathetically, without covering his mouth. "I can't prostitute myself like Cyril and his crowd. They think he's Che Guevara, the Marilyn Monroe of Marxism, but he's nothing but a political symbol whose emptiness mirrors the emptiness of his demonstrations and his pro-gay stance. He's an unfilled receptacle for fantasy, sex, and lust. It's unsustainable behavior. God will seek revenge for Cyril's perversion."

"What's really bothering you?" demanded Prudence. "It's not Cyril, is it? You don't have to succumb to sex if you view it as immoral. You can be celibate and serve God. You know that." She was caressing his long fingers in slow, soothing motions.

I imagined her fondling and stroking the hands of Fabian with him reciprocating the advances: his dark, hairy hands around her shoulders. Unbuttoning her blouse to reveal a black lace brassiere, he'd reach his hands behind her to unfasten her restricting garment, cupping his hands over her blanched breasts. He'd massage them tenderly before enveloping them with sweet kisses, sucking and licking her smooth flesh while his Italian hands delved lower down her back to her firm buttocks and thighs. Rubbing his large hands across her flat stomach, he'd unzip her skirt and let it fall to the ground. Passionate kisses on her mouth, her ears, her Roman nose and slender neck would make her swoon and murmur for more. Pressing his body close to hers, she'd feel his warmth, his pounding heart, and his hairy chest. I had lost myself in the intensity of the emotions when Prudence's clearing cough disturbed my erotic daydream. I sighed. At least Cyril had passion. Where was Fabian's passion? Where were the romantic gestures Italians were famous for? Wasn't he ever going to proposition Prudence? Instead of Fabian, the epitome of manliness, or Cyril, the model of seduction, there was before me an insipid waif-like boy.

"But professor, my one and only professor, I adore you, but can't you see that indulging in pluralistic ideas is like drinking alcohol. Some people can drink moderately without harmful effects, but there's a danger that drinking will become excessive. Becoming a devotee to liberation and liberal views is like becoming a heavy drinker. I can't delineate the difference when I'm subsumed in it. Sexual thoughts and tendencies overwhelm my mind before I'm able to rationally cope with them. I must renounce all sins and sexual thoughts and live wholly within the principles of God's laws. That way, I know that I won't stray toward evil." His eyes had turned gray, washed out, devoid of the color of life.

"Please have something to eat. You're looking emaciated. I worry about you," said Prudence, moving the platter of food closer to him.

Innes ignored her and abstained from eating. "Because of sin and feminism and emancipation, men and women are tempted to live selfishly. This selfishness is the root of all sexual evil. I have chosen a celibate vocation through the ministry. Celibacy within today's society is impossible for me; I cannot cope without the sanctity of the ministry. Celibacy transcends traditional categories of masculine and feminine. It's directed to oneness. True chastity neutralizes the power issues of sexual domination."

"You can have chastity in your life as a scientist," Prudence pleaded.

"Professor, I cannot live among the temptations of society. I'm tormented daily by sexual thoughts of you. I cannot bear to be near you for fear that I'll weaken and lust after you. I endlessly dream of ravishing you. You are all I desire. I must live a celibate life within the ministry to remain pure to you and to God."

I conjured up thoughts of Innes ravishing Prudence. It was impossible and improbable. Prudence had no sexual thoughts for him in any way. Of that I was perfectly sure. Images of the frail schoolboy physically overpowering my daughter were ludicrous. This pathetic, limp creature could be overcome with a feather. I was certain Prudence had also realized the folly of his thoughts. Nonetheless, she accepted the futility of pleading for him to pursue a scientific vocation. It was pointless to waste her energy getting water from a dry well.

Prudence leaned forward and gently kissed Innes on the forehead. "I understand. You will excel in the ministry, I'm sure. I know you'll be a brilliant bishop. Good luck, Innes." She again glanced at me as if to indicate that she had tried and failed.

Instantly, Innes was greatly relieved that he had the blessing of his beloved professor. Color returned to his cheeks and eyes as he helped himself to the luscious, red strawberries. In my mind, I could not imagine Innes as a bishop facing a congregation of worshippers leading them to divinity, but I could be wrong.

I heard the whistle of the postman as he cycled along his delivery route, heralding the arrival of the day's correspondence. I walked around the side of the house, along the brown and white gravel driveway, and onto the paved path that led to the bottle-green, metallic mailbox. I returned with a flat, brown parcel, bearing American stamps, and addressed to Prudence.

"Prudence, it's a parcel from Luis Alvarez. Wasn't he last year's Nobel Prize winner?"

"Yes, for his studies on subatomic particles. What is it? Open it."

I opened the parcel, being careful to save the stamps for Franco. It was a bundle of papers and a letter written in scrawling handwriting. I took my glasses from the pocket of my shirt and read his notes. "He has a query and wonders if you had a point of view about it. He said that Raup and Septoski think that massive comet catastrophes occur on Earth periodically every twenty-six million years. Alvarez says that can't be right and he wants to know what you think. He thinks that it can't be periodic. He's got Raup and Septoski's papers here and some notes on why it must be a mistake. He thinks these guys are wrong."

"Raup and Sepkoski, not Septoski. They are extremely well-known paleontologists. Knowing Alvarez, he's probably right. He's been doing some work on asteroid collisions and dinosaur extinction." She picked a dried apricot from the platter and nibbled gently on it, testing the taste for sulfur dioxide.

"Is there something wrong with the apricots? I dried them myself naturally. They're not bought ones," I explained.

"Good. The sulfur dioxide gives Innes asthma attacks. Innes, you can eat these." She turned the platter to place the dried apricots in front of him.

"Thanks professor, but I'll just have a few strawberries. Alvarez? I've read some of his work," he said. "I've seen some photos of large asteroids and comets floating in space in orbits that crossed Earth's path. Some astronomers think disastrous impacts have taken place previously on Earth and Alvarez was working on that theory. Remember, we talked about it some time ago? You agreed with his workings then, but we didn't have proof." The color of the red strawberries reflected in his cheeks in a flush of excitement.

"Yes, I remember. Let's have a look at it." She set the papers in between herself and Innes. His eyes danced over the writing as he absorbed and digested each word. This provided more nourishment and sustenance to his starving, emaciated body than a punnet of strawberries. I folded the torn, brown parcel wrapping and placed it on an empty seat.

"Raup and Sepkoski's analysis shows that there were intense periods of extinctions every twenty-six million years," said Innes. "It's odd that they are periodic. You wouldn't normally expect them to be regular, would you, professor?"

"It's incredible," acknowledged Prudence. "I know a bit about astrophysics, but this has me puzzled. Earth is such a comparatively small target in the universe, so it seems odd that there's a regular hit of such proportions. What could make comets hit Earth so regularly? Get to the end, Innes. Keep turning. What does it say?"

"Nothing. There are no conclusions, just some data. What a letdown. Here, look at these graphs. They've plotted the varying extinction rates for the last 250 million years. Wow! The peaks are exactly spaced at twenty-six million years apart. What do you make of that?" I had never seen him this animated before.

"I've been reading Alvarez's notes," answered Prudence. "He thinks some peaks should be removed from the data because of their low statistical certainty. He's taken out the Cretaceous and Eocene extinctions too because they were due to asteroid impacts and therefore are random in time."

"He's right there. Yes, it's obvious professor. Alvarez is right. It's so simple really. If you take them out of the equation you can definitely see that the comet disasters aren't periodic, there's too many gaps. Obvious." Innes was as convinced as I was.

"Wait a minute. It's convincing, but let's re-plot the data," she said flicking the pages back and forth from the data to the graphs.

Re-plotting the data was completely unnecessary. Alvarez, the Nobel Prize winner had clearly spotted the mistake. I placed paper and pencils on the table in front of them. Without acknowledging me, they scribbled their calculations and graphs on the notepad. I stood behind them to see their formulations. Their rapid hand movements were too fast for my feeble eyes, and I seemed to be a few coordinates behind them. Prudence and Innes appeared to assign each extinction peak an uncertain age and intensity. Prudence arranged arrows at the regular twenty-six million year intervals. The final graph was impressive. Eight of the ten arrows pointed exactly at the extinction peaks. Remarkable, I thought.

"There are eight out of ten, Prudence. Maybe the paleontologists are right," I said but, in my mind, I doubted it. Alvarez was a brilliant man, and he was not likely to be wrong.

"Why did he exclude the Cretaceous and Eocene extinctions? We don't know for certain that they're random," said Prudence. "What do you think, papa?"

"Of course they're random. You can't cheat and leave them in," I said.

"I agree with your father. You can't ignore something you know to be true," said Innes.

"No, no. We don't know that it's true," insisted Prudence. "It's speculation based on presumptions."

"Now, Prudence, use your logic. I agree with Alvarez. The theory is flawed. It can't be periodic," I said adamantly.

"Alvarez is a Nobel Prize winner, professor," said Innes in my defense. "You can't compete with that. Alvarez and your father are right."

Prudence turned her head to glare at me with her combatant, green eyes. "Neither of us are experts in astrophysics, so we're even and, at this stage, all theories are to be considered." She had an effective command of the English language. Her words could either soothe or burn, but they never failed to leave an impression.

I was perplexed by Prudence's approach. This wasn't social science, or art, or indeed politics or sport. This was data analysis based on mathematics. *Problemi e metodi di analisi.* How can there be any discrepancy in statistical facts? We debated the facts for some time before I asserted my patriarchal authority. "Prudence, I've been doing mathematics and data analysis for a long time. I taught you, remember! It's useless to argue the point any longer. The impacts are random. The information has been skewed to include data that shouldn't be there. Innes is an expert on astronomy and he agrees, as I do, with a Nobel Prize winner!"

"Alvarez wasn't a Turing Award winner for mathematics, though. And I was, dear papa."

"And Turing committed suicide in 1954 after having been convicted of homosexual behavior," I added.

"Get off your perch, papa. What the hell has that got to do with Turing's genius ability? Don't answer that! Let's get back to the facts. What I meant was that the burden of proof rests with you and Innes, and of course Alvarez, not with the paleontologists, or me. Where's the proof that the impacts are random? Maybe the paleontologists are right and that the comet impacts are periodic. You don't have a case." She was forthright and frank, but I was not about to concede defeat.

"And you don't have a model!" I was even more determined to win this argument.

"You've got to have a model, professor. Your father is right. That's what you've been telling me for years. Your father has a point. Unless you can come up with a model, professor, our argument is justified and your father, Alvarez, and I will have the upper hand."

I liked Innes after all. He wasn't as insipid as I had previously thought. How courageous he was for affirming his beliefs and opinions. Good lad, I thought. I wanted to perform the Australian tradition of slapping him on the back, but it was not my way and he was, indeed, a very frail boy.

"Okay, what about this?" said Prudence. "What if there's a companion star that orbits the Sun, and every twenty-six million years it approaches Earth in such a way that it makes the comets hit Earth? Remember, it's in orbit. It's a regular orbit." She looked at both of us, her eyes darting from one to the other.

"You can't have dust and rocks from outside the solar system, I believe," I said proudly. "Isn't that right, Innes?"

"You're right, Dr. Bari, but that's not what Prudence, I mean professor, is talking about. She's talking about a companion star from within the solar system. If it's born at the same time as its Sun then it will have the same isotope ratios as the Sun. She has the upper hand, Dr. Bari, but there's still a problem with professor's model. I think the orbit would be too large, and the companion star would be pulled away from its Sun by the gravity of any nearby stars. I don't think her model would work, not from my experience anyway. So we may have won this argument after all, Dr. Bari, sir."

Prudence put her hand to her mouth, rubbing her forefinger across her bottom lip, deep in thought. She looked at Innes, watching his gaunt face, nodding her head slightly and deliberately as if acknowledging a known fact. With a sudden snap of consciousness, she said, "We can calculate that. We can calculate how big the orbit would be using Kepler's laws of gravitational motion." Prudence began the computation. "The major diameter of an elliptical orbit is the period of the orbit; in this case it is twenty-six million years raised to the two-thirds power and multiplied by two."

"Let me, I'll be quicker than you two," I said. I had the answer of 176,000 astronomical units; that meant a distance 176,000 times as far as the distance from the Earth to the Sun. "That's 2.8, almost three light years. What do you think, Innes?"

"Dr. Bari, that puts the companion star close enough to the Sun to stop it from being pulled away by other stars. It's a perfect solution, Dr. Bari. She has her model. Professor Bari has her model. Amazing! Even Alvarez won't be able to fault her model. He can't fault that. Isn't she divine? Where does her inspiration come from? It must come from God."

"Let me do the calculation again," I said, wondering if I had made an error. "I'm not usually wrong, but I'll do it again." I reached the same answer. "I still get 2.8 light years. I suppose I'll have to concede that one." Where did her inspiration come from? It was a creation from within. It was spontaneous and miraculous. Was it a dream in a wakeful state? To dream is to fancy improbable realities, to bypass limits and logic, and to arrive at a moment of inspiration. It was not the inspiration of a common person in everyday life. It was the inspiration of a genius. And yet it transpired only because the challenge was placed in front of her; she did not seek it. She had inner determination to persist with the problem and the innate pursuit of perfection. It was a victory over approximation and haste. It was a victory over acquiescence.

"Well then, Innes," said Prudence. "You have a job to do before you quit studying to join the ministry. Write up a response and send it to Alvarez. Before you do though, check all the calculations with Richard Muller. He's an experimental physicist in America and he'll know what you're talking about. I've got his address at work. He's a year younger than you and the two of you will get on famously together."

I had never seen Innes as animated and as enthusiastic as he was at this moment. The excitement and thrill of a challenge revitalized his pasty skin and lifeless disposition. Prudence had found the perfect solution to two problems and, even though she had trumped me, I had to admit that I was proud of her.

# COMMISSIONER'S COMMENTARY

Innes was cooperative in a quiet and nervous way. It was obvious from the start that he was a scholar of considerable intellect. I wouldn't say he was composed because it was clear that he was highly distressed over the loss of his mentor. In fact, apart from Leonardo Bari, Innes appeared to be the person most affected by the incident.

With his eyes downcast he provided short answers, giving us glimpses of his studious and monastic approach to life. Rigid and obsessive about learning and loathsome of failure, he seemed to put the weight of success on his fragile shoulders. He spoke of progressing from science to theology, and of helping humanity in a humbling way, due mainly to his desire for peace and harmony in the world. I wondered whether he had the confidence to fulfill his desires on a large scale because he appeared too sensitive and timid to me. I couldn't image him giving a speech or sermon to one person, let alone a whole congregation. Yet his compassionate heart may surprise the skeptics, like me, one day. When I expressed sympathy for Innes, Constable Hallett suggested he was sedated. Constable Collins said he was the suicidal type. My mother agreed with Collins. She said an ill wind and depression would be the end of him. At first I almost dismissed him as pathetic, but by the end of the interrogation I felt a sense of sorrow and sadness for the young man.

# CYRIL SILVERMAN

"For goodness sake, you parasites, you bludgers, when are you going to bear me fruit?" I heard myself snap at the flowerless clump of geraniums in their heavy terracotta pots. "When are you going to be productive? When are you going to flower?" I was frustrated at the inaction of my dawdling garden. Perhaps the orthodox, nature-worshipping gardener that I used to be was progressively vanishing? I was annoyed with the geraniums whose blood-red flowers should be blossoming profusely. I was annoyed with the pugnacious noisy honeyeater for chirping stridently as it pillaged my apricots. And, as I looked at the honeyeater, it took on my appearance and my mannerisms: rushed, anxious, and stressed. And quite probably, like me, there was nothing of any substance to be stressed about. Gardening should be a pleasure that depended on the ability to appreciate the gradual opening of a bud, the slow passing of time, the deliberation of every phase of growth and decay in God's garden.

I tried to ignore the telephone, but it rang annoyingly. With much to do in the garden, I resented the intrusion. Irritating though the telephone was, I was more aggravated by traipsing grass and soil into the house. Pulling off my garden gloves, I picked up the receiver. "Leonardo here," I answered bluntly.

"I want Prue. Get Prue on the phone. Now!" The voice was aggressive, insistent, and agitated.

"She's not here, Cyril. Is there anything I can do for you?"

"Fucking hell, Leon! Get the bitch on the phone," Cyril yelled with such hatred I was taken aback. His voice broke with rage. "Sorry Leon. I, I have to speak to Prudey. Darren's dead. Darren's dead," he sobbed. "He killed himself because of Prue.

192

I know he did. I hate her. I hate her. Where is she? I'll kill that bitch."

"Cyril. Listen to me. Calm down. Don't say things now that you'll regret later. You're upset. Calm down. Why don't you come here and we can talk about it? Prudence is with Arlene in Melbourne for the weekend."

"What am I going to do? I've lost Darren." He sobbed convulsively into the phone. He was heartbroken, devastated, and desperate.

"Cyril, listen. Darren was an angry man. He was also very sensitive. You know that. He wanted everyone to like him, and he was paranoid when they didn't. You know Prudence wouldn't hurt him. Prudence will be terribly upset when she hears of Darren's death. She cares about you. She really does. Tell me what happened, Cyril."

"The police, the police rang this morning. They just said Darren slit his wrists and was dead when the warden went to his cell. That's all they said. I visited him only a couple of days ago. He hated jail, but he seemed okay. He was upset, sure, but he was okay. He was only going to be in jail for a few months. He knew that, but he said the inmates were bashing him because he was gay. He said it was hell, but I thought he was coping. I thought he'd be out soon. I thought he was okay." Cyril sniffed back the tears and mucous. The convulsions decreased.

"Cyril, I'm so sorry. He was too intense, Cyril. He took everything to heart. Don't torture yourself. You couldn't have helped him."

"I could have and I should have! I should have helped him, Leon. Prudence should have done something too, at the restaurant. We should've stopped him fighting. He just lost it. He hated Arlene and he hated seeing Prudence with me. I wish Prudence hadn't been at the restaurant. Why was she there? Why was she at the restaurant? Why did I talk to her? I swear I didn't know Darren was after Arlene, I swear. Why did this happen, Leon?"

"Cyril, calm down. Where are you? Do you want me to come and see you?"

"I'm at home. No, no, I'm okay. I'm angry at Prudey. I'm upset. I'll be okay."

"Cyril, you need to speak to someone about how you feel. You must speak to someone."

"I'm tired. I need to sleep." His voice dissipated to a whisper.

"Cyril, Cyril? Are you all right? You haven't taken any drugs, have you? Cyril?"

"No, no, I haven't. I didn't do them as much as Darren did. I'm okay. I just need some sleep."

"Can you ask someone to be with you? I don't want you to be alone right now. Cyril, can you hear me?"

"I'll call someone. My sister, Carla, maybe. I dunno. I'm okay."

The phone was silent. I was concerned for his welfare. What if something happened to him? What if he was to commit—? I didn't want to think of the consequences. I looked in the notebook next to the telephone for Polly's number. What was Polly's surname? Finally, I found it and rang three times before I dialed it correctly. "Polly, Polly, this is Leon. Polly, listen to me."

"I know. Darren's dead. I heard about it. The whole city knows about it. I've been trying to ring Cyril, but his phone's always engaged. I can't get through." She was a different person. Her usual flippant voice was serious and sober.

"Polly, we don't have time to talk. Polly, listen. Please do me a big favor and go to Cyril's place. Get him to let you in; bang the door down if you have to. Get the police if you have to, just let yourself in and stay with Cyril. He's taking it very badly, Polly. Can you stay with him? Do you hear me, Polly?"

"Sure. I'll go there now. Does Prue know?"

"I'll ring her. She's in Melbourne with a friend. Go to Cyril's place and I'll try to ring Cyril after I've spoken to Prudence. Good girl." For once, I knew I could trust her to be the comfort that Cyril needed.

Arlene Bernie's name was written in red ink in the telephone notebook. Five times I rang before she answered. "What? What is it? Who's calling?" she yelled into the telephone. Arlene had no telephone manners.

"Arlene, it's me. Leonardo. Is Prudence there?"

I tried to calm down as I spoke with Prudence. She was audibly upset when I explained the events of the morning. She must have said "Oh no!" a hundred times.

"Is there anything I can do, Prudence?"

"No, papa, nothing, Wait, there is something you can do for me. Michael's in Adelaide. Did I tell you? I forgot to give Michael the maps I promised him. Have you got time today? Can you take the maps to his hotel? They're on the dresser in my bedroom. I'll ring Cyril and see if Polly's there. I'll make sure he's okay."

"Sure, I'll take the maps to Michael. By the way, Philip Brownley rang. He was hoping to interview you. What shall I say if he rings again?"

"Let Fabian handle that. Tell Fabian that I'll do the interview in a few weeks. Fabian will arrange that. Philip should've known to ring Fabian. Never mind. Just worry about getting the maps to Michael." Her voice was agitated and distracted. "I've got to go." She must have dropped the phone. All I could hear was an eerie echo.

# COMMISSIONER'S COMMENTARY

Cyril Silverman was a different person from earlier interviews. My first meeting with him revealed a discourteous, uncooperative, disheveled bundle of irritability. He rarely spoke, and if he did, it was with a brusque, abrupt manner. During the later interviews, after Darren's death, he was alert, cooperative and almost polite, answering questions in sentences.

He adored and admired Prudence, but was always in awe of her. Secretly he wished that she were younger or he older because she was the only woman he had any respect and love for. Why then did he choose to be with an unemployed bad-tempered drug addict? Cyril sighed then looked straight at me before answering in a reflective voice. He looked ashamed and disgusted with himself. Acknowledging his own creative and artistic mind, and his teaching ability, he admitted to being stupid in love, attracted to "bad boys." He knew his life was spiraling downward, and he knew it was due to Darren's influence, but he couldn't pull away from the irresistible hypnotic force of the younger man's control. He vilified Prudence to please his lover, knowing full well that Prudence did not hate homosexual men. Nor was she excessively puritanical in her sexual views, he confessed. Darren had influenced him to the point where, in his presence, Cyril would malign the people he loved. There was nothing about Prudence he did not like, despite his comments to her and the public. Poisonous was the word he used to describe his relationship with Darren.

The desire to please him had resulted in a caustic relationship with others, but not with Prudence. Cyril strongly believed that Prudence knew his inner turmoil and tolerated his destructive relationship with Darren. He maintained that her friendship for him was deep and true.

It struck me that Cyril was an astute man caught in the clutches of a vile person. Why? He liked the passion, the extreme intensity with which Darren loved him. Over time, love turned to obsession. Obsession manifested itself into jealousy and rage, squeezing the hold over him with an ever tightening grip. He missed Darren after he committed suicide in jail, but revealed that inevitably it was for the best.

Had he killed Prudence to exact revenge for Darren's premature death? Again, he eyed me directly and defiantly, uttering one word: No!

# MICHAEL McSHANE

I was anxious. I could tell because my breathing had shortened and I couldn't control it. The more I tried, the more I gasped for air. I had let the trauma of the morning affect me.

I was in a hurry to deliver the maps to Michael as Prudence had requested so, for the first time, I did not catch a bus into the city. Light rain fell as I dashed to the waiting taxi. The journey was calming and it gave me time, in solitude, to re-order my thoughts. With a few deep breaths I forced myself to think of something, anything but the day's events. I visualized Prudence at the beach. She was happy and carefree, the waves gently and rhythmically washing over her. The waves rose higher and sprayed mists of salty water onto my black trousers. Wind whipped up grains of sand that clung to the wet streaks on my trouser legs. I would have to wash them. They needed a thorough washing.

The taxi driver repeated his words, forcing me out of my daydream. "Rain. It's raining. God knows we need it, hey?"

"Yes, yes," I stammered. "We need the rain."

I had never met Michael, nor spoken to him on the telephone. A new wave of panic overcame me, but I was at the reception desk before I could change my mind. A woman with a beautifully styled chignon telephoned Michael. He was in room number nine, which in a strange way, made me more relaxed. I didn't like the number four. To me, it was an angular number, not rounded like the others. Seven, I supposed, was also angular, but less so. For many, seven was a lucky number, so in my mind, four was my least favorite numeral. I knocked on the door of room number nine in the three-star hotel.

"Hello, there, Dr. Bari." Michael outstretched his hand. "You must be Leonardo. Prue talks about you a lot. She rang to say you'd be coming. Please come in."

"How are you? Prudence forgot to give you these maps. She's in Melbourne for two days, so she couldn't come here herself. She went to see Arlene Bernie's play. I'll be off now. Prudence just wanted you to have them today." I thrust the maps into Michael's willowy hand. It was an elegant, artistic hand, quite unlike my hard gardening hand, and I felt embarrassed. Surely he would notice the feel of sandpaper against his smooth skin. If so, he didn't show it.

"Come in and have a cup of tea with me." The lyrical lilt of the southern Irish brogue was soothing and inviting. "Sit down on the sofa. You look tense. You haven't been rushing, have you? Take your time, sit back and relax. Life's too short to be fussing and worrying." His voice was the relaxant I needed.

I stayed with Michael for a few hours, talking to the son of a poet. He was an intellectual, creative, handsome, and placid man. His clothes were relaxed and comfortable, clothes that wore him: simple, soulful, and serene. I could understand Prudence's attraction to him. It was in his sorrowful eyes, his beautiful hands, his mellifluous voice, and his entire manner. He was devastatingly handsome in a dark, bewitching, atmospheric way.

He inserted a cassette tape in a machine and joined me in the slow, deliberate sipping of black tea. The tape was Faure's *Requiem* and the infinite, repetitive sadness of the piece hung low in the sparse but comfortable room like impending bad weather. We talked of Ireland, his birthplace. We talked of England, his living place. Mostly we talked of his frequent travels in his search for a place that defined his soul and his spirit: a place to settle.

"Prudence is the only person who understands me," Michael said. "She knows what home is and how important it is to have a sense of place. Years ago I lost my belief in what home represented. Through a passage of time, I'd seen the astonishingly rapid disintegration of two households where I grew up: my parent's house and my grandparent's house. Both of them lost through poverty. I came to think of the concept of home as an elaborately constructed false front. A façade, really."

His black hair covered his intense eyes and he made no attempt to push the thick strands from his face. The locks, clumped together with sweat and grease, safeguarded his eyes like prison bars. He rolled a cigarette deftly between his fingers and licked the paper with the flick of his tongue, beguilingly and sensually. His smiling eyes and the upturned crook of his lips were mesmerizing, even to me, an aging man. It was as if a strong magnetic force-field filled the room, pulling me closer and closer toward him. I couldn't take my eyes off this striking man whose every lilting word lingered like music in my ears. He was more seductive than Cyril. Cyril was raw, rough, and rugged. Michael was more tragic in the poetic sense. Painful memories etched into his face as constant reminders of past struggles. There was no anger, only a haunting pain. The attraction was logical and real, not supernatural in any sense. There was no black magic, no hypnotic magic, none of that sort of Svengali darkness that surrounded Cyril. It was plain and simple common sense submission to Michael's heavenly aura.

"We were poor, Leonardo. We were poor, but we had our dignity."

I could relate well to this because his stories were tales similar to my own past.

"But," he continued, "there was death everywhere: the death of animals on the farm, the death of crops such that we could no longer eat, the death of my parents, too early, from a hard life, and the demise of my grandparents. Death was everywhere. All human action, including inaction, carries an element of risk, of death perhaps. You could be sitting watching television and have a heart attack, but the act of watching television isn't the cause of death, is it? Who knows when and why death happens. I've known a lot of death, yet I don't fear it. I've known fear too. When Prudence told me about Africa, when that rhino chased her, I told her my story of fear. I was on a sailing trip with friends when the boat ran into a powerful Atlantic storm. Everybody got sick and I had to steer the boat through eighteen-foot waves by myself, with virtually no experience. At first I was terrified, but I knew it was a 'do or die' moment: a moment of decision. If I did nothing, the whole boat would be fated. In a split second, I knew I had to do something, even if I failed. Once I accepted the situation, some greater power took over, and I lost my sense of fear. I recited poems in the face of the storm and felt total exhilaration. No, life isn't dangerous, nor should it be feared, but it's full of death. That's the law of averages. You'd know about that, Dr. Bari. My father was an elegant man, a poet, and he taught me to find beauty in everything, even death. Prue talks to me often of aesthetics and beauty in science and mathematics. I know what she means."

"Yes, there's a simplicity and beauty in mathematics, particularly nature," I answered wistfully. "It's an almost frightening simplicity and wholeness that nature spreads before us. Poincare attributed great importance to mathematical beauty, to the 'harmony of numbers and forms' and to 'geometric elegance.' Linked with the revealing power of beauty, though, is nature's capacity to unsettle the ideas that we humans habitually need and the theories we need to make sense of the universe. Apparently Buddha, when his disciples asked him many complex metaphysical questions, just took a flower and placed it in front of them, revealing nature's inexpressible truth. Beauty discloses to us that which is beyond thought. It lightens our greed. It's the way to liberation. It lightens our fears too. Prudence went through the same thing in Africa. She was so in awe of the rhino's sense of beauty that she almost forgot its dangers. She said that in the face of danger life was, in a strange way, liberating."

"Precisely! Yes, I agree. You said it so eloquently. It must be the Italian in you. That's why I had to leave Ireland. For my liberation. For my freedom. The freedom of detachment. In England, at university, life seemed worth living again. It seemed to be an endless, decadent party. I hung out with students of the avant-garde French director, Didier Dubois, at Avignon. *Vous parlez francais, Monsieur Bari?"*

*"Oui, tres souvent."*

"*Bon,*" He smiled. "I slept outside the walls of the *Palais des Papes.* I had little money. I still have little money, but enough to travel the world and live in hotels. I get paid for my travel stories. I don't know why I continue to live in England. It was wonderful at first, but it got duller and duller and more expensive. My God, at times it was terribly depressing. I needed to travel. Travel is good for me, but because I travel so much, I find it easier to be myself in the company of strangers than with friends. I'm constantly running away from intimacy. I admit that. I can say that to strangers. I can be my true self to people I hardly know. Prue's an exception, of course. I can always be myself with her. It's easy for me to talk to her. She's a good listener, as you are. Have I kept you too long?"

"No, no. Are you working on anything at the moment while you're in Australia?" I wanted to extend the afternoon for as long as possible and, for the first time since I can remember, I was content not to rush home.

"I'm working on a travel story. It's just in the research stage. It's about the South Pacific. I think it'll only be a limited edition because the publisher wants it to be illustrated. I'd love to write something on the shipwrecks off the Australian coast. There are some treacherous reefs out there. But—who knows." He shrugged his shoulders indifferently as he looked out of the window toward the parklands.

"Do you enjoy the craft of writing?" I asked. Writing about mathematics was always difficult for me.

"Sometimes I do. Sometimes a piece of narrative will come easily, but when it doesn't flow, there's no use forcing it. With me, it has to flow. When you were a mathematics lecturer, if you didn't feel like lecturing, you still had to do it. With writing, it's not like that, except if I'm writing a piece for a newspaper and there's a deadline, then I write, but I'm usually not happy with the outcome. Then it's a matter of inspiration versus obligation. Sometimes I just have to prostitute myself though." He fiddled with his empty teacup, swirling the dregs in an anti-clockwise motion.

"Do you write every day?"

"Not unless I have something to write about. I'm not disciplined. I keep a dream diary. When I get an idea from a dream, or I find myself dreaming of a place I've been to or a place I'm going to, I write notes to see if my visions reflect reality. I find it an interesting game."

"Do you subscribe to the idea of the Muse?"

"That the Muse might possess me, you mean? Absolutely! Artistic inspiration, whether for poetry, or prose, or painting, or song, or any form of creativity, comes from a Muse; for me that's a certainty. Isn't that the derivation of the word music? Weren't the Muses described as 'the keys to the good life' and, if so, you're possessed by the Muses when you're lucky, if you're lucky. The Muses were sure to bring both prosperity and friendship. Prudence was my Muse; her friendship inspired me to write my best work, to be my best being. Was it Shakespeare in Henry V who wrote "O, for a Muse of fire that would ascend the brightest heaven of invention, a kingdom for a stage, princes to act, and monarchs to behold the swelling scene!" Some writers believe that the Muses are merely the vessel through which their work flows. It's not good to force creativity. Who was it that said forcing creativity was akin to bathing a cat? Prudence said lighting a candle brought her inspiration. Light and color enhanced it, she said. She said gardening inspires you, Leonardo. Music and poetry inspire me. Some people have a creative space, but I travel too much for that. My creative space is in my mind; it's critical for my soul's survival. It's not good to force creativity, I believe that," he said looking intently at the tea leaves in the base of his cup.

"What do you see, Michael?"

He seemed surprised that I asked. Perhaps he wasn't aware of his actions. "Oh, um—separation," he stuttered. I had caught him off guard, and both he and I were embarrassed by it. "I see separation. In what connection, I don't know. Maybe it's the separation of science and religion? Scientists are too impacted with spiritual ignorance: maybe not you, Leon, but certainly the majority of scientists. Or maybe it's the separation of the ruling classes? It seems to me that the so-called ruling classes are moving to a hermetic circle that has nothing to do with what's going on in society. Maybe I saw in the tea leaves the separation of people with their environment. I'm very distressed by the destruction of the world's rainforests. I hope someone will put a stop to it. Well, let's not get into all of that. I can see a separation of some sort in the tea leaves, that's all: not that you believe in such nonsense, Leon. I believe in it. My grandmother was a great reader of the leaves. It might represent me going back to England. Perhaps that's all it is. I have kept you too long, haven't I? Thank Prudence for the maps. Perhaps I'll see her when she gets back from Melbourne? She wanted to see me. She said that she had some ideas to discuss with me. It sounded important."

"I'm sure she'll want to see you, Michael. Are you staying here long?" I wanted to see him again. I longed to discuss the beauty of science, the beauty of death. I wanted to understand his pain.

"A week maybe, then I go to Melbourne or Sydney. Maybe I can see Prudence next week?"

"I'm not sure. She's had some bad news this morning. A friend, Darren, killed himself last night. I imagine she'll want to pay a visit to Cyril to see that he's coping with the loss. Cyril was Darren's best friend, you see."

"Yes, of course. I understand."

I reluctantly rose to leave.

In parting, Michael said, "When your number is up, it's up. Life is over. That's destiny: another day, another death." It was meant as a sort of light-hearted answer, I suspect, but the lugubrious atmosphere of the room had taken over.

# COMMISSIONER'S COMMENTARY

Not in a million years could I envisage Michael McShane killing anyone. He appeared not to have a violent bone in his body. My constables used the phrase 'emotionally balanced' when describing him. He was not a meek man, not by any stretch of the imagination. Rather, he was a gentle, softly-spoken, calm person. It was easy to take an instant liking to him.

I asked the usual questions and there appeared nothing untoward about this man. Before questioning him, my officers had investigated the time when he was picked up by Prudence, when they left the hotel, and when he checked-in at the airport. All appeared above board, leaving no time for him to follow her back to the location where she was attacked—it was on the other side of the city.

As part of the investigation, I ordered Constable Hallett to collect the clothes that Cyril, Fabian, Oswald, and Leonardo were wearing on the day Prudence was killed. Our laboratory scientists analyzed the garments. Because of the nature of the crime scene, and by that I mean the burning of the upper part of Prudence's body, we wanted to test for fire residue. It would seem logical that ash and soot would appear on the killer's clothing and body.

The results surprised me. No trace of fire residue, soot or ash, appeared on the samples of clothing provided by Cyril, Fabian, or Oswald. Amazingly, there were particles of soot on Leonardo Bari's trousers and shirt. In fact, there were carbon streaks across them. I say amazingly because I sincerely believed Bari had nothing to do with his daughter's death. However, evidence was evidence. To be certain, I had the samples tested a second time, at an independent laboratory, but the results were the same. I admit to not ordering tests on Michael's clothes, but the flight log clearly showed that he left Adelaide.

This left me no choice but to re-examine Dr. Bari's testimony. In a way I felt sorry for him. How anyone could endure the thought of a daughter being killed so maliciously, I'll never know. If he did it, there must have been a compelling reason, beyond anything that I could imagine. And that's the point—I couldn't imagine him killing her at all, not even accidentally. Bari as a murderer had not been a serious possibility to me.

Before questioning Leonardo Bari, I summoned Constables Hallett and Collins into the interrogation room with their notebooks for a re-cap of the whole investigation to that point in time. I asked my constables for a rundown of every suspect's feelings toward Dr. Bari to compile a glossary, so to say, of the man who appeared to be the center of the victim's universe.

Words and phrases were shouted out randomly by the two officers, as I requested, of course. Here's the list: responsible, compassionate, sympathetic, kind, generous, wise, balanced, can span the generation gap, his life revolves around his home, overly-critical of himself, often exaggerates, can be meddling, worries too much, wants his daughter to be married with children, wants his daughter to be happy, wants to lead and direct, wants to be recognized for his abilities, overly sensitive, idealistic, obsessive about order and symmetry, but not driven by power and wealth. No one mentioned aggressive, insane, jealous, violent, or any other phrase that might suggest that he despised his daughter or had any reason to kill her so sadistically.

Bari seemed to be in his own world: not crazy but disengaged. I'm not sure that he recognized the gravity with which this case could unfold. Displaying my most authoritarian manner I questioned him relentlessly. The more I did so, the more his mind drifted inwardly. I didn't know what to make of his answers or actions.

The first sentence he uttered was an admission of his guilt. More to the point he said that he failed to protect Prudence. Several times he claimed that he did it. Whenever I asked him to detail what in fact he did, he avoided the question. He spoke only in generalities, nothing specific. We needed details, but they were not forthcoming.

Desperate for a respite, I left the room to grab something to eat. When I returned, Bari was doodling in a notebook, scrawling what looked to me like a series of letters and numbers. I put it down to him seeking relief and comfort in the world he knew: mathematics. Awkwardly, for I know nothing about numbers, I asked him what he was scribbling. An effusive answer ensued. Not knowing exactly what he was talking about makes it difficult for me to explain here in these pages. All I can remember were phrases about numerology; it was supposed to determine a person's destiny. It sounded like hocus pocus to me. I think he was confused because he kept saying that numerology was more accurate with birth dates because birth dates never change. He said that names change. Hence, a person's date of birth was more accurate than a person's name, in terms of numbers. And I admit that's what confused me because a date is comprised of numbers, but a name is comprised of letters. I didn't know what he meant by saying that a date was more accurate than a person's name.

Bari said he didn't know when Prudence's friends were born. He said something about names changing or that he had changed someone's name, after which he added that everything was his fault. I'm not patient with the mentally handicapped, and even though I believed that Bari wasn't actually weird, he sure acted like he was. This made me very nervous because I had no idea what to do with him. I let him ramble on and on.

One name that Bari mentioned many times was a female's name, Greek I think, comparing it with the name Prudence. Again, I can't write what he said with any great clarity because it seemed insignificant to me at the time. It's only since reading his journal that I realize that some importance should be attributed to what he said. It was as if he was arguing with himself, saying that this Greek person was a more compassionate person than Prudence. This Greek person, fictitious or real, I don't know, was more inclined to give comfort and solace to the underprivileged, more community-minded, and with a more delicate ego. I remember that phrase well: a more delicate ego. This Greek person was not interested in leadership, he said. It was as if he thought the Greek woman would have assumed a humanitarian role in life. At the time, I thought he was talking about his wife or a second daughter. At one point Bari said the name Florence. His wife's name was definitely not Florence.

To be honest, I got my nationalities mixed up. I thought Italians and Greeks were the same. I knew Leonardo Bari was Italian, but I was confused when he mentioned a Greek woman. Who can blame me? I know people who think the English and the Irish are the same, or that the English and the Scots are the same. My constables gave me a geography lesson and set me right. At least I won't be making that mistake again.

Constable Collins became increasingly impatient with Bari and banged his fist on the table, startling us all. He screamed at the old man, telling him to "get a grip" and to put his notebook away so he could concentrate on the questions. Surprisingly, Bari shoved his notebook into his pocket. Secretly, I was grateful to Constable Collins. At no point do I consider violence a method of coercing answers from suspects, and I would never condone an officer of mine bullying a suspect in custody. Constable Collins merely banged on the table, but, my word, it was an almighty wallop, and it produced the desired result.

Taking the opportunity so spectacularly presented to me, I asked Dr. Bari again whether he had killed his daughter. He said "indirectly" and clarified it with an admission that he was partly, if not wholly, to blame. Collins questioned him about his sooty clothes, to which Bari answered that they were his gardening clothes, and he often burned leaves and debris. Hallett and Collins looked at me. At least it seemed as if we were making progress. I, myself, do the same thing. I burn autumn leaves and other rubbish in my incinerator. The municipal council is considering banning incinerators from people's back yards because they say that the smoke pollutes the air, but I think this is poppycock and absurd. Everybody burns things in their incinerator and the air looks fine to me. What Dr. Bari said he was doing was quite normal. Quite frankly, we believed him.

Unprovoked, Bari offered the following information. He maintained that the person who killed Prudence was knowledgeable of the great female mathematician, Hypatia, because the slaying was a replica of her death. He added that there was one exception, and it was that Hypatia—who was Greek apparently—was murdered in March and not September. Actually, there were a few other differences, but I don't think any of them were important.

Hypatia was a famous figure of antiquity, the head of the Platonist school in Alexandria, with a father called Theon, an unusually liberated person who encouraged his daughter to achieve success in the male-dominated field of mathematics. It is generally believed that she never married and that she, as Dr. Bari put it, was wedded to truth. Antagonism grew between the Christians and pagans with Cyril, the archbishop of Alexandria, accusing Orestes, the Prefect of Alexandria, of performing pagan rites. I thought the names were interesting. Cyril and Orestes were similar to Cyril and Oswald. And Theon was similar to Leon. It fascinated me. My constables didn't react when I looked at them. They merely shrugged their shoulders.

Bari declared that Hypatia was murdered for her association with Orestes and because she was an influential woman. Apparently, she was a strong advocate of unorthodox pre-Christian traditions and was therefore a focus for those wanting to eradicate the old order. A group of Christians followed Hypatia on her way home, threw her from her chariot, dragged her into a cathedral where they killed her, and cut her body into pieces which they burned. What Bari said next was quite enlightening, and the first time he had attempted to place the blame on someone. It seems clear, he said, that Hypatia was the victim of the aggressive and fanatic ideals of Cyril, whether he ordered her death or not.

My officers and I all spoke the same name at the same time: Cyril. We nodded. Everything seemed clearer at that point. Instantly I thought of Polly Smith's theory about Charles Manson. He wasn't present at the massacre at Roman Polanski's house, but he was charged with inspiring, or masterminding, the killings of the actress Sharon Tate and others. Could it be true of Cyril Silverman also? How were we going to obtain evidence of that? Obviously we had to coerce Cyril to confess to ordering the killing. It was necessary to obtain as much foolproof evidence as possible, through hard facts or a confession, before any court could convict someone who wasn't at the murder scene but, undoubtedly, was the mastermind behind the killing. I sighed out of frustration. That, in my mind, was unlikely. In fact, it seemed mighty impossible.

# SEPTEMBER 28, 1969

On Sunday September 28, 1969, Melbourne police raided the theater where Arlene's play was performed. It was front page news. About a homosexual's birthday party, the play was controversial in its content, but it was the liberal sprinkling of profanity that caught the attention of the vice squad. Three actors from *The Boys in the Band* were convicted on nine charges of using obscene language in a public place.

I remember the day, not only for this occurrence, or the 35th birthday of French actress Brigitte Bardot, but also because an auspicious omen marked another more devastating incident. In Murchison, Victoria, in southeastern Australia, a huge fireball burst into the atmosphere as a result of a disintegrating comet. More than a hundred kilograms of meteoric rock crashed through the atmosphere toward Earth.

The local newspaper reported the following:

*The Murchison rocks contain amino acids, carbon compounds known to be 'building blocks' for life. "We still don't know how life emerged from these compounds," said Dr. Hatton, "but the find provides a clue that the ingredients for life on Earth may have come to Earth from space.*

Meteorites from the Murchison comet were highly significant for Australian scientists, and, in fact, scientists around the world. They were found to be virtually unchanged since they had formed in the solar system 4.57 billion years before the comet smashed to Earth. The Murchison comet was not from an asteroid belt; scientists knew this because it contained twelve percent water and over eighty different amino acids. Eighty different amino acids! The importance of that piece of knowledge was monumental. On Earth there are only ever nineteen differ-

211

ent amino acids that comprise all living creatures. To be sure, the Murchison comet contained those nineteen amino acids, but also another sixty-one or more. And of course, it was the same for all the pieces of the comet's meteoric rocks that were found. If I were younger, I would have endeavored to join the team of scientists studying the characteristics of the meteorites: Prudence would have too.

Prudence knew of the comet because it arrived in the morning—at 10:58 a.m. Radio announcers and newsreaders made such a commotion about the event, but they knew little about the science of it.

Jonathan Swift said old men and comets have been revered for the same reason: their long beards and ability to foretell events. It was even said that the word comet derived from the Greek for long-haired, or stars with hair. For me, comets were the precursor to the return of Phaethon. Comets were an omen. There was generally little good that ever came on the day of a comet.

I'm an old man and I failed to predict the events of that fateful day. The Murchison comet was surely a good omen for, scientifically, it brought critical information to Earth about the origin of life. However, every positive element has a negative element—equal and opposite forces—call it what you will, for it was also indeed a bad omen: the worst possible day on Earth. It was the day that my daughter died. In one day I was to learn of the origins of life and of the realities of death.

Prudence flitted in and out of our home, leaving me with few connections and understandings of our disjointed conversations. Our exchanges seemed to join sentences between long absences in a surreal way that lacked coherence throughout the whole day, bewildering me with half-answered questions, misinterpretations, and misunderstandings. There was no beginning, middle, and end, and if there were, I could not differentiate them.

"Gotta fly, papa. I'm late. If Fabian rings, tell him I'm on my way," Prudence said as she slammed the front door on her way out. Seconds later, the banging of the brass knocker surprised me. It was loud, determined and incessant. I ran with short steps to the door. As I swung the door open, my daughter pushed passed me and ran the length of the hallway to the kitchen. "Keys? Got them! You must listen to the radio to hear more about the Murchison comet and meteor rocks. Let me know what they're saying. You do realize today is Brigitte Bardot's birthday, don't you? We should call it Bardot's Comet. That's a suitable name, papa, isn't it? So I declare I'm officially changing the name, Murchison Meteorites, to Bardot's Comet. And it'll be a lucky omen this time: not a bad luck one. Mark my words, papa! You'll remember the date forever. No one will ever remember Mr. Murchison, but they'll never forget Brigitte Bardot. I really must go." Again, she ran passed me and out of the door. I hadn't said a word. There wasn't time.

She was right. Murchison was not a name I would remember, nor the date of this auspicious comet, except that it occurred in my birth month. At a pinch I might remember that it occurred three days after my 75th birthday, but I would always remember Brigitte Bardot's birthday. It was a fitting change of name.

I continued tidying my garden. It was a day when the warm scent of northerly breezes heralded the first flowering blooms of spring: flowers blooming merely to make seed to ensure another year's survival. Frustrating the blossoms, I removed the seed-heads to enable greater flower production. I cleared the winter debris and top-dressed the soil with a mixture of loam, leaf-mold, and manure to protect the garden during the driest months of the year. It was a task I dutifully performed every spring, and I religiously watered the plants before and after fertilizing to prevent the rich, fertile mulch from burning the delicate roots of the flowering annuals. I snipped away the excess and tangled dead growth of winter allowing the new life-buds of spring to emerge triumphant. Prune and feed. Prune and feed. It was a simple formula for success in the garden.

I heard the Fiat return to the driveway. Prudence erupted from the back door, and the metallic clash of the screen door reverberated raucously throughout the yard.

"Here's some lawn food. I saw it on special at the plant nursery down the road. There was a big red sign. I had to park the car up the road and carry the bags back. Did I buy too much? I'll leave the bags on the back veranda. Have you heard any more about Bardot's Comet?"

"No, they just keep repeating the same information. A piece of meteoric rock fell into a haystack or something, apparently— on a farm. That's all I know."

"Okay, papa; keep listening. Do you need anything else?" She remained on the veranda and we continued our conversation by shouting to each other.

"No thanks. I thought you were going to Fabian's place?"

"Not yet. I went to see Michael first. He's going to Sydney this evening. Has he rung?"

"Michael? No. You just said that you were with Michael."

"No. I meant that I want to see Michael first, not Fabian."

"You were with Fabian? I thought you were with Michael." I wished she would come closer, so we wouldn't need to raise our voices. I was at the compost heap, reeking of decaying foliage, an odor I did not want inside the house.

"I meant did Fabian ring? Did he phone while I was gone? Has he arranged an interview with Philip? Did he mention that?"

"No. The phone hasn't rung. I didn't hear it."

"I'd better go. I'm on my way to Fabian's house." She skittered off towards her car.

The delivery of lawn food was perfectly timed. How did Prudence know I would need it today? Patches of dead brown lawn, compacted hard over winter, were in need of repair. I struck the tines of the garden fork into the toughened areas. With every prod, I swung the fork back and forth, leaving tiny wedge-shaped holes to aerate the soil. Sprinkling the lawn food over the spiked areas, I then watered liberally. Inspecting the azaleas, I examined the leaves for fleshy pale or white ones that indicated leaf gall, a fungus disease. I snipped off the affected diseased leaves and piled them neatly on top of a concrete slab next to the compost. Petal blight was common at this time of year, so I scrutinized each petal closely for pale, circular spots.

I removed dead flowers and placed them on top of the diseased leaves which I set alight to prevent the spread of fungal spores. It was a small fire, and I watched it burn safe in the knowledge that this preventative measure would lead to a more perfect garden next year. It was what every good gardener strived for. The diseased bundle smoldered, emitting a trail of white smoke weaving its way upward. Was that Prudence calling out? I saw her standing by the back door. I couldn't hear her.

"Okay," I yelled. "No, I haven't heard any more about Bardot's Comet. *Ritorna a me.*"

Prudence blew me a kiss goodbye. Her long curls framed her smiling face. I saw her wave; her orange fingernails caught the late afternoon sun and streaked through the air while her topaz ring flashed its brilliance. In tight, black pants and orange, short-sleeved shirt with its neat Peter Pan collar, Prudence stood in the entrance of the cavernous, dark hallway. The last image of her was of her flat, black plimsolls as her body twisted on its heels and the door closed behind her. She looked just like Brigitte Bardot, only ten years older.

The bulbous sun disappeared beyond the horizon, casting long, inky shadows across the yard. When I discarded my gardening gloves and removed my boots, I entered the back door. I brewed a pot of tea and investigated the refrigerator and larder for dinner ideas, deciding to cook Prudence's favorite mushroom fettuccini. With stocking-feet, I padded to the telephone to make a call.

"Ah, hello, Fabian. How are you? Everything well? Good, good. Can Prudence come to the phone, please?"

"She left some time ago to take Michael to the airport. He's off to Sydney."

"Good, it means she'll be home soon. I'm just preparing dinner. I'll call you tomorrow. *Ciao.*"

I replenished my teacup and sat at the kitchen table with the newspaper spread before me. Underneath the paper were Prudence's rosary beads. It seemed odd to me that they were on the table. I hooked the string of beads on the back of a chair where they clattered several times before dangling limp and still. A small, pale green oblong piece of paper caught my eye. I turned it over. I was startled at the picture. It was Prudence's mother in a black and white photograph taken in her teenage years, before the birth of my daughter. Faded and yellowed, it was a picture I had not seen in nearly fifty years. She was hardly recognizable. Her hair was shorter than I had remembered, clinging to the form of her head, finishing at the lobes of her ears. For some reason, I had thought her hair was curly, but now I see that it was wavy. With longer hair, the waves would be more prominent, just like Prue's. I had forgotten how much Prudence resembled her mother: the curve of her chin, the long Roman nose, and the shape of her face. My fingers traced the lines of her features, stopping at her lips. I caressed the tiny mouth, kissing my thumb and imprinting it onto her chromatic image. With only her head visible, I imagined the shape of her body, the rounded belly, the unshapely thick legs, and the fine, dark hairs that covered her limbs. That's where mother and daughter differed, for Prudence was slim and shapely without the inherited hirsute Italian physique. I placed the photograph on the table. As I turned the pages of the newspaper, the photograph spun aloft and drifted silently to the floor. I sipped the last drop of tea and idly stared at the teacup. Unlike Michael, I had no such imagination. I saw nothing.

# THE MEMORIAL

I had not cried at all. It was as if my mind and body had collapsed within themselves and had shut off a valve to the senses. All emotion was gone. I was a depleted man.

Reporters and journalists crowded outside the stately, austere cathedral, amid the crowd of sightseers and well-wishers. Police tape formed a preventative barrier and security staff guarded the cathedral entrance, admitting only invited guests.

I was protected from all this. Like Roman pillars, Fabian and Oswald held my elbows and guided me to a pew in the front row. I was wrapped in a cocoon, impervious to the wailing of the congregation. It seemed that everyone was there: the known and the unknown. Faces peered into mine and spoke consoling words. Fabian answered for me. I could not speak, but I took it all in—silently. It was as if I was outside the whole process, but somehow within it.

Cyril Silverman sat quietly among Prudence's university colleagues and students: Dr. Stewart Gorrie, Professor Jack Garland, Professor Bobby Chemsley, Julia Lamond, Raphael Milano, and Innes Cartwright. Innes was as pale as chalk with rubbed-red bulging eyes. He was frail and tormented. Philip Brownley was there, immaculately dressed, gripping his wife's hand in tight restraint. Julie Brownley's powder blue dress was most becoming. Even Arlene Bernie and her partner Jade Palmer were there. I recognized Prudence's friends from overseas, the ones I had seen in photographs: Professor Dante Zollo, Rosie Morgan, Gilbert Wales-Cochrane, Mario Rinaldi, Marie Claire Rotrosen, Andre Dystel, Jon Fletcher, and Stefan Pikarski. I was surprised to see Constables Bruce Collins and Peter Hallett, both in navy blue uniforms next to the commissioner of police. I did not know the old woman sitting next to him, but she seemed like a shriveled, faded version of the commissioner. None of them smiled, and for a brief moment, I wondered whether they were there out of empathy or whether they were watching me, waiting for me to admit my sins. I had already done that; I had already told them that I was to blame for my daughter's death. I would have pondered their presence further, but I was distracted by the movement of a red handkerchief. My neighbor Franco Visconte and his wife Maria smiled when I looked at them. In Franco's hand was a large red handkerchief, crumpled into a ball in his fist. He dabbed his eyes unashamedly. Franco and Maria were my best friends; I loved them like I would love a brother and sister. My gaze returned to Cyril and I felt immense sympathy for him. He gave me a slight wave and smiled. His eyes were clear and sparkling, just the way I remembered when I first saw him.

Fabian handled the invitations, so I was unfamiliar with the many faces behind me. From them I turned to the Catholic house of God. The imposing dignity of the cathedral's façade paralleled its rich, golden interior. A feeling of awesome power welled within me. A theatrical creation of statues and angels combined to produce a dramatic backdrop to Prudence's finale. Her mahogany coffin was draped in roses elegantly entwined together: soft cream, pallid pearl, baby pink, and sea coral, blending into the strong colors of fuchsia, crimson, and scarlet. In the middle of the elliptical floral shroud was a velvet black-red rose of exquisite hue: a ruby jewel in a velvet cloak of tenderness. They were Fabian's roses. I could not control the tears, and I allowed them to furrow into the creases of my face and drip down my chin. Fabian embraced me tightly, reassuringly. He shuddered next to my body and I knew that he too was crying a quiet, persistent sob. I sat with my sentinels and comforters as the church filled with mourners.

High on the red brick wall, behind the altar, hung a gilded picture-frame surrounding the face of my daughter. The border glinted with the flickering of lit candles making Prudence appear angelic. The muted, creamy tones of her cheesecloth dress added to her pious and feminine expression. An alabaster replicated

Pieta, of the dead Christ lying on the knees of the Virgin Mary, stood imposing and impressive beside Prudence. Christ's body, with its polished surface, reflected a golden aura around my pure, immaculate daughter. As Fabian stood to address the audience, he squeezed my hand in solace and support. He was as distinguished as ever in his dark Italian suit as he ascended the pulpit.

"Thank you everyone for your presence here today. Dr. Leonardo Bari thanks each and every one of you: overseas guests who have come from England and Italy, prominent and eminent professors, local guests, and friends. Thank you for sharing with Dr. Bari the memory of his beloved and treasured daughter. Professor Prudence Bari died on September 28, 1969, murdered brutally in the city of Adelaide. Born in Adelaide on August 3, 1924, she was proud of her Australian-Italian heritage. She was educated at Adelaide High School before studying at the Milan University and the University of Italy in Rome. She was an extraordinary person: a passionate scientist who will be forever remembered as the youngest chair of the prestigious Cabrini Mathematical Institute in Milan and the 1966 Turing Award winner, a highly prized honor bestowed upon eminent mathematicians. Professor Bari was a true professional in a fast-changing world, confident in her own abilities, but simply never grasping quite how brilliant she was. For all of her accolades, in some ways Professor Bari only scraped the surface of her talent, writing a number of books that inspired many young men and women to take on a career in the sciences." He looked up at the congregation before bowing his head. He took a deep breath and continued.

"Tributes have come from all over the world. They have described a woman of intense will and unswerving faith in the ability of science to find solutions to societal issues that change the lives of ordinary people for the better. The classically educated scholar believed that gifted people had an obligation to serve their local community. She did this to the end with grace, serenity, sincerity, and passion unmatched by her peers. It was an honor and a privilege to have worked with her and to have celebrated her achievements. She was the epitome of intelligence and modesty. Professor Prudence Bari was a creative and mathematical genius beyond comparison." He bowed his head as he swallowed his emotions. "She was—she was the greatest and most attractive woman that I have ever known. I share with you all my devotion to her genius and to her spirit as the pianist performs *You Belong to Me* by Dean Martin, a song that had a special place in her father's heart."

The sobbing increased and Fabian hesitated at the pianist's last note. "Her father, Dr. Leonardo Bari, also a former prominent mathematician, would like it known that Prudence's original name was Hester, after Hestia, the goddess of the hearth in Greek mythology. The hearth is the symbol of the fireside, of house and home, and of the security and love that resides within it. It is therefore fitting that Prudence returns to earth as Hester as she remains in her father's heart forever—hearth-bound, as he would say. Dr. Bari specifically requested that her gravestone show her name as Hester Prudence Bari. Thank you. Professor Dante Zollo from the University of Milan has prepared a eulogy."

A white-haired man rearranged the microphone before speaking. "Friends of Professor Prudence Bari, I speak to you now in not-good English, I think, but with words of praise and love for my dear, dear student." His wiry hair was as unruly as his crumpled white shirt beneath a somber jacket. Washed-out eyes were set inside deep chasms lined with circles of darkness. The thin, frail body stooped over the lectern and his skeletal hands gripped it tightly. "You do not know me, but I know Prudence. I know her from a young girl with the brain of an old man. She studied hard and was the best student. She laughed hard too, but with an Australian accent. I love her work in mathematics because it was beautiful like Prudence. Her work was inspiring to all students in my classes and she helped them very much. When she graduated, she inspired her own students and students all over the world. Australians are lucky to be in this country with the memories of Prudence. At my university we have collected money for a marble bust of Professor Bari to place in the science hall so we too can have memories of her. Thank you for inviting me to share my admiration for Prudence with you. She will be remembered a long time in our country. Thank you."

Fabian assisted him to his seat while Polly exchanged places. I did not recognize her because she was in black. An understated dress clung to her lithe body respectfully. A string of bulbous pearls choked her pale neck, her celestial looks clouded in morbidity. The pink lipstick smiled a crooked, quivering line. She bit her bottom lip before she began.

"Hi. I asked Fabian if I could say something and he said I could. I'm not anyone special. I only did one subject of mathematics because I wasn't very good at it, but Professor Bari was patient with me. I think it was the only mathematics subject I ever passed. All the other students said that she was the best lecturer and so was her father, Dr. Bari, in his time. I wasn't at uni then, but it was like an honor to say that you were taught by one of the Baris. Everyone knew the Baris." She hesitated as she looked directly at me with the familiar look of freshness and youth. "I think Prudence was lucky having such a wonderful father. He was like an uncle to me and I liked visiting him. They were like family in a way, and I guess Prudence was like a big sister to me. I wanted to be like her and to look like her. I even begged my mother to buy me a pair of white boots like hers because I thought they were real groovy. I just want you all to know that she was the best, that she was real good to me and to all her students. She made us want to learn and that's not easy when we just want to party all the time. Sometimes I even forgot to turn up to class and she'd give me the lecture at lunchtime when I was eating my pie and chips. It was no good hiding from her because she would find you, but she never yelled. She just said it was her job to teach everyone in her classes. Before I finish this eulogy, I'd like to recite one of her favorite Shakespearean sonnets: Sonnet 14. She used Shakespeare to interest me in mathematics because she knew I liked his poetry. Here's the one I chose to represent Professor Bari:

*Not from the stars do I my judgment pluck,*
*And yet methinks I have astronomy,*
*But not to tell of good or evil luck,*
*Of plagues, of dearths, or seasons' quality;*

221

*Nor can I fortune to brief minutes tell,*
*Pointing to each his thunder, rain and wind,*
*Or say with princes if it shall go well,*
*By oft predict that I in heaven find:*
*But from thine eyes my knowledge I derive,*
*And, constant stars, in them I read such art,*
*As, truth and beauty shall together thrive,*
*If from thyself to store thou wouldst convert;*
*Or else of thee this I prognosticate:*
*Thy end is truth's and beauty's doom*
*and date.*

"This poem is one of Shakespeare's procreation sonnets. To some people, the phrase 'to each his thunder, rain, and wind,' means that each of us hears, sees, and feels only what our own souls want us to hear, see, and feel—no more. But to me, they are symbolic of bad times. You know, like good weather means good times and bad weather means bad times. That's what I think anyway. I think the poet says he has the power to predict the future, not from astronomy or reading the stars, but from the eyes of his loved one. By looking at her eyes, the poet predicts her death. He says it's in fact the death of truth and the death of beauty. To me, it predicts the death of Professor Prudence Bari. It was her beauty that was doomed. Anyway, that's what I think. Thank you Dr. Leon Bari and thank you Prudence wherever you are right now."

Fabian stepped up to the lectern. Polly had made me smile and I was thankful for that. "Father O'Healey will lead us into prayer," announced Fabian.

Emptiness washed over me at the end of the service. The tide of black attire stymied individuality and creativity, replacing them with funereal traditions of uniformity and decorum. Even Oswald had borrowed a dark suit from Fabian and had polished an old pair of patent leather shoes. No one wore the appearance of familiarity; they were strangers cocooned in veils of darkness. I had never hated black so much as on this day.

# COMMISSIONER'S COMMENTARY

Cyril Silverman was always the front-runner at the top of the suspect list at police headquarters. To most of the officers he was a fair bet. At the memorial I watched him closely, searching for gestures and tell-tale signs that might expose the mind of a crazed killer. Frighteningly, he actually looked rather normal.

At headquarters we were planning our interrogation strategy before questioning Cyril. He was waiting impatiently when the strangest thing happened.

Constable Hallett announced that Innes Cartwright was at the reception desk claiming that he had new information about the killing of Professor Prudence Bari. I really couldn't bear time-wasters and almost dismissed the puny young man if it weren't for Hallett. The constable, keen for the process to be thorough and professional, suggested that we listen to him. For all we knew, the information could've been about Cyril. Well, it could have been, but it wasn't.

Innes didn't dither about. Sticking out his scrawny chest, he confessed to killing Prudence Bari, his professor, adding that it was an accident. He wanted to scare her, no more. My first reaction was to laugh. It seemed absurd that a weakling such as Innes could commit the most heinous crime I'd ever encountered. All I said to him was that I wanted details. It was details I got. In fact, a few minutes after he started, we realized the enormous importance of his testimony, so much so, that we had to stop him. I wanted to be sure that the tape equipment worked and that my officers were fully prepared.

When we were ready, to my astonishment, he continued in a quiet, methodical manner to recount the moments leading to, and resulting in, the death of Professor Prudence Bari. Nothing was omitted. When he finished, I asked him to tell me again, which he politely did, never wavering from his first account. My two constables and I questioned him persistently and uncompromisingly, but he did not falter. Repeatedly, whenever we backtracked to ensure that we understood a point, Innes provided the same amazingly specific story. That is, with one exception.

Innes, the student with the scientific mind of a genius, could not recall slashing Prudence with a knife, maintaining that he must have been in a frenzied state at the time. Everything else he said matched the forensic evidence accurately. Furthermore, he was unremittingly remorseful.

We temporarily released Cyril Silverman and detained Innes Cartwright overnight in a holding cell, on suicide watch for precautionary reasons, before further questioning him the next day. Fresh from a sleep-filled night, my first in many months, I was eager to determine the motive. Admittedly I was as baffled as my officers. Some suspected Innes wanted notoriety and thus fabricated the confession. My mother, over breakfast, warned me not to let Innes out of my sight. She insisted that he would suicide in the holding cell or in the interview room in order to bring attention to himself: to have his moment of fame. My mother refused, point blank, to believe that Innes had committed the crime. Quite firmly she told me to detain Cyril and, through any means possible, get a confession from him. She was two hundred percent certain that Cyril did it, whether he was actually at the crime scene or not. Initially I had come to the same deliberation as my constables—that Innes fabricated the confession—yet he convincingly recounted all the bloody events, fact by fact, detail by detail.

Had he despised his professor so much? Had he been enraged by something she said? Was he trying to molest her? Was he a pyromaniac? Was he aware of the Charles Manson killings in America? Did they influence him? Did he know of Hypatia and her demise? Why did he choose to be so vicious? Nothing made sense.

When Innes continued, he did so calmly and methodically. It was not an opportunistic event, he said. Innes had been stalking Prudence throughout the day. Plainly and calculatingly he followed her to the point where he felt compelled to talk to her, forcing her vehicle into a disused abandoned parking allotment. However, while the desire to see Prudence was calculated, the act of murder was, apparently, not.

It was an impulse, Innes said, an urge of immeasurable force that he could not control. He had stalked her many times, but on this occasion a satanic strength controlled his actions, making them devilishly uncommon. That was his phrase: devilishly uncommon. Strange, I thought. I asked if there were voices in his head. No, there were not. It was not an act of a crazed man, he said, because he was not told to do it. Rather than a mental fixation to harm her, it was a disability to control his actions, as if his body were not his own. That was his reasoning. What I wanted to know was whether he carried weapons. This, to me, would indicate that, in fact, he did have intentions to kill Prudence. If so, the act of murder would not be an impulse, as he put it, but a deliberate action. It would confirm that it was a pre-meditated deed, and not one of impulse.

I asked Innes whether he was aware of the Charles Manson murders of a few months prior to Prudence's attack. Charles Manson was familiar to him although he vehemently denied any influence or intended copy-cat undertakings. Constable Hallett asked whether Innes owned a thin-bladed knife. Innes said no. Constable Hallett asked whether he borrowed one on the night of the murder. Innes recollected nothing about a knife. He could not recall whether he owned, borrowed, carried, or found a knife at the time of the murder. He could not recollect slashing Prudence with intent or out of frenzy. He shook his head several times. We decided to change the direction of the questioning.

Innes acknowledged awareness of Hypatia, her pagan friend, Orestes, and her Christian antagonist, Cyril. Both Prudence and Leon had mentioned the famed mathematician and astronomer because she had also devised a gadget called a planisphaerium. I firmly believed that my constables and I were on track in finding the true motive for the killing. The fact that he was aware of Hypatia and her demise would seal the case.

I asked him how Hypatia met her end. Innes shrugged and said he had forgotten. It was not important, he said. He admitted that he had studied Hypatia's ancient inventions, but he believed that his work was so far advanced that there was nothing to be gained from studying the ancient scientist beyond noting the dimensions of her planisphaerium.

Constable Hallett digressed briefly when he asked Innes, "What the heck is a planisphaerium?" Simplistically, Innes answered, it meant "star chart," but Innes preferred the term "celestial plane." Two flat disks, one with a complete 24-hour time cycle marked around the rim, and the other with a full 12-month calendar around the rim, rotated on one pivot to display the stars and constellations in the sky for any time and any date. If you hold it above your head, aligned with the eastern and western horizons, you can determine planetary positions, he explained. It was widely used by Islamic astronomers, but he was aspiring to modernize it to three dimensions to produce stereographic projections. It would preserve the property of circles, he said. I'm not sure whether Constable Hallett fully understood, but he nodded and said thank you.

When I reminded him of Hypatia's fiery death, Innes nodded. Instead of elaborating on the Greek woman's murder, Innes asked if we, my constables and I, had read Ray Bradbury's novel, *Fahrenheit 451*. He added that it had recently been adapted as a movie. We didn't answer, of course, but we knew it was about the burning of books. Pursuing this line of questioning, Innes eventually divulged a powerful attraction to fire, although, he maintained, there was no time in the past when he had maliciously and willfully committed senseless arson. However, he acknowledged that the allure of fire and its combustible qualities gained momentum in his mind. At the time of the murder, he had recalled Hypatia's death and had a fervent inclination to scare Prudence by setting her hair alight.

Was he emotionally or sexually aroused before the act, Constable Collins asked? Thoughtfully Innes answered that he was, but that he felt repulsed at the thought of sex. Instead of sexual gratification he described it more as a failure to control or resist his impulses, similar to the urges of a kleptomaniac or a pathological gambler. He had an urge to do something and could not stop.

Constable Collins asked how he intended to light a fire, if indeed it was an act of impulse. Innes asked for a respite to go to the bathroom and, of course, we permitted him to do so. I asked a junior officer to accompany Innes. His absence gave Collins, Hallett, and I the opportunity to discuss our interrogation tactics.

On his return, Innes seemed more relaxed. He politely thanked us and sat down. Rather than leaning back in the chair, he sat forward with his hands clasped together on the table. Constable Collins repeated Innes's last statement to him. He asked Innes whether he carried any flammable or combustible liquid on him at the time of the murder. Before Collins could give examples, Innes insisted that he was not in possession of oil, brake or transmission fluid, mineral turpentine, kerosene, or gasoline. He admitted to having lighter fluid, but only in the form of a cigarette lighter. What he said was consistent with forensic investigations, but I found it hard to believe that a cigarette lighter could be the cause of such a heinous crime.

The science student insisted that he only had a cigarette lighter in his possession on the night of the murder. He did not know why he had it because he did not smoke. He knew that one was in his pocket. And he used it. He remembered trying to light it several times and Prudence scoffed at him. The moment flame burst from her hair, he stared in fascination and intense curiosity, because, he said, he found it difficult to distinguish between the redness of her tresses and that of the fire. He said an angel appeared to him from the flames, just as an angel had appeared to Moses from a burning bush. God subsequently appears, and instructs Moses to lead the Israelites out of Egypt. Moses saw that, though the bush was ablaze, it was not consumed by the flames. Like the holy bush, Innes believed Prudence wouldn't burn. Expectantly, he waited for God's instructions. He was so in awe of her beauty, and the splendor of the flame, that he forgot its danger. The fire ignited quickly and intensely, exploding in front of him. Realizing his actions, he attempted to extinguish the flames, but could not. And just as Moses did on the Mount, Innes hid his face for he was afraid to look at God. Unlike Moses, Innes fled in fright. I must admit, I was enthralled listening to him.

Quick-thinking Constable Collins asked Innes for his theory on why the fire was intense. Innes blamed modern clothing material, such as acrylic and rayon which were highly combustible. Even cotton ignited easily and burned rapidly, he said. He noted that women were wearing more acrylic sweaters and blouses these days. Fabric construction, he said, was a factor. Open knits and fabrics with uneven surfaces were also quick to burn. Flames from matches, cigarette lighters, and candles could effortlessly ignite clothing, he said with conviction. I don't know whether this was fact or not, but Innes said that hospitals in Australia reported about two hundred clothing fire deaths in the previous year. I didn't expect him to know so much about clothing fires. I made a note to check his theory with our forensic scientists.

What was the motive? It was my aim to determine why he did it. I led this phase of the interrogation. He aspired to no financial gain, and he was neither angry nor revengeful. He shook his head when I suggested that he did it for recognition. No, he said, in a quiet tone. By his own analysis, he was not relieving boredom, he was not making a political statement, nor was it done in an intoxicated state. He was not delusional, nor was he hallucinatory. Looking at his pathetic face, I wanted to shake the motive out of him. Constable Hallett expressed his frustration verbally, shouting "What the hell did you do it for? Are you psychotic?" in such an aggressive tone that I had to order him to back off.

At this point, Innes cried.

Dismissing a diagnosis of insanity, he said he thought he was perfectly sane, but he admitted to having anti-social tendencies, making him a loner. Only Prudence made him feel confident and worthy as a person. Honestly, he said, he did not intend to kill her. He simply could not control the powerful urge to scare her. But for what ends? To make her notice him: to show her that he was a man and not a boy: to gain her love and respect, not only for his scientific intelligence, but for his total being. Innes wanted her to love him as much as he loved her.

How would scaring her make him attractive to her? Did he seriously think she would love him when he confronted her and scared her? Did he realize his logic was flawed? What he was trying to attract was, by his very actions, being repelled.

I'm not sure of the science of magnets, but surely Innes was. I told him that when magnets are near each other, they will not be attracted to each other unless they are also oriented in the same way—facing the same direction on the same line or axis.

Innes stared at me for a long time—at least a couple of minutes—without saying a word. Can't you see that you were driving Prudence away, I asked him. Weren't you aware of that? In fact, I asked the questions several times.

For the first time in two days, Innes looked straight into my eyes. "No," he said, in almost a whisper. "No, I wasn't aware. I must have forgotten that. I must have forgotten. That must be what the professor was trying to tell me. How could I have been so, so—how could I have been—so, so stupid?"

Innes stood up, approached me with his hands outstretched, begged me to hand-cuff him, and asked to be locked up for eternity. In the loudest, most confident voice I had ever heard from him, he said to me: "Write this in your notebook commissioner: do not throw your pearls to swine for they may never reach the spiritual capacity to respect that which is valuable. I despise myself and repent in dust and ashes."

# CLOSE

A fter the memorial, I did nothing. I was incapable of thinking clearly. Fabian spent much of his time with me, taking
telephone calls, and attending to correspondence. He was a rock
of comfort when he helped me to apportion Prudence's clothes
to charities and friends. It was a distressing period, one that
was extended over time due to my fragile and emotional state. I
did not want to part with any of her things—clothes, or books,
or cherished souvenirs—and, in the end, Fabian retained a few
keepsakes as a shrine to her memory.

On a day when Fabian was not with me, I sat on her bed and
recalled images of Fabian fawning over Prudence's new clothes
in jest. I held her baby-blue jacket against my chest and paraded
in front of the full-length mirror just as Fabian had done. The
scent of *Cuir de Russie* wafted around me, filling my nostrils
with her perfume. I closed my eyes and inhaled the fragrance.
The brass knocker tapped gently against the wooden door. It was
a hesitant knock, the sound of Innes or Philip.

"Oh, Michael, I, I wasn't expecting you. Come in." Michael's
visit was a relief and I was thrilled to see him.

"Leonardo, I had to see you before I left for England." His
dark figure stood in the doorway, a poetry book clutched in his
delicate hands.

"Come in, son." I led him silently to the living room. "This
is my daughter's home. We'd sit here amongst the books and
magazines and talk about many things. She bought me books from
everywhere. She always found an interesting book for me to read."

Michael placed the poetry book on the coffee table. "Here's
another for your collection. Prudence mentioned that you liked

Gerard Manley Hopkins. This is an antique copy that I travel with. I'd like you to have it."

"I, I don't know what to say. Thank you. I, I don't know how to thank you. Shall I make a pot of tea?"

Michael slowly wandered the room, touching and caressing items that caught his attention. As I entered with a tray of tea and biscuits, he was in front of a large gild-framed painting that commanded the room. Italian artist Francesca Guarina's study was of a woman, her right hand touching the folds of a white vestment over her left breast. The subject's skin was the same translucency as my daughter's, but with stained yellow hues of antiquity. I watched Michael move to the bust of Michelangelo. He softly slid his finger along the brow and down the side of the face to the neck. With the same finger, he ran it along the length of the marble top of the Vincenze console table until it stopped at a jagged broken corner that had been damaged on its way from Italy to Australia. It now stood in a dark nook to hide its flaw. Michael had traversed the entire room.

"It's a beautiful room. It's dark and decadent—aged, I mean. For a minute I thought that large painting was by Guarini, the geometer and architect. His mathematical fantasies and spatial complexities were extremely influential in Spain and Portugal, but I suppose you know that. But no, I didn't think he painted. No matter. I like this room. It tells me your story." He unfolded himself in my armchair, letting it wrap him in leather. I watched him close his eyes. Minutes later, he opened them, slowly sat upright and leaned forward. Fingering the ancient poetry book he had placed on the table, he picked it up and felt its leathery cover. He replaced it on the table languidly. "This is a good home for my book. It will not be out of place here. I'm glad about that." Abruptly, he leaned closer to me and said intensely. "I'm sorry, Leonardo. I desperately wanted to attend Prue's service. I'm so sorry I couldn't make it."

"She would've liked you to be there. She knows that you were there in spirit."

"There in spirit, but not in body," he sighed. "To tell you the truth, I was scared. I didn't want to go. I thought I would get too upset. Really upset, you know? I couldn't face it." He looked at me with misery in his dark eyes.

"I understand perfectly. I do understand." After some silence, I asked, "Did you love her, Michael?"

"More than you know. More than you know."

"Did she know?"

"It was not my way. She wouldn't have known, although she may have guessed." His head dropped, and he rested his right elbow on his leg while placing his head in his handsome hand.

"Did anyone tell her, do you think?"

"Tell her what, Leon?"

"That they loved her."

"Probably not," said Michael. "That's the tragedy, is it not?"

"A tragedy of the highest proportions," I said.

Michael's face showed the pain of the past and the tragedy of the present. His voice resonated with suffering. "Prue lived with the gentle modesty and grace of the darkened chartreuse that matched her eyes. *Je ne sais quoi de la beaute*—an indefinable touch of beauty. She had many male friends; she adored their company. Don't get me wrong. She loved you. You can be sure of that," Michael said. "She was a jewel—no, she was more than that. She was the fire in the jewel, like the fire in an opal, and in my dark life she lit the way like a lover's candle. *Ma chandelle est morte. Je n'ai plus de feu. Ouvre-moi ta porte pour l'amour de Dieu.* It's a poem for her. My candle is dead. I have no more fire. Open your door for me for the love of God. *Mon Dieu, elle est mort. Elle est mort.* I loved her."

It was true. Michael did love Prudence. *"Oui, c'est vrai. Qu'est-elle devenue?"* I said sharing his pain, his sorrow.

"Yes, what has become of her? What has become of your daughter, her body, and her spirit? *Heureux, comme Ulysse, a fait un beau voyage.* Happy is the one, who like Ulysses, has made a good journey."

I stood up and moved toward Michael. He stood tall and straight, outstretching his arms. We embraced. For me, a hug was more soulful than a handshake or even a kiss on the cheek. It was a long, heartfelt embrace, both of us swaying gently, rocking each other in comfort and peace, neither one of us wanting to let go.

Printed in Australia
AUOC011406300112
251295AU00002B/1/P